T0274573

GIRLS LIKE HER

GIRLS LIKE HER

MELANIE SUMROW

BALZER + BRAY

An Imprint of HarperCollins*Publishers*

Balzer + Bray is an imprint of HarperCollins Publishers.

Girls Like Her

Library of Congress Control Number: 2023943948
ISBN 978-0-06-334328-3

Typography by Corina Lupp
24 25 26 27 28 LBC 5 4 3 2 1
First Edition

For each and every girl like her

THIS STORY WAS INSPIRED by the many criminal cases I reviewed during my time as a lawyer with the Dallas Court of Appeals. To honor the real experiences of the children and teens involved in these cases, it was important to me to be authentic in the telling of Ruby Monroe's fictional story. Because of this embedded reality, please be aware that *Girls Like Her* incorporates content that may be triggering, including drug and alcohol abuse, physical and sexual violence, tense exchanges with law enforcement, suicidal ideation, and graphic descriptions of death. My hope is that, in telling the story of girls like Ruby, those who have experienced these traumas feel seen and those who have not experienced them will begin to see.

Melanie Sumrow
June 2024

Millionaire Found Dead Outside Dallas Home

BY GRANT LATHAM
Staff Writer

Dallas police are investigating a deadly shooting after local million-aire and philanthropist Eric Hanson was found outside his home in the Preston Hollow neighborhood yesterday. Police were called to the 9800 block of Walnut Park around 9:00 p.m. after a neighbor reportedly heard shouting and "something like firecrackers."

Officers said they found Mr. Hanson lying face down in his back-yard with multiple gunshot wounds. Dallas Fire-Rescue pronounced him dead at the scene.

A neighbor, Francine Whitaker, called 911 when she heard noises coming from the victim's backyard. "I thought it was kids playing with leftover fireworks from New Year's. I was worried they were going to start a fire." Ms. Whitaker added, "This kind of thing just doesn't happen around here." Home to at least five billionaires, several pro athletes, and the forty-third president of the United States, Preston Hollow is typically characterized by its high-ranking private schools and low violent crime rates.

In a statement to the community late last night, spokesperson for the Dallas Police Department, Alicia Williams, said, "We intend to use the full force of the law to convict the perpetrator and bring justice for this family." Williams noted police have already identified a suspect, who has been located and taken into police custody for questioning. Because the suspect is a minor, the Dallas Police Department is not providing their identity at this time.

OCTOBER 15, 2022

Dear Maya,

You asked if I was okay last time I saw you. I know I told you I was, but that was a lie.

    You're probably wondering why I'm writing this letter instead of texting, but the thing is, I'm in trouble. And not like the kind you were in before. I know you probably figured something like this would happen—you told me so and all that—and maybe you don't even want to hear from me right now. But I don't know where else to turn.

    I'm in juvie. Please don't be mad.

    I get that it's been a while since we talked. Almost 13 months. And I know a lot has happened since then. But Mr. Tate (he's my new lawyer) thought it would be a good idea for me to write to someone. He said, "It might help you remember what happened before if you talk to a friend."

    It's funny how a guy with puffy eyes and a comb-over can slice my life up like that. "Before" and "after." Like the day the cops caught me is some giant knife.

    I don't really understand why the public defender's office sent Mr. Tate except that the other lawyer was a real prick. He didn't believe me when I said I couldn't remember everything that led up to that day, so I was like, forget it, I'm not answering this stuck-up asshole's questions. So they sent Mr. Tate. Now he's saying the prosecutor wants to move me to the women's jail, where the real sickos are. I figured he was just trying to scare me. I thought they have to keep me in juvie because I'm only 15. But it's kind of freaking me out.

Ever since Mr. Tate said I need to remember, I've been thinking about that time we went to the party at Bachman Lake. Remember that? I didn't know anybody because school hadn't started yet. But you told me to stick with you and I'd be fine, and I was. I'd never met anyone like you. I guess I really screwed that up, didn't I?

Mr. Tate is making me see a social worker tomorrow. He thinks maybe I'll talk to her, give her something to help him "prepare my defense, just in case the prosecutor is serious about trying you as an adult," he said. But you know how much I hate social workers. I'm not talking to anybody.

You may be saying, "Then why are you talking to me?" That's fair. Especially after everything I said to you the last time I saw you. But I need someone on the outside to know where I am. And to know that prosecutor has it in for me. It's been 10 months since they arrested me and suddenly the prosecutor is wanting to throw me in jail with a bunch of psychos? That's bullshit. I hope this new lawyer gets me off.

Maybe I'll keep writing and you can decide if you open my letters. Or you can throw them away or burn them or whatever. But that doesn't seem like something you would do. You always were a good listener. At least before I told you to fuck off.

Anyway, I'm glad everything turned out okay for you. Really, I am.

Your friend (I hope),
Ruby

4

MEMORANDUM

Dallas County District Attorney's Office

TO: Nick Vanelli, Assistant District Attorney
FROM: Audrey McCaslin, Fall Intern
DATE: October 17, 2022

Question presented:

Whether a minor may be tried as an adult and charged with capital murder in Texas?

Facts:

Fifteen-year-old Ruby Danielle Monroe is currently awaiting trial in the Dallas County Juvenile Detention Center for the alleged murder of a local businessman, Eric Hanson. On January 7, 2022, the thirty-two-year-old was found dead on the grounds of his Preston Hollow home after having suffered multiple lacerations and gunshot wounds. At the time of Monroe's arrest, the police discovered she had stolen Mr. Hanson's wallet and truck.

Based on the horrific nature of the crime, the State would like to certify Monroe as an adult in order to transfer her case from the juvenile system to the adult system and charge her with capital murder.

Law:

Under Texas law, a juvenile may be certified as

an adult if they were fourteen years old or older at the time of the capital felony. *See* Tex. Fam. Code §54.02. The Juvenile Court will hold a certification hearing and make the determination whether the accused should be certified as an adult.

Conclusion:

Because Ruby Monroe was fourteen years old at the time of the offense and the murder was committed during the commission of a robbery, the crime meets the requirements of capital murder. *See* Tex. Code of Crim. Pro. §19.03. Thus, the State may seek certification of Monroe as an adult. *See* Tex. Fam. Code §54.02. The process can take several months, so I recommend requesting a certification hearing as soon as possible.

Mtg scheduled 10/18/22, 3:15 p.m. via Brian Tate
Ruby Monroe (Inmate #22-TX2873)
@ Dallas County Juvenile Detention Center
** Reserve Rainbow Room
Possible transfer: juvenile detention to adult jail
DA under pressure—victim's family has $$$

*Ruby
—Charged w/ capital murder
—15 yrs. old (14 at time of murder)
—CPS file requested
—Tate need help w/ viable defense
—Trauma likely
—Previous psych eval?

*Victim: Eric Hanson
—32 yrs. old
—$$$
—Family history?
—Connection to girl?

Motive???

OCTOBER 18, 2022

The girl stares up from her bunk bed to the water spots on the ceiling. She inhales the scent of fresh Pine-Sol, and within seconds, misshapen faces materialize in the brown stains overhead. She shudders and squeezes her eyes shut, willing the faces to disappear.

"Ruby Monroe," a woman's voice barks.

The girl quickly turns her head to the side, the cheap fill of her pillow deflating under the weight of her head. She peeks through the slits in her eyelids.

It's just the guard, the white one everyone calls "Mama." Ruby manages a breath.

"What on earth are you doing up there?" Mama asks. "I've been looking for you everywhere."

Mama's hands are perched angrily on her wide hips, but Ruby still can't help noticing that she looks relieved. Mama is a big softy, inside and out, unless you push her too hard. Do that, and she won't hesitate to drag a girl from the top bunk and beat her ass. Not that Ruby has seen her do it in the ten months she's been in juvenile detention, but that's what the other girls say.

"Don't just lay there smiling at me."

Ruby sits up and quickly judges the slipperiness of the floor she's just mopped before she jumps. She skids a bit, catching herself on Mama's fluffy arm.

"Good grief, girl. You're going to kill us both."

"Sorry," Ruby says, quickly letting go. Mama's only a tiny bit taller than Ruby's five-foot-even frame, but she still commands respect. Ruby quickly gestures to the floor. "I finished early, so I thought I'd take a break."

"You mean you thought you'd skip class again. When you weren't in the rec room, I was worried maybe . . ." Mama shakes her head.

Ruby knows exactly what Mama was worried about. It's why they won't let her have anything sharp in her room. Why Mama made sure they let her sleep with the door open to the hallway even though it drives her roommate, Ashlyn, nuts with the light always streaming in.

But it's the only way Ruby can sleep. *If* she sleeps.

Ashlyn is getting released today, and Ruby was hoping to say goodbye. After all, it was Ashlyn who shared her Flamin' Hot Cheetos when Ruby was equal parts scared and hungry and already deep in the shakes from withdrawal when she arrived that cold day in January. Ashlyn's been looking out for Ruby ever since. She reminded Ruby of Maya that way.

"The social worker is here," Mama says.

Ruby's nose wrinkles.

"Don't give me that face. She's here to help, and from what I hear, you could sure use it."

Ruby's hands clench at her sides. She hates that the guards are always all up in her business. "I just wanted to see Ashlyn one more time."

A squeak against the clean floor startles them both. Mama spins and points to a lanky Black girl who is attempting to sneak into her room. "Freesia, you better be going to class."

Freesia turns and smiles guiltily. Her gum pops as she gives a dramatic salute. "Was just going," Freesia says in a singsong tone.

Ruby laughs. She could definitely learn a thing or two about lying convincingly.

"And you better have finished your essay. Ms. Carter isn't going to give you another extension."

Freesia grabs a worn notebook from her room. "Was just getting it," she says, and then retreats back the way she came.

When she's gone, Mama turns to Ruby, her expression soft. "No time for goodbyes, honey. Dr. Ware is here. I'm sure Ashlyn will understand."

"But—"

Mama raises her hand.

With a sigh, Ruby steps onto the edge of the bottom bunk, pushing up on her toes and swiping her hand across the mattress until she can reach the far corner of her bed, where she retrieves a small bag of Flamin' Hot Cheetos. It took her a whole week of mopping to afford it. "I got these out of the vending machine as a going-away present."

"I'll tell her you left them," Mama says. "Now, come on. You know it's time for my break."

Ruby gently places the small bag on Ashlyn's bed, already stripped and ready for the next girl.

"Don't make me miss my break," Mama threatens, "or you'll be doing a lot more than mopping."

Ruby decides not to test Mama's patience and lifts her hands in surrender. She carefully tiptoes across the remainder of the wet floor. When she reaches the dry linoleum where Mama stands, they move into the stream of traffic.

Girls in the same faded V-neck T-shirt and sweatpants run toward their classrooms. If they're late, it can mean anything from revoked privileges to added chores. The bell rings, signaling the start of afternoon classes, and there are a few squeals as girls duck behind doors.

"You better hurry," Mama says to the stragglers.

Out of view from everyone except the security cameras, Mama and Ruby's pace slows to a stroll, arms swinging freely by their sides. "You're going to be meeting with Dr. Ware in the Rainbow Room," Mama says.

Ruby rolls her eyes. Someone painted the story of Noah on the walls of the Rainbow Room, probably thinking it would give the girls hope. Maya once told Ruby the rainbow is a symbol of God's promise after the flood to never destroy man again. At the time, Ruby thought that was a pretty fucked-up promise. If anyone should know man would do a fine job of destroying themselves, with or without His help, it was God. Ruby sometimes wonders if that was the plan all along.

Ruby's Crocs squeak quietly against the shiny floor next to the thud of Mama's boots until they reach the last yellow door on the left. "You be polite now, understand?" Mama takes a step back.

Ruby raises her hand to knock, but then hesitates. Maybe she can fake a stomachache and Mama would take her to the infirmary instead. Lying on a cot for an hour has to be better than sitting with some social worker.

But before she can say anything, the door opens in front of her.

"Ruby?"

The woman is tall, dressed in a blue suit, with wavy hair cropped close to her face. Her skin is so pale under the fluorescent light, Ruby can see the tiny veins in her forehead. A flowery silk

11

scarf wraps around the woman's long neck from the base of her throat up to the knot at her jaw. It reminds Ruby of a noose.

The social worker smiles slightly. "I was starting to wonder if they'd lost you."

Mama huffs her disgust. "No, ma'am," she says, her gaze unwavering. "I know where my girls are."

Ruby bites down a smile, not daring to mention Mama admitted less than five minutes ago that she didn't know where to find Ruby.

"Well, you're here now," the social worker says, looking to Mama. "Will you be right outside?"

Mama shakes her head. "I'm on my break now, but this one won't cause you trouble." She glares at Ruby to make sure she understands. Trouble means no more open door at night. "When you're done, you can call for a guard on this phone." She points to the one on the wall nearby. "Just lift the receiver and someone will answer."

"All right, then." The woman pushes the door again, holding it open. "Ruby, won't you sit down?"

Ruby leaves Mama behind and moves into the bright room. The mural has been chipped in several places where people have knocked chairs against the walls. She yanks back one of the plastic chairs from the table, smashing another dent into Noah's face before sitting.

The door slams shut as the social worker lowers herself into the chair opposite Ruby. "My name is Dr. Cadence Ware. Please call me Cadence. I'm the forensic social worker who has been called in to assist with your case."

Ruby folds her arms over her chest.

"You're from Northwest Dallas, is that right?"

"Yeah."

"That can be a rough neighborhood."

"What do you know about it?"

"I grew up there." Cadence smiles. "A few blocks off Stemmons Freeway."

Ruby smirks. "What, you think that's going to make me want to talk to you? Let me guess: Next you're going to tell me how much you want to help. Because you *genuinely care*. Then you're going to follow up that bullshit with a bunch of open-ended questions. Nothing too personal, just enough to get me to start talking."

If Cadence is surprised, she doesn't show it. "I take it you've spoken with a social worker before."

Ruby shrugs.

"All right, Ruby." Cadence leans across the table, her smile gone. "Since it seems like you're someone who likes to get to the point, I'll be straight with you. I'm here because Brian—Mr. Tate—asked me to be. I believe he's told you that the prosecutor on this case has asked the court for a hearing so that he can argue that you should be tried as an adult. It's called a 'certification hearing.'"

Ruby shrugs again, but her insides are churning. Late yesterday, Mr. Tate stopped by to let her know the prosecutor had made a decision: a hearing has been scheduled for the end of December. He said if the prosecutor wins, she will be moved to the adult jail to await trial there. And if the prosecutor wins again at trial, she could get life in prison.

"I'll ask Brian to go over it with you again so everything is clear," Cadence says as she pulls a lined notepad and a pen from her messenger bag. "But there's no time to waste. I'm going to be taking some notes to help me remember everything. Is that okay with you?"

Ruby looks everywhere but at the social worker's waiting expression. The yellow door. The bars of fluorescent light overhead. The rainbow over Cadence's shoulder. The box on the floor beside the social worker's chair. She wonders what's inside.

"Do I have your permission to take notes?" Cadence asks again.

Ruby pulls her gaze from the box. "I guess."

She scratches something on her notepad. "Thank you. It helps when I go back and write my report for the judge." Cadence tilts her head, examining Ruby. It's all Ruby can do not to squirm. "Brian did tell you I was coming, right?"

"He said something about it."

Cadence nods her approval. "I think you'll like him. If you can get past his horrible taste in ties." She laughs to herself. "But more importantly for you, he's a really good lawyer."

Ruby smiles for the first time. "You're dating."

Cadence doesn't give her the satisfaction of looking offended. "What makes you say that?"

"Hooking up," Ruby tries again.

"We're colleagues."

"Whatever."

Cadence scribbles something else before propping the notepad on her lap. "I've started reading through your files and—"

"Files?" Ruby asks, her gaze returning to the box.

"Your case files. I've read your court file, of course. I haven't had a chance to go through everything yet, but I asked Brian to request all of the records Child Protective Services had on you as well." Cadence pulls the lid off the box and removes a large stack of folders. She spreads them across the table like a dealer daring Ruby to pick a card.

Ruby's muscles tighten.

"Looks like you've been through a lot." Cadence holds her pen above her pad expectantly.

Ruby presses her lips together.

"Listen, Ruby, we want to help you."

There it is, Ruby thinks. "We?"

"Brian and I," Cadence says. "I know it might not be easy to trust us yet, but we're on your side."

Ruby shakes her head.

"Can you tell me what happened with Eric Hanson?"

She tries not to think of the contents of those files. "I thought you were here to tell me what to say at the hearing."

"I don't know why you'd think that." Cadence uncrosses and recrosses her legs. "I'm here to discuss what happened on January seventh, 2022, and the events leading up to that day. It will be much easier if you're willing to give us your side of the story." She taps her pen against her notepad. "It will be better for your case."

Ruby huffs. "Like you give a shit."

Cadence doesn't blink. "I can understand why you don't believe me. You have every reason to be cautious—"

"Just because you read some file doesn't mean you know me." Ruby pushes away from the table, banging her chair into Noah's crumbling face.

"Where do you think you're going?" Cadence stands.

15

Ruby moves toward the door. She doesn't want to think about what's in those files, especially when it has absolutely nothing to do with what happened to Eric.

"Are you hungry?" Cadence moves from her chair and comes close. Too close.

Ruby's right fist clenches, but then her stomach growls, betraying her.

"Because I can get you something to eat."

Her hand loosens.

"A Coke? Some Oreos?" Cadence suggests.

A Coke *and* Oreos? It would probably take Ruby two weeks to earn enough for that. But she knows this woman has an angle. Everyone has an angle. "I don't like Oreos," she lies.

"No Oreos, then," Cadence says. "I think I saw some Twizzlers in the vending machine last week."

Ruby considers a moment. Even if the woman buys her food, it doesn't mean she has to talk. It doesn't mean anything. She shrugs. "It's your money."

"Good," Cadence says with a satisfied smile. "Let me get those for you, and then we can talk a little more." She returns to her messenger bag, grabbing her phone and wallet, and then opens the door, carrying her pen and notepad with her. "I'll be right back."

When her footsteps fade, Ruby contemplates going back to her room to wait for Ashlyn. But then her gaze catches on the faded rainbow stretching across the wall. She looks from the rainbow to the files and back again.

She doesn't know how much time passes before she hears footsteps. Ruby shakes her head. She can't trust anyone. Especially not a social worker who says most of the same things all the other ones did.

Even if she does bring her food.

Cadence returns to the Rainbow Room, dropping into her seat and placing the Twizzlers and soda on the table between them. She gestures to the candy. "You know the second thing Neil Armstrong said after landing on the moon?"

Ruby stares blankly.

"'I could go for some Twizzlers right now,'" Cadence says. "No joke."

Ruby greedily snatches the bag, ripping it open and shoving a twisted red rope into her mouth. Her eyes close at the taste of the sugary goodness.

"Better?" Cadence asks.

Ruby opens her eyes and sits, suspicious of the notepad that is now back on the table. "It's okay," she mumbles.

"Then let's get started." Cadence picks up her pen. "Tell me about the day you met Eric Hanson."

10/18/22

Tattoo—RD?
Victim

Ruby + sex
$$$

OCTOBER 18, 2022

Dear Maya,

So, turns out I'm REALLY not okay.

Remember when I said that prosecutor had it in for me? Turns out I have to go to this hearing where he's going to try to convince a judge that I should be tried as an adult. That means if the trial goes bad and I lose, they could lock me away for life. LIFE. That seems pretty fucked to me, but Mr. Tate says, "That's what happens when you have a DA trying to look good for voters." I really don't know what that has to do with me.

Cadence (she's the social worker they made me see) says it's not my job to worry about all that. She says I should focus on taking care of me. Like I haven't been doing that for pretty much as long as I can remember. And anyway, she's not the one who might have to live behind bars with a bunch of wackos for the rest of her life.

You'd think being a social worker she'd be all soft and nice and smiley to get people to talk to her. But not Cadence. She's one of the buffest women I've ever seen and has this super-short hair tucked behind her ears. Even her jaw has muscles. I found that out today when I pissed her off.

After telling me all about how fucked I probably am, she asked all these questions and then waited for me to answer even when it was obvious I wasn't going to talk. She'd just sit there in silence like it didn't even bother her. And they think I'M crazy.

There was one good thing about it all. SNACKS. I know that sounds stupid, but you have no idea how much I miss food in here. I'd literally give anything for one of your cookies 'n cream milk-shakes with extra whipped cream and three cherries. My mouth is watering just thinking about it. I had a dream last night that I was in a tub full of macaroni and cheese and eating a whole chocolate cake. I'm not even kidding. There was a fire-breathing dragon, but he was friendly. Just there to melt the cheese. And it was the good kind of mac and cheese, not like the boxed frozen shit they gave us for dinner tonight. Luckily I'd had some Twizzlers and a Coke, which Cadence bought from the vending machine to get me to talk.

She said she'd come back. She was a little strange, but it was nice how she got me something to eat and didn't look at me like she thought I was trash. She seemed more worried I wouldn't trust her. Can you believe it?

We'll see. I'll probably go when she comes again. I'm not going to pass up a chance at real food.

Is it weird I miss hearing Ashlyn's snores? She was my room-mate. Did I tell you about her? I say she was my roommate because she got out today, so I guess she's not my roommate anymore. She had been here almost 3 years. I just wish I'd had a chance to say goodbye, but I had to talk with Cadence.

Thinking about that makes me think about how I wish I'd said goodbye to you, too.

Anyway, I know I won't be able to sleep tonight with all this legal stuff and everything that happened with that social worker *and now with it being so quiet. I guess neither of us could ever really sleep, could we? Or maybe you can now, since he's gone?*

Okay, don't be pissed at me for asking, but have you seen Redd? I haven't seen him since I got arrested, and I'm starting to get worried. Could you tell him I'm thinking of him if you see him? I know you're thinking "No way" while you're reading this, but maybe you could do it for me anyway.

Your friend,
Ruby

NOVEMBER 29, 2022

Inside the Rainbow Room, the social worker tightens her scarf as she waits for the guard to bring the girl. Cadence scans the list she's compiled of previous cases she'd worked that share similarities to Ruby's. She even pulled a few of those files to help her recall any mistakes she'd made when interviewing her clients for their initial evaluations. The same evaluation she's about to administer to Ruby.

She runs her finger down the list of names. While Ruby's situation is not unlike that of many young people Cadence has been asked to evaluate over the last sixteen years—raised in poverty, incidents of abuse and neglect, forced to grow up too soon—none of those cases were quite like Ruby's. In fact, this is only the second she's had where the DA was angling to try a minor as an adult—and the other kid pled out before his certification hearing ever took place.

Here, there is no plea deal on the table. She'd asked Brian again this morning just to be sure. The prosecutor is determined to make an example out of Ruby, especially since the victim's family has money and influence, and Ruby's, well . . . Typical political bullshit.

Cadence knows the pressure she's under today. What she's able to get out of the girl could mean nothing—the prosecutor's case is strong, and she's painfully aware that Ruby is not the sort of girl the court tends to give the benefit of the doubt. But it could also be Ruby's only shot at avoiding a trial that could end in life in prison.

She looks again at the highlighted names in the file in front of her—*Jacob Alvarez, Caitlin Taylor, Noah Thompson*—and hopes this case doesn't come back to haunt her.

The door to the interview room pops open, and there the girl is. Cadence gets a read on her immediately: anxious eyes, bordered by the deep purple of exhaustion beneath them, a stark contrast against Ruby's fair skin. The girl is obviously tired, and given how stand-offish she was at their last meeting, Cadence knows she's going to have her work cut out for her getting Ruby to cooperate. She's had clients like this shut down before.

As the girl approaches, Cadence puts the list away and writes the date at the top of her notepad. The guard closes the door, leaving them alone. "It's good to see you again," Cadence says. "How are you?"

Ruby slumps in the chair across from her. "You said last time that you wouldn't write down anything I say if I don't want you to."

"I won't. This is just here for me to jot down a few reminders of my own thoughts while we talk." Cadence pulls a stack of index cards from her messenger bag and pushes them to the center of the table in front of her client. "This is in preparation for the certification hearing so I can testify on your behalf."

Ruby blinks, her icy glare now aimed at Cadence.

So this is how it's going to be, Cadence thinks, taking a deep breath. "My job at the certification hearing will be to make the case to the judge for why you should remain in juvenile detention instead of being transferred to the women's jail."

"I told you what happened with Eric Hanson," the girl shoots back. "You said I wouldn't have to worry about being tried as an adult anymore."

Cadence shakes her head, unsurprised by the girl's twisting of her words. It could be Ruby misremembering—or, in her experience, it could be the girl testing her.

"I never said that," Cadence says plainly. "The State has requested a certification hearing. We talked about it, remember?"

The girl tilts her head. "So, how are you going to convince the judge I should stay in juvie?"

From what Cadence has seen in her files, the girl has enough street sense to detect when someone's overpromising, so she doesn't. "You and I will chat, and based upon whatever I learn from you, I'll prepare my recommendation for the judge. I can't know exactly what it will entail until I complete my initial evaluation here."

Ruby crosses her arms over the letters spelling *DETENTION* on her sweatshirt. "Will I get to talk to the judge?"

"That's up to Brian," Cadence says, which isn't a lie, though he will likely follow her recommendation. She takes the stack of cards with both hands, and as she taps them on the table, she feels the silk of her scarf slip. Ruby's gaze immediately flits to the exposed skin beneath her jaw. Cadence can already sense the questions forming in the girl's mind. She casually works the scarf back into place, fully covering her neck again. "Let's not worry about your testimony now." She gestures to the stack of cards. "Just tell me what you see."

But Ruby doesn't look at the cards. "What makes a grown-ass woman take a job like this?"

Avoidance, Cadence thinks. She knits her fingers on the table. "I wanted to help people," she says with a nod. "Still do."

"Why?"

"Why not?"

Ruby flips one of her long braids over her shoulder. "I just know I wouldn't come here if I had a choice."

"You have a choice now, whether you talk. Though," Cadence says, leaning forward, "legally speaking, it will likely be better for you if you do talk to me. It could help me fill in the gaps in what you've already told me."

Ruby frowns. "All I'm saying is someone must've fucked you over pretty good to make you want to come to a place like this."

"If you're suggesting I have personal reasons for doing this work," Cadence says, leaning back with a half shrug, "of course I do."

"Like what?"

"It would be unprofessional to discuss them with you."

"Whatever."

Cadence glances at her watch. She needs to get this meeting on track. Otherwise, she'll have nothing to tell Brian when they meet later today except what he already knows about the girl: she's difficult.

But then, Cadence has worked with difficult before. More importantly, she knows what it's like to put on a mask—hard, tough, defiant—in order to survive. She just needs Ruby to relax enough to drop it.

She takes a deep breath and exhales slowly, hoping Ruby will do the same, but the girl only squirms. "I'm not sure what will matter to you more," Cadence says. "That I'm doing this because

I care, or that I'm doing it because it's my job. But the truth is, I want to help you."

The girl scoffs. "Yeah, I've had people tell me they wanted to *help* me before. It only meant they wanted something from me." She sucks her cheek for a moment and then releases. "So, what do you want?"

"The truth," Cadence says, thinking of her mentor's old adage: *If you're honest with me, I'll be honest with you.*

"You can't handle the truth," Ruby says with a dry laugh.

Deflecting with humor, Cadence notes to herself. *Interesting.* At least the girl isn't shutting down. Yet. "What do you—"

"Forget I said it. It's from a movie."

"No, I know what movie it's from. Do you like movies?" she asks.

Ruby's Crocs nervously tap against the floor. "Can't we skip this part, and you make something up for your report?"

"No, we can't." For a moment, Cadence considers whether Ruby is too afraid to be honest with her, or whether she's covering for somebody, or if she's even willing to be honest. She watches the girl in silence—the roll of her eyes, the pressed lips. When it's apparent Ruby isn't going to speak, she decides to pivot once more. "I'm not asking you these questions to waste your time. I'm asking because I really think talking to me can help you."

"What do you want from me?" Ruby shakes her head. "You have some kind of savior complex? Some save-the-world, one-girl-at-a-time bullshit?"

Cadence can't help but smile. "Where did you hear the term 'savior complex'?"

"Some magazine," the girl says with a shrug. "It was in a

waiting room my mom dragged me to while she talked this asshole doctor into writing her another scrip for Demerol or some shit."

Cadence blinks. She's read about Ruby's mother in her files. But she's not about to go there yet. The girl isn't closing off, but she's not exactly opening up either, and Cadence has a feeling that if she tries to push too hard too soon, Ruby will shut down for good. She can't afford to waste an entire session, not when the certification hearing is less than a month away.

Instead, she says, "I'm actually hoping this girl here will save herself."

Ruby snorts. "Original."

"Let's find out, shall we?" Cadence edges her chair closer to the table and slides the cards toward Ruby's clenched hands before picking up her pen. "Now, why don't you stop trying to figure out every reason I could possibly have for asking you these questions and look at the cards and tell me what you see?"

Ruby presses her lips into a tight line.

"You know, for this to actually work, you have to let me get to know you a bit."

Ruby eyes Cadence and then nods at the stack. "And that's what these cards are about?"

"They're . . . a start," Cadence says.

"I don't see the point of any of this," the girl says, but Cadence knows she's only attempting to stall again.

"You don't have to see the point. You just need to know it's a necessary piece in a puzzle—one the judge uses to decide whether you remain in juvie or not." *So let me fucking help you already*, she wants to add.

"And if I lose?"

Cadence takes a calming breath. There's no reason to go through every possibility at this stage when there will likely be more meetings between them, especially if the prosecutor wins at the hearing and decides to bring her to trial as an adult. Which is feeling more likely to Cadence every second.

"Let me tell you what's going to happen at this hearing," Cadence says, taking a different approach. "The State will have their own story to tell the judge. They're going to argue that you're a girl who's always looked for trouble. That you're an addict and a thief who killed Eric Hanson in order to rob him."

"I'm not an addict." Ruby's eyes drop for a brief moment.

"Okay, then," Cadence says, making a mental note of Ruby's objection. "It's my job to give the judge insight into who you *really* are, which might make him think twice before transferring you to the adult system." She tries to catch Ruby's eyes, hoping her sincerity will convince the girl to start talking. "You told me what happened the day you met Eric Hanson, and I believe you. But I also have a feeling that what happened with him isn't the whole story."

Ruby rubs her forehead.

"We can't know unless you try."

After a few seconds, Ruby picks up the top card again. "This one?"

"Yes, the one with the three girls walking down the street."

Ruby studies the card for a moment. "I see three girls walking on the sidewalk. Two are walking next to each other. The third is a couple of steps behind."

"I'm sorry," Cadence says, shaking her head. "I didn't explain very well. I want you to tell me a story about what's happening in the picture."

"A story?" Ruby says, irritation creeping back into her voice. "Is this some bullshit they taught you in social-worker school?"

Cadence points to the illustrated girls with her pen.

Ruby examines the card once more; a line of concentration forms between her thick eyebrows. "Um, I think these two girls here are cutting that third girl out."

"Why?"

"Like, they probably were all nice to her before and then cut her behind her back."

Cadence looks at the card and then up to Ruby's face, questioning.

"*What?*" Ruby asks, tossing the card onto the table again.

"The third girl is smiling."

"So what?" Ruby says. She yanks off her sweatshirt and drops it into her lap. "She's acting all happy because she has to."

With the shift in Ruby's T-shirt, Cadence notices a scar, exposed and crawling over Ruby's right shoulder. She quickly looks down, marking the girl's response on her notepad.

Ruby slaps the table. "What the fuck are you writing?" She quickly adjusts the fabric of her shirt, pulling the V closed.

"I'll advise you not to hit the table." Cadence looks up from her notes. "As I already mentioned: I'm taking down a record of my thoughts."

Ruby purses her lips before lowering her voice. "Did I say something wrong?"

There it is again, Cadence thinks, *that vulnerability.* "There are no right or wrong answers." She offers a smile of encouragement, which seems to have the opposite effect of what she intended. Ruby looks angry, her mask back up. "I just want to know what you see."

Ruby snatches the card from the table again. "I hate when girls act all fucking nice to your face and then cut you behind your back."

Cadence pauses. "You have experience with that?"

"Haven't you ever faked a smile before?"

"I don't know a woman who hasn't."

"I do that sometimes," Ruby says, her expression loosening. "Fake it."

"How so?" Cadence holds a breath.

Ruby hesitates and then a moment later pushes the card with the girls aside. Whatever Cadence had briefly seen in the girl is gone. She silently berates herself for pushing too hard as Ruby yanks the next card from the deck. "This one?"

"Sure," Cadence says with a sigh. "Tell me another story."

Teen Will Be Tried as Adult on Murder Charge

BY GRANT LATHAM
Staff Writer

A judge has ordered that Ruby Monroe, fifteen years old, will stand trial as an adult after being accused of fatally shooting a Dallas millionaire outside his home in January.

Following a hearing on Tuesday, the Honorable Chris Leventhall, of the 106th Juvenile District Court, granted the State's request to transfer Monroe's case to adult court. Transfer from the juvenile detention center to the Dallas County women's jail is expected to take place early January 2023.

Monroe faces capital murder charges for the January 2022 death of local businessman and philanthropist Eric Hanson. Officers involved in the case allege Monroe shot the victim multiple times in the commission of a robbery. Monroe did not testify at the hearing, relying instead on an expert witness, Dr. Cadence Ware. Ware claimed Monroe was too young at the time of the crime to be considered an adult and noted her sealed court files indicate a history of trauma.

Dallas County Assistant District Attorney Nick Vanelli disagreed and said the State will be seeking the harshest punishment under the law in this case, a life sentence. During the course of the hearing,

Vanelli argued Monroe is a "cold-blooded killer who premeditated the robbery and murder of Mr. Hanson." In states such as Texas, crimes by adults charged with capital murder are punishable by death. But the United States Supreme Court case from 2005, *Roper v. Simmons*, banned the death penalty for juveniles.

The victim's ex-wife, Charlotte Hanson, called the juvenile court's ruling "a small victory for Eric" and hopes the upcoming trial "will give this girl exactly what she deserves."

A spokesperson for Judge Leventhall's office stated the case will be transferred to a new court within the week. Monroe had previously been assigned new counsel familiar with the adult justice system. A trial date will not be set until the transfer is complete.

JANUARY 31, 2023

Dear Maya,

We lost. The judge wouldn't listen when Cadence said I'm too young for jail, that I won't be safe. He just let the prosecutor say all this horrible shit about me. Even though Mr. Tate tried to make him stop, the judge didn't care.

So now I'm alone. The judge had me placed in a cell by myself, saying they can't put me with anyone until I turn 18. He said it's to keep me safe. But I don't believe him. How can you feel safe trapped in a concrete box with iron bars? The guards walk by my cell and stare at me like I'm something wild they want to tame. I never thought I'd say this, but I miss the guards in juvie, especially Mama.

I'm scared. I haven't heard from you or Redd or anyone, so I was wondering if you got the letters I sent before? I was told the guards here might read them before they send them, but it's been almost a month since I got here and I don't care anymore. If they are reading this, I wish they'd give me back my blankets since I'm shivering and can't ever get warm. I also wish they'd give me a job like some of the other women have so the days would go faster and maybe I could stop thinking about all this shit. There's not really anything I can do about the nights, though.

I don't know. Maybe you haven't written because you're still

33

mad at me for leaving or because you didn't hear from me until my first letter from juvie. Or maybe you're pissed because I didn't answer you when you asked me if you were a bad person for what you did, and now you don't trust me anymore. I hope you still trust me.

Remember how Jade and her friends thought I was all tough? You saw through me from the start. You knew it was an act because you had to pretend, too. They probably could've given us one of those Oscars for how good we were at lying. Anyway, I'm doing it again. I don't have any choice. Now I'm trying to act tough so I don't stick out so much. I asked them to cut off my braids last week so I'd blend in. I know you always liked my hair since it was thick and straight and yours was so curly. But I always liked yours more. I told you, right?

I can't look in the plastic mirror over my sink anymore. That girl isn't me.

There's a guard everyone calls Dickhead because he's bald and pink like the top of a cock. Dickhead asked why I wanted to cut off my hair and look like a boy. When I didn't answer, he said, "Okay, fine. I'll take you to cut your hair. But you'd be a whole lot prettier if you didn't."

Isn't it fucked how guys want us looking young and pretty and women don't? I know my mom didn't. Even with everything that happened, I used to like it when guys looked at me. You know I did. I can almost see you now, shaking your head at me with those curls getting into your eyes like they do when you forget to wear your favorite headband.

It's 155 days until trial (I've counted 3 times to be sure), and I don't know how much longer I can play this part. The problem is

34

Cadence doesn't want me to. She told me we have to prepare for the trial now, and the next time she sees me I'm going to have to start "facing what's happened to me" and "how I feel about it." Whatever that means. She has no idea what it's like for the women who let their feelings happen in here. They get their asses kicked. I don't know if I should even talk to her anymore. It's not like she really cares. This is just her job. She keeps wanting to bring up all this shit, and I'm trying to forget like you did.

It's hard to believe, but if I'd made the same choice as you, I'd be finishing up 10th grade soon. You'd probably be telling me all about where you're going to college. You still plan to go to college? I'm sorry I won't be there for your last summer before you leave. I'm sorry for a lot of things. But it was Redd. I loved him too much to stay. You may not believe me, but that's the truth.

I hope you're getting my letters. Can you at least write back so I can know? I'll try to write again soon.

Your friend,
Ruby

FEBRUARY 1, 2023

Ruby steps from the padded elevator and scans the hallway with haunted eyes. It's empty. Dickhead presses his fingers between her shoulder blades. His touch lingers on her back and every one of Ruby's nerve endings is alert. She twists her wrists against the edges of the metal cuffs, but it's no use.

"Straight ahead," the guard says. His pink face hovers above her. The meat of Dickhead's hand pushes, shoving her forward. She stumbles into a shuffle, and that's how she moves along the concrete floors and around a corner, where she spots a pair of vending machines filled with sodas and sweets. Her mouth waters in spite of herself. She bites her tongue, just short of drawing blood, to ward off the incessant hunger.

Ruby knows not to ask for sweets or sodas because there's always a price. Not that she's above paying it. But she doesn't want to think about that now.

They take a turn down a hallway she hasn't seen before and pass a guard with a boyish face that doesn't match his muscled arms. *Steroids*, Ruby assumes. The boy-guard gives her a cautious but knowing glance, followed by the tip of his tongue wetting his bottom lip. "Have fun," he says to Dickhead.

Ruby can't help it: she flinches. With her wrists bound to a belly chain, the ends of the chain clink between her legs, announcing her vulnerability.

Dickhead moves his hand from her back to her arm and squeezes a grunted warning. Ruby nods in submission. *I won't cause any trouble*, her body says. *I'll cooperate*. She wants to savor every moment she has outside Cell Block A, since she rarely gets out of her cell except to go to the showers. Sometimes outside to the yard. But it's always just her and the guards. That's how it is for a girl in a jail built for dangerous women.

Ruby can't stand the thought of being alone in her cell right now. She can't have the guard turn her around and march her straight back—she just can't—so she ignores the pounding of her heart, reminding herself that Mr. Tate arranged a meeting for her with Cadence today. That's why Dickhead is taking her to this unfamiliar part of the jail. That's all.

Ruby straightens her back, complying with the guard's silent instructions, and tries to focus on the newness of the place—the solid green walls in lieu of bars and the blessed quiet, broken only by the rhythm of their whispered steps. She tries to concentrate on something, anything, besides the moist heat of his hand that has now slipped to the small of her back. His musky smell mixes with the light scent of cigarettes, and she can almost taste the smoke—Camels, not Marlboro Lights, which were Redd's favorite—as they round the corner to another long hallway, flanked by a series of doors.

He veers them to the right. "Here," Dickhead announces and points to a door marked in stenciled black letters: INTERVIEW ROOM 2B.

Through the tiny window in the door, Ruby spots Cadence and manages a breath with the realization she won't be trapped in this room alone with him. Too far away from listening ears.

Dickhead knocks, and Cadence stands with a ready smile, her hair tucked behind her ears emphasizing her wide nose and sharp jaw. She's wearing a cream-colored suit that somehow warms her pale skin and a different silk scarf around her neck, this one pink with tiny red hearts. Her smile fades when she sees Ruby.

"You the social worker?" Dickhead asks.

Cadence's gaze darts from Ruby to the guard. "Well, I'm certainly not here to do her taxes."

The guard laughs uncomfortably; Ruby shifts, making the chains rattle again.

"Those won't be necessary," Cadence says, pointing to the handcuffs.

Dickhead's face scrunches with disapproval. "You sure?" he asks. "You know what she's in for?"

"Yes, of course," Cadence says with a firm nod. "Now, please remove them." Cadence tries to smile again. It's fake—a tight, worried grin. Nothing like the crafted smiles Ruby has seen on the faces of men who lie for sex.

For a moment, the three engage in a silent standoff on either side of the metal table that's much too large for the small space. It draws a shiny dividing line between the towering social worker on the one side and the hulking guard and the small inmate on the other.

The guard hesitates for a second, but when Cadence crosses her arms over her chest, Dickhead relents. "Don't say I didn't warn you." He fumbles for the key on the ring at his hip, first detaching Ruby's cuffs from her waist. The chain clinks as he releases the cuffs and frees her hands.

Ruby's muscles clench their readiness. The temptation to elbow the guard and make a run for it is still high after all of these months behind bars, but she knows she wouldn't get fifty feet before three guards were on top of her. She'd be put on lockdown for sure, not able to leave her cell for at least a month. They warned her any trouble would result in lockdown here. They didn't care how old her birth certificate said she was. She was just another wild thing in a cage.

She rubs where the bracelets of bruises have already started to form and glances around the windowless eight-by-eight room. There's a cat poster on one wall and a caged clock above the door.

"Thank you," Cadence says with another nod, dismissing the guard.

Dickhead juggles the handcuffs and chain between his hands. "I thought—"

"You are, of course, aware this is part of her defense preparation covered by privilege." Then she offers him a condescending nod. "You are welcome to wait in the hallway. We'll call you if we need you."

Dickhead nods feebly. "I'll be outside," he mutters before slinking out of the room.

Cadence gestures to the chair opposite hers and then takes her seat.

Ruby pulls the empty chair from the table. It scrapes loudly against the concrete. With Dickhead out of the room, her relief immediately shifts to annoyance over the fact this is the first time she's seen Cadence since they lost the certification hearing. Ruby has been stewing about it for over a month: What was the point in talking to Cadence before when it didn't make any difference? The judge obviously didn't care what she had to say. And now Ruby could be locked up with these sickos for the rest of her life.

She's about to go off on her when Cadence says, "You cut your hair."

Ruby's stomach sinks.

"Looks good."

No, Ruby thinks, *it doesn't*. She self-consciously brings her fingers to the base of her skull before forming them into fists. "I told Mr. Tate he should've let me tell the judge my side. Maybe I'd still be—"

Cadence shakes her head, interrupting. "You weren't ready."

Why is she only telling her this now? "So why bother meeting with me before if you weren't even going to let me talk to the judge?"

"It was to prepare for my own testimony."

That's not how she remembered their conversation. She thought the whole point of meeting with Cadence before was so she could tell the judge her story, but that must've been a lie too. "You know what? You both should've saved me the trouble and told me the judge was going to send me here to die."

There's the slightest tremor in Cadence's jaw before her expression returns to neutral. "At least now we'll have more time to prepare for trial."

Ruby assumes that means more talking. She crosses her arms over her chest. "Great."

"It is great, actually."

"Is that why you're here?" She shifts in her chair. "To tell me how lucky I am? I wasn't supposed to end up in adult jail. You promised."

"I told you I can't promise you results. I still can't." Cadence doesn't look away. "But I'm here now, and unless the prosecution objects, I will be allowed to testify as an expert witness at your trial." She pulls out a notepad and scribbles something at the top. "That's why I'm here. To get to know you a bit better and obtain a deeper understanding of what led to the events of January seventh."

"You already talked to the judge at the hearing, and I ended up here." Ruby wipes the cold sweat from her forehead. "You think if you testify at my trial, it's gonna turn out different?"

"I think, given the time for me to learn more about your past, it might allow Brian and me to prepare a more thorough defense."

Here we go again, Ruby thinks. *More bullshit.*

"The judge will probably allow me to remain in the courtroom for the length of the trial. If that's the case, I can help you through the process, too. Sitting through your own trial can be . . . tough." Cadence gives a half shrug. "Though I'll admit sometimes experts are only allowed in the courtroom when we're on the witness stand. The judge will decide."

Ruby presses at the bruises on her wrists. "Yeah, knowing my luck, he'll say I have to do it alone."

"You won't be alone. Brian will be in the courtroom with you the whole time." Cadence gestures across the table. "And depending on how open you are with me, maybe Brian will agree you can testify, too."

Open? She never agreed to this. "I thought it was my choice." Ruby pops her chest with an open palm. "*Mine*, not his." She clenches her jaw, determined to avoid any more talk about digging into her past. "I think he's on something," she says, trying to deflect.

"Who?" Cadence asks.

"Mr. Tate. Why else would he talk so fast? And he doesn't stop moving. Ever. Have you noticed? That guy can't keep still."

Cadence's face breaks into a grin.

Ruby stiffens. "Really? You think it's funny that my lawyer is always walking around half-baked?"

"I can assure you, if Brian's on anything, it's just too much coffee. He's overworked and there are only so many hours in the day." Her smile softens. "I think the only thing he's guilty of is being a Yankee. He's been here for years but never quite picked up on our more relaxed speech patterns. I can promise you, though, he's taking this as seriously as you are—"

Ruby rolls her eyes.

"—and I think he made the right choice, not having you speak at the hearing in December, even though we lost." Cadence nods toward Ruby. "Whether you testify at the trial ultimately depends on you."

Meaning it depends on how much she's willing to talk in the meantime. Ruby shakes her head. "And if I lose at trial, that's it, right?"

"Let's not think about that now." Cadence tries to write something, then scribbles circles with her pen. It's out of ink. She opens her bag and begins to dig.

"It's all I think about," Ruby admits. She's quiet for a moment while Cadence continues to search through her bag. *Seriously? Here she is, actually letting her guard down, opening up like she asked, and Cadence is too worried about finding another fucking pen?* Ruby slaps the table. "You don't know what it's like in here. I haven't been able to relax since I got transferred. Everyone's always looking at me."

42

"Who?" Cadence asks, finally finding another pen.

"Everyone," Ruby says, her voice dropping to a whisper. Like if she says it too loud, they might find her, come after her. "It's like at the zoo when they release those little mice in the snake's cage, and everyone's watching, waiting for the snake to strike."

"Are you saying you're the mouse or the snake here?"

Ruby glares, unamused by her attempt at a joke.

Cadence sighs. "It sounds like you don't feel safe."

"Locked in a cage with a bunch of psychos? Oh yeah," Ruby says. "Totally safe."

"Has something happened to you that I should know about?"

"They haven't had the chance to do anything yet," Ruby concedes, hoping by admitting as much Cadence will realize she's not crying wolf. She truly is worried about what could happen to her in here. "When the trial ends, I'm just going to be sent to prison to die, and you'll walk out and go on with your life."

Cadence props her notepad against her lap. "Let's try to focus."

"Yeah, sure." *Avoidance*, Ruby thinks. *Typical.*

"All I'm saying is that we're going to have a bit more time before the trial than we did before the hearing, which means we can talk about your past and build a better defense. There might be a chance we'll uncover something regarding your circumstances that Brian can use."

But Ruby doesn't want to talk about her past, with this woman or anyone else. Only Maya and Redd ever really understood what she's been through, and look how that turned out. "Like what?"

Cadence shrugs. "I don't know. Like who's Redd?"

Her heart jumps to her throat as she wonders how Cadence found out about him. She *knows* she didn't mention his name before, not when Redd specifically told Ruby never to mention him.

"You might find talking actually helps."

"And what if it doesn't?" The girl can hardly breathe. "What if you find out things about me you don't like? What then?"

Cadence tilts her head. "What sort of things?"

"No," she says, her whole body tight. "I'm not doing this."

Candence's lips part, as if she's going to say more, but then she closes them, nods. "All right. If that's what you want." She collects her things into her bag and stands. She's always taller than Ruby remembers. "But the trial is going to start in July. That's five months from now. And if you want my help, you're going to need to start talking."

Ruby scoffs, but her stomach is turning.

"You know what I think?" Cadence adjusts the strap of her messenger bag across her shoulder. "I think you're not the bad girl they're painting you out to be. And I think you know it, too. But none of that is going to matter if you won't accept my help."

Ruby is silent as Cadence moves to the door and knocks for Dickhead. Before it opens, Cadence nods. "Your move."

IN THE 141ST DISTRICT COURT

DALLAS COUNTY, TEXAS

HONORABLE FRED AMBROSE, JUDGE PRESIDING

THE STATE OF TEXAS

V.   CAUSE NO. 23-061504-S

RUBY DANIELLE MONROE

****

JURY TRIAL

OFFICIAL REPORTER'S TRANSCRIPT OF PROCEEDINGS

JULY 5-22, 2023

DALLAS, TEXAS

****

APPEARANCES:

For the State: NICK R. VANELLI, Deputy Prosecutor
For the Defendant: BRIAN S. TATE, Public Defender

Reported by: Nicole Stanford, RDR, CRR, CRC
                        Official Court Reporter

Transcript produced by Reporter on computer.

45

THE COURT: Is the State ready?

VANELLI: Ready, Your Honor.

THE COURT: And the Defense?

TATE: Ruby Monroe and I are here and ready to proceed, Your Honor.

THE COURT: All right. Sorry for the late start today. It seems I always have an emergency motion right after the Fourth of July holiday that has to be sorted out. So, thank you for your patience as we got that motion heard.

VANELLI: Of course, Your Honor. I think we're all getting a little bit of a late start after the holiday weekend.

THE COURT: True. Did you get out to the lake with your new boat?

VANELLI: No, Judge. My wife took the kids up, but I had some final preparations for today.

THE COURT: I think we all can relate to that. The law is a jealous mistress, right?

VANELLI: I'm afraid so, Your Honor.

THE COURT: Well, I've reviewed your motion, and I'm going to allow the social worker to testify.

VANELLI: Judge, we contend the social worker—

THE COURT: I know what you contend, Counselor, but that is my ruling. If you want to raise your objections for the record when we get there, that's fine. We can address it again then.

46

VANELLI: Yes, Your Honor. I'll do that. Thank you.

THE COURT: And through your pretrial filings, we've agreed there are no objections to State's Exhibits 1 through 37; is that correct, Mr. Tate?

TATE: That's correct, Your Honor.

VANELLI: That sounds right, Judge.

THE COURT: Thank you. I've found the parties coming to an agreement on as many exhibits as possible makes things run more efficiently. Any other pretrial motions before we get started?

TATE: Yes, Your Honor. I have not yet received the Court's ruling on my motion.

THE COURT: Remind me, Counselor.

TATE: It was our request that the State be prohibited from making any mention of alleged written notes the social worker took during her initial meeting with Miss Monroe when she was being held in juvenile detention and within the exclusive jurisdiction of the juvenile courts. The forensic social worker in question is Dr. Cadence Ware.

THE COURT: Oh, yes. I remember now. I tend to agree it's irrelevant.

VANELLI: Your Honor, the State contends the lack of notes calls into question the veracity of Dr. Ware. Whether she failed to take the necessary notes at her first meeting with the Defendant or she's not being truthful about the fact that she didn't take them, we argue she is not qualified to testify as an expert.

TATE: Are we really going to get into this again?

THE COURT: All right, gentlemen. Mr. Vanelli, you've already received my ruling. This court has found Dr. Ware is an expert, and you have received the entirety of her written notes that she states form the basis of her report, correct?

VANELLI: Yes, Your Honor. That's what they're saying. But I still would argue it goes to the veracity of the witness.

TATE: Good God. He doesn't know when to quit. Your Honor, as I'm sure you recall, this court indulged the State with a lengthy hearing on this issue a few months ago, and Dr. Ware was clear in her testimony then that she decided not to take notes at her initial meeting when she found Miss Monroe was uncomfortable with it, as is her prerogative. The Court has already ruled in our favor, yet the State continues to insist on rehashing it here.

THE COURT: Gentlemen, the jury has been waiting all morning, and we need to get started. So here's what I'm going to do. I am going to grant the Defendant's motion insofar as the State must notify the Defense before referencing Dr. Ware's alleged notes. Mr. Vanelli, you bring it up without warning, you're looking at a mistrial. Understood?

VANELLI: Yes, Your Honor.

TATE: Thank you, Your Honor.

THE COURT: Anything else before we get started?

TATE: Yes, Your Honor. One more item of business. Because the Court agrees Dr. Ware is an expert, we ask the Court to exempt her from the Rule and allow her to be present in the courtroom for the duration of the trial, as it may inform her testimony.

THE COURT: Does the State have any objection?

VANELLI: Yes, we object again on the basis we do not believe Dr. Ware is an expert.

THE COURT: Overruled. Dr. Ware may remain in the courtroom. Anything else?

VANELLI: No, Your Honor.

TATE: No, Your Honor.

THE COURT: Okay, then. Let's bring in the jury.

HERE ENDS THE EXCERPT

FEBRUARY 6, 2023

Dear Maya,

It's 5 months until trial, and I think I might be going crazy from all the gray. The walls. The floors. Gray everywhere. Even the bars are gray. Actually, they're more white but with the paint worn off where women put their hands. But no color anywhere except for these baggy green-and-gray-striped uniforms with "Dallas County Jail" stamped in red across our backs.

The noises in my head are getting louder. My cell block is finally quiet, but I still hear everything. The hum of electricity from the bulb outside my cell. The scratch of someone's fingernails against the cinder block a few cells down. Someone crying. The inmates cry at night, and the sound crawls into my ear like a roach ready to lay its eggs.

I can't blame them. They cry at night because that's when it's safest. It's when no one can see how weak they really are. But I can still hear. I've been counting in my head trying to block everything out like you taught me, but eventually I lose count and have to start again, over and over, until I fall asleep or it's morning.

And in the morning, the women act all tough again, like the night never happened. I guess we're all lying to survive. But when the guards take me to the showers, the women stare at me in a way that makes my stomach hurt. *I pass all of them—women so thin I can see their bones, so fat their uniforms can't hide the dimples on their asses, some with long hair, dyed hair, braids, shaved heads, brown skin, white skin. But they all have the same desperate look in their eyes.*

The guards won't take me to shower when everyone's asleep. I asked twice already. "You can't change the schedule," they said. "Just because you think you're special, you're not." But I don't think I'm special. I just want to disappear. But I can't, not when they're constantly telling me where to move, how to move, when to move, when to sleep, when to eat, when to pee, when to bend over and separate my cheeks and cough.

Sometimes the women's boyfriends or families come to visit, which breaks up all the sameness. I wish you would come see me. Please don't be mad I said that. I know you probably haven't visited because you're still pissed. But I have to tell someone what's happening to me, and I don't have anyone else. There's this guard (I think his name is Steve) who's been giving me looks. Tonight he brushed his hand against my ass when he brought me back to my cell and smiled like it was an accident. You know the type. He reminds me so much of Clay, my stomach hurts just thinking about it. He even has the same crooked front tooth.

Have you heard from Redd? I haven't since before I got arrested and I'm really worried. Even if you don't want anything to do with me, maybe you could ask him to visit me instead? Only if you see him around. I really need to see him. I know you don't like him, but Redd always did like you. Maybe you could ask around for me?

I've put my return address on the envelope again so you can tell him where I am if you see him.

Your friend,
Ruby

P.S. Can you let Redd know I didn't say anything about him to the cops or anybody?

THE COURT: Ready to call your first witness?

VANELLI: The State calls Detective Les Martinez.

After being duly sworn, **DETECTIVE LES MARTINEZ** testified as follows:

VANELLI: Please state your name, employer, and the kind of work you do for the record.

MARTINEZ: My name is Les Martinez. I have worked for the Dallas Police Department for twenty-six years. I started out as a beat cop and worked my way up to homicide detective. I've been doing that for about twelve years now.

VANELLI: And how did you come to be involved in this case?

MARTINEZ: I had just come onto my shift when I was called to investigate a homicide at a residence in the 9800 block of Walnut Park.

VANELLI: Is that in the city of Dallas?

MARTINEZ: It is.

VANELLI: And what did you discover when you arrived at the home?

MARTINEZ: After being briefed by one of the officers who had secured the crime scene, I walked around the residence, through a side gate, to enter the backyard. That's where the body was located.

VANELLI: And where exactly was the body?

MARTINEZ: The body was in a prone position near the pool. On the south side of the pool.

VANELLI: And by "prone," you mean the victim was found on his stomach?

MARTINEZ: That's correct.

VANELLI: And was the victim already dead?

MARTINEZ: Oh, yes. He'd been shot multiple times.

VANELLI: Detective, did you know that Mr. Hanson had been shot as soon as you saw him?

MARTINEZ: Yes, he was bleeding out of the left side of his head. Brain matter was also visible.

VANELLI: And was there any blood?

MARTINEZ: There was a lot of blood surrounding the trunk of the body, on his shirt, on the coping along the pool. In addition, there was a trail of blood from the bedroom inside the house to the concrete patio to the edge of the pool where we found the body. It was dripping over the edge of the pool and into the water as well.

VANELLI: So a lot of blood, then.

TATE: Objection. Asked and answered.

THE COURT: Overruled.

VANELLI: Thank you, You Honor. Detective, there was a great deal of blood at the scene?

MARTINEZ: Yes, more than average for a single gunshot, which made me suspect there were multiple wounds. I also saw several lacerations across the victim's arm and the side of his face that were bleeding.

VANELLI: Lacerations?

MARTINEZ: Small cuts all over the victim's arms and face. There was a broken sliding glass door that the victim likely either fell through or walked through after being shot.

VANELLI: There was glass on the ground?

MARTINEZ: Just outside the house. And some glass pieces were stuck to the victim's clothing and scattered near the edge of the pool. But most of the glass debris was against the house.

VANELLI: You indicated you thought he fell through the glass door after being shot. Why do you say that?

MARTINEZ: Inside the house, there was blood splatter against the wall and on the chest of drawers near the bed, a little on the white comforter. All indicative of a gunshot injury.

VANELLI: Did you locate anything else inside the house indicating that the victim had been shot there?

MARTINEZ: Yes, we found a bullet lodged in the interior wall to the left of where the sliding glass door would have been.

VANELLI: And, I'm sorry, what room was this again?

MARTINEZ: It was inside the home's main bedroom. The downstairs bedroom.

VANELLI: After you located the bullet in the wall of the primary bedroom, what did you do next?

MARTINEZ: We followed the blood trail along the

ground through the broken glass door to the body by the pool.

VANELLI: And you said you found the victim on his stomach?

MARTINEZ: That's correct.

VANELLI: Oh, I'm sorry, I forgot to ask. Was the victim fully clothed?

MARTINEZ: Yes, he was wearing khaki pants and a polo-type shirt, loafers. Fancy watch. Rolex, I believe.

VANELLI: Now, did you move the body after you arrived?

MARTINEZ: After I confirmed photographs had been taken of the body in the position in which the victim was first found, I put on my gloves and turned him over.

VANELLI: What did you discover when you turned the victim onto his back?

MARTINEZ: That he had also been shot in the chest. There was a hole in the fabric and bloodstains along the front of his shirt consistent with a gunshot wound. I also saw that his other arm had multiple lacerations and there were more cuts across his face.

VANELLI: And did you locate anything inside the victim's pockets?

MARTINEZ: Yes, after we searched him more thoroughly, I discovered a folded Taco Bell receipt in his front right pants pocket, along with a couple of dollars and some loose change.

VANELLI: What about a wallet or keys?

MARTINEZ: No, the victim did not have a wallet or keys on him.

VANELLI: What did you do next?

MARTINEZ: That's about when forensics arrived and began to collect evidence. Blood samples, DNA, et cetera.

VANELLI: And as the forensics team took their samples, what did you do?

MARTINEZ: One of the officers notified me that we had a lead on the victim's stolen vehicle. It had been located in a grocery store parking lot in Northwest Dallas. So I left the scene to go to the location of the vehicle in question.

HERE ENDS THE EXCERPT

FEBRUARY 14, 2023

Ruby rushes into the interview room. "I knew you'd come back."

Cadence glances at the guard, waiting for him to unshackle her client. After a few moments, he steps into the hallway, closing the door behind him. "You told them you wanted to see me, and I'm here."

Ruby drops into the chair opposite Cadence, but the woman doesn't move. Ruby notices she is still wearing her coat. "Are you hoping to make a quick exit or something? You have an early Valentine's date?"

Cadence clears her throat, ignoring the question. "That wasn't really as noticeable before you cut your hair," she says, nodding toward Ruby's collarbone. "Your tattoo."

Ruby instinctively brings a hand to her chest, covering the letters and everything they mean.

"What does it mean?"

And here she was, almost relieved to see Cadence today. Almost. "I don't want to talk about it."

"So what do you want to talk about?"

Nothing really, but she can't tell Cadence that when the whole reason she's here is because Ruby told the guard she needed to see her social worker. Ruby, of course, didn't mention the actual reason she wanted to see her: she's in desperate need of contact with someone from the outside who looks at her like she's a real person and not a thing meant for their consumption or disposal.

Cadence sighs. "I didn't come all the way down here to do this with you again," she says. "If I'm going to help you, you need to talk to me. That's how this is going to work."

Ruby should've known Cadence would never just let her *be*.

"Otherwise I have other clients to see."

The girl stiffens at the thought of returning to her cell so soon. "Is that supposed to be some kind of a threat?"

"Do you feel threatened by me?"

Ruby considers the woman across from her with the clear eyes that aren't afraid to look too long. *No*, Ruby thinks. "If the trial is anything like the hearing, you know I'm already fucked, so what does it matter whether I talk to you or not?"

Cadence gives her a disapproving look. Ruby can't tell if it's because she cursed or because Cadence doesn't agree.

"Tell me, Ruby: Am I wasting my time here?"

This was a mistake. Ruby should have never started talking to her. What's that thing her mom used to say? *Nobody buys the whole loaf when they can have a slice for free.* No, not that. *Give them an inch, they take a mile.*

Cadence pulls out her pen and notepad, probably preparing to take another mile.

"What more do you want from me?" Ruby rubs her hands across her pants, the green stripes bleached in spots to a dull mint. "I've already told you all my shit."

"I'm not talking about what happened with Eric Hanson. I'm talking about *you*." She scribbles something on the page. "I need more information about whatever you were doing that led you to meet him that day. We both know you weren't just in the neighborhood."

Ruby sneers.

Cadence looks from her notes to Ruby's tattoo. "That's an *R*, and—what is the other letter?" she asks. "Is it a *D*?"

"Fine," Ruby says. Talking about *something* has to be better than returning to her cage. "R. D., yeah. My boyfriend."

"I see. And your boyfriend's name?"

"Redd Dogg." Ruby closes her eyes. It's been so long since she's said it out loud. She remembers the feel of his hands, both tender and rough. Ruby opens her eyes to the pale green room. "It's not his real name, but it's what everyone called him. I thought it was dumb when we first met, but it kinda grew on me."

"Tell me about him."

On the wall behind Cadence, a poster with a gray kitten dangling from a tree branch tells her to "Hang in There."

"You could start with how you two met."

Ruby pulls her gaze from the doomed kitten. "Why do you want to know that?"

"It's a perfectly normal thing to ask about. Is there a reason you don't want to talk about him?"

She hates when Cadence cuts to the root so fast. "I didn't say that. I just want to know your angle."

Cadence shrugs off her coat. "No angle. It's like we've discussed before: Now that we have a little more time before trial, I'd like to get to know you better. And I know it's sometimes easier to talk about the people in our lives. Easier than talking about ourselves."

Ruby brings her fingers to her temples and starts rubbing small circles around the indentations in her skull. She figures Cadence probably thinks she's elicited some difficult memory from her past, but all she's thinking about is something she overheard an inmate bragging about: how easily a skull can shatter between skilled hands. Hers fall to her lap. "You seriously want to know where I met Redd?"

Cadence nods.

Despite trying not to, Ruby thinks of Redd's dark eyes that she thought she could stare into forever. "You'll think it's stupid."

"Do you think it's stupid?"

"No."

"Okay, then, neither will I."

Ruby hesitates and then nods to herself, deciding it should be okay if she can keep things on the surface. "Sonic."

"The best," Cadence says, making a note. "Ever tried one of those ice creams with candy mixed in?"

"My friend Maya used to work there," Ruby says. "Maybe she still does. I don't know. She'd make the best cookies 'n cream milkshakes. *Those* are my favorite." Ruby's stomach gurgles loudly.

Cadence flips the page. "Did Redd like milkshakes too?"

"I really never saw him eat much when we were there," Ruby says, already sensing what Cadence is doing, asking seemingly meaningless questions to get her comfortable. But if she wants her to talk, maybe Ruby could get something in return. She thumbs toward the door. "Speaking of something to eat, do you think we can get something from the machine?"

"Were you hanging out with Maya when you met Redd?" Cadence asks.

"I'm pretty hungry."

Cadence nods.

Ruby doesn't know what the nod is supposed to mean. "Maya was working that day, yeah. But I was there with this girl Jade. We were hanging with some of her friends." She looks toward the door and can see Dickhead's sweaty profile at the edge of the small window. "I know you have all these really important questions to ask, but seriously: Food? I'm starving."

Cadence's lips form a straight line as she lowers the notepad to her lap. "I can't buy you snacks just because you show up to talk to me. That's not how this works."

Ruby clenches her hands against her lap, questioning for the fiftieth time why she ever agreed to *this* in the first place.

"I'm more than happy for you to eat a snack while we talk, but you're going to have to get it for yourself."

"And how the hell am I supposed to do that?"

The door suddenly flies open, smacking against the wall. Ruby startles in her chair. She wonders if she screamed. She didn't mean to scream.

Dickhead's beady eyes flick between Cadence and her. "I heard trouble." His face is redder than usual.

Cadence shakes her head and waves him off. "Clearly, we're fine."

But Ruby doesn't feel fine. Her heart thuds as she watches Dickhead's hand against his nightstick, ready to pull it out and strike. She eyes the door, considering her odds. How many other guards are within earshot? The idea of several men holding her down makes her stomach turn.

"I told you before, if we need you, I'll call," Cadence says and knocks on the table. Ruby turns to find Cadence eyeing her. Somehow she knows what the social worker is telling her:

He's already on edge. Don't give him an excuse.

Ruby manages a breath, trying to slow her pulse. Her fists loosen slightly.

After a moment of stillness, the guard marches into the hallway, slamming the door closed behind him. Ruby can see him through the window, swiping a handkerchief across his face.

The social worker returns to the conversation as if they were never interrupted. "Most of the women find some kind of a job to earn money for the things they want. You worked in juvenile detention, didn't you? Could you get a job here?"

Ruby checks, making sure Dickhead doesn't change his mind. "They say I'm too young to work."

Cadence shakes her head. "It's just that if I buy something for every client for every session—"

"Forget it," Ruby interrupts, not wanting Cadence's sympathy. She'd rather starve than have anyone feeling sorry for her. She pinches the skin between her thumb and finger, attempting to mask hunger with pain.

"So, where were we?" Cadence scans her notepad. "You met Redd at Sonic."

Ruby releases the whitened skin between her fingers. "There was this song playing on the radio, 'Watermelon Sugar.'" Ruby watches the color flush back into the skin of her hand. "I was singing pretty loud."

"I didn't know you sang," Cadence says, a smile to her voice.

"I used to." Ruby grabs the cold edge of her chair. "I guess Redd heard me, 'cause that's when he came over. He was wearing

63

this white T-shirt that fit tight around his arms and showed off his tattoo. These really nice jeans." She thinks of Redd's dark eyes again, his long eyelashes, his lightly stubbled chin.

"You really like him, huh?"

"Yeah." Ruby tries to suppress a grin, but she's only half-successful. "He was so cute; I couldn't believe he was coming over to talk to me. And Jade was giving me the side-eye like she was all jealous."

Cadence nods, but it doesn't seem like she's being fake.

"He started to sing with me," Ruby continues, remembering how, at the time, she thought it was like in that movie *Grease*. She'd watched it with her mom at least a dozen times, and meeting Redd was like the part when Danny and Sandy sing a duet for the first time. Except without the wind machine and cheesy split screen. She breathes in the memory. "Redd couldn't sing, but it was really sweet he tried. When the song was over, he said I had a beautiful voice. He wasn't like all the other guys I'd met, trying to be all cool and tough. Redd's voice was soft. He asked if he could buy me something to eat."

"And did he?"

Her stomach growls again; Ruby covers it with her hand. "Yeah, I wasn't getting real steady meals then. He bought me some of those chicken popper things and a cookies 'n cream milkshake."

"Your favorite." Cadence makes a note. "Would you say it was love at first sight?" she asks, not in a mocking way but in a dreamy sort of way. Like someone who has known that feeling.

Ruby shrugs. "I knew he was special. He just had this way about him, you know. Like he wouldn't take crap off nobody, but he had this real sweet side underneath it all." She thinks again of

Danny in *Grease* and how she was a version of Sandy, but without all the prude bullshit getting in the way.

Cadence scribbles something else on her notepad. "So you started dating?"

"I'm not sure if we were *dating* or whatever. But yeah, I guess we were. I didn't want Redd to know how I was living, since I could tell he had a little money. But when he found out, he didn't care. He didn't treat me like trash. I think it's because he knew what it was like. He told me he'd had some problems—" She cuts herself off. She doesn't want to betray Redd's trust, even in here, even after everything. "Anyway, he told me he had this friend from school who was a talent scout and also knew some of these music producers. I'd heard of one of the girls he'd gotten singing gigs for."

"So what happened next?"

"Some stuff went down with my mom, and I needed a place to live. I thought he'd find a reason to break up with me, but he didn't. He said I could move in with him." Ruby shifts in her chair. "I figured he'd take better care of me than any of my mom's boyfriends had ever taken care of her."

"And did he?" Cadence raises an eyebrow. "Take care of you?"

Ruby hesitates and then nods.

"You don't seem sure?"

"He did," Ruby says. She doesn't want Cadence to get the wrong idea about her and Redd. Like Maya had.

"I'm sorry, I believe you," Cadence says, and, as if she were reading Ruby's mind, then asks, "What did Maya think of him?"

"She . . . didn't like him." Ruby swipes a hand across her mouth. "It kind of pissed me off. I mean, we'd been through some shit together. I'd been a good friend to her, didn't boss her around

65

like she was trying to do me with Redd. She'd never really had a boyfriend, so she didn't know what it was like. Besides, she knew I couldn't be with my mom anymore, and it wasn't like she could help me out. She didn't get it." Ruby sighs. "I think she's still mad at me."

"What makes you say that?"

"I've been writing these letters to her. Mr. Tate thought it might be a good idea to write to somebody to help me remember stuff."

Cadence nods like she already knew about Mr. Tate's suggestion.

"She hasn't written back." Ruby mindlessly presses the bruises on her wrists. "I don't even know if the guards are mailing them."

"Why did you choose Maya?"

"Because she's a friend," Ruby says, like the answer should be obvious.

"You must feel like she's still a good friend for you to want to write to her."

Ruby isn't sure if Maya would agree. She shrugs.

"So Maya's your age?" Cadence says, leaning back in her chair.

"A couple years older. We went to the same school. She's a senior now."

"I see." Cadence makes a note. "And what do you like most about her?"

"I don't know." Ruby shifts again. It's impossible to get comfortable in these metal chairs. "Lots of things. She looked out for me when things got bad. She's a good listener. Everyone liked her."

"And she liked you."

Ruby scratches the back of her neck, considering. "She did stuff for me when she didn't have to."

66

"Like what?"

"Bring me those milkshakes and told me they were free, even though I knew her manager took them out of her paycheck. She didn't expect anything in return when she did stuff like that."

"Sounds like Maya is kind."

"Yeah." Ruby doesn't bother hiding her smile this time. "She's smart, too. Writes for the school paper, that sort of thing. And she's funny without trying. We like the same kind of music. She gives good advice. Mostly." She nods to herself. "We just clicked as soon as we met. Maya likes Tex-Mex, probably even more than me. She's a queso addict."

"She *is* smart."

Ruby actually lets out a genuine laugh at that. "Yeah. She wants to be a doctor or nurse." Her smile fades as she remembers the tears in Maya's eyes. "Last time I saw her, we had a fight."

"About what?"

"Something she did." Ruby gives a small shake of her head. "She was in a bad place for a while, but she's better. She lives with her sister now."

"Who did she live with before?"

Ruby bites her lip. There's no way she's going to tell another person Maya's secret. She's learned her lesson. She clears her throat. "So. That's Maya."

The woman watches her, allowing the silence to lengthen, but Ruby is determined not to crack. After what seems like forever, Cadence apparently decides to move on, because the next thing she says is "And you've been giving your letters to the guards?"

"Yeah, they told me to do that. I figure they might be reading them, but . . ." Another guard's footsteps thud outside the door and stop when he reaches Dickhead. It's the guard with the dandruff flakes and shifty eyes; Ruby stiffens. "Why do you ask?"

Cadence's gaze darts, as if checking to make sure the guards aren't listening through the door, before she lowers her voice. "Nothing, really. It's only that I've heard stories about some of the guards skimming from the mail." She shakes her head. "I know you're probably not sending anything of value to Maya, but if you want, I could mail your letters. I'll even add the stamp."

Ruby wonders if the guard put a stamp on her letters like he said he would or if he even mailed them. "You won't read them if I give them to you?"

"Only if you give me a reason."

She wonders what would constitute a reason.

"Up to you." Cadence scribbles something else on her notepad. "You're welcome to keep giving them to the guards if you prefer."

Ruby glances past Dickhead to the scruffy guard. He's the one who took her last letter, saying he was doing her a big favor. If she keeps asking him to help, she knows he'll eventually expect something in return. They always do. "Yeah, okay."

"Great," Cadence says and slips her notes inside her messenger bag.

"What are you doing?" Ruby points to the caged clock, her stomach plummeting at the thought of having to return to her own cage so soon. "Time's not up."

"I didn't get a chance to eat lunch." Cadence buckles the latch on her leather messenger bag. "Perhaps we could share something from the vending machine since you said you're a little hungry too?"

Ruby almost laughs at Cadence's obvious ploy to get her to talk more while she eats. She notices the dandruff guard is now gone, but a familiar panic still twists in her stomach. Redd won't like it if Ruby tells the social worker any more than she already has.

"Of course, if you aren't hungry now . . ."

She tries a breath and wonders if she could talk about him. The good parts, anyway. It *did* feel really nice to talk about him before. Like he was real, and she hadn't just imagined him. And maybe Cadence could even find him for her. Or bring him to visit her? She seems like the type of person who would be able to track somebody down.

Ruby's heart beats with possibility as she nods. "Do they have Flamin' Hot Cheetos?"

History of violence?

Possible

FEBRUARY 16, 2023

Dear Maya,

I put the jail's address on my last letter again, so I thought I might have heard from you by now. Are you pissed I asked you to talk to Redd? I shouldn't have done that, but I didn't know where else to turn. I won't do it again, okay?

I'd still like to hear from you. Maybe you could tell me something about your new life. Are you writing for the school paper still? Or what about your sister's apartment? Do you still want to be a nurse like her? Or did you decide to become a doctor? I liked when you said you wanted to help kids who've been through shit like we have. I think you'd be good at that. Do you have a boyfriend?

Now that I'm thinking about it, maybe you're too busy to write with studying and everything.

Did you hear what they're saying I did on the news? Is that why you're not writing? Cadence (the social worker, you probably remember that) tells me to "tune it out." Maybe if you can tune it out too, you won't be so mad and will remember the me who used to bug you on your shift at Sonic instead. The one you would sneak free milkshakes and fries to because you knew I hadn't eaten in days. If you think of that, maybe you won't be so mad when you get my letters?

I really hope you're reading them at least, because I wanted to tell you my good news. You'll never believe it, but I got a job here! They've got me mopping floors and cleaning the cafeteria tables and stuff. And now they'll put money in my account and I can buy from the vending machine when Cadence visits.

The best part is I get out of my cell. Today was my first day of work. There's other inmates in the kitchen area, but they all left me alone. They probably don't want to get in any trouble. This is one of the better jobs, and they sure as hell don't want to end up scrubbing shit out of the toilets instead. There's a guard who is there just to watch me. I'm supposed to call her by her last name (Harrison), not her first name. I think she wants me to call her that so she blends in with the guys. I've seen how they tease her for being short and try to touch her like they do to us, but I think if it came down to it, she could kick most of their asses.

God, I miss real food. Mostly they make this tasteless shit, even worse than in juvie. The cooks really can't help it, though. You should see what they have to work with. Swear to God, dinner tonight was a hot dog between two pieces of crappy white bread with some brown shit smeared on top. Thankfully, I snuck some sugar packets from one of the tables during my shift. Now I'm pouring them onto my tongue and letting the crystals melt. It's almost like candy. So good.

The work made today go faster, but there's still nothing I can do about the nights. I keep flipping through the wall calendar Mr. Tate gave me with pictures of different kinds of dogs for every month. I decided to hang it above my bed to give me something else to look at besides all the gray and the cross. He gave it to me so I wouldn't have to wonder how many days it is until my trial. I counted 4 times tonight so far. My trial starts on July 5, and it's 139 days until then. I thought counting over and over might help. Remember how you used to tell me to count when it happened? You said it was like you left your body if you counted and that shit wasn't happening to you anymore.

The problem is there's too much time to count. Funny how time seems all stretched out in here. I never paid that much attention to it before. But now it's like I can feel every second. Sometimes it's so much, I think I might choke myself. . . . They took away my blankets and pillow so I couldn't. Cadence says I shouldn't think like that, but she doesn't know what it's like for girls like us.

Anyway, I really would like to hear about your new life. I'll try to write again soon.

Your friend,
Ruby

VANELLI: Detective Martinez, was the truck you located Mr. Hanson's truck?

MARTINEZ: Yes. The victim's truck was parked in front of a Tom Thumb grocery store on Maxwell Boulevard.

VANELLI: Did you use the license plate number to make that determination?

MARTINEZ: No, it was a brand-new truck with paper plates, so we had to run a search based on the VIN.

VANELLI: Once you determined you had, in fact, located the victim's truck, what happened next?

MARTINEZ: After asking around, we were told by one of those kids who collect the carts that a girl had been seen walking from the truck in the Tom Thumb parking lot to the nearby Super 8 motel. He said she looked pretty shaken.

TATE: Objection, hearsay.

THE COURT: Sustained.

VANELLI: Did you go to the Super 8 motel?

MARTINEZ: Yes, I first talked with the motel's front-desk clerk and described the suspect—by that time we already had a picture of the suspect, too.

VANELLI: How did you obtain a picture of the suspect?

MARTINEZ: The victim's home had one of those video doorbells that captures footage of folks as they approach the front door. It was part of the victim's home-security system, and we captured a still from that footage.

VANELLI: So you captured a still photo from that video footage of the suspect?

TATE: Objection, leading.

THE COURT: Sustained. Mr. Vanelli, rephrase.

VANELLI: Yes, Your Honor. Detective, you had a picture of the person who you believed to have been in the house with Mr. Hanson when he was murdered from Mr. Hanson's home-security system?

MARTINEZ: Yes, there's video footage of them entering the home together. She left alone.

VANELLI: And when you say "them," who do you mean?

MARTINEZ: The victim and the suspect entered the home together at around 1700.

VANELLI: They entered around 5:00 p.m.?

MARTINEZ: Yes, the camera was triggered by motion, so anytime it sensed motion, the camera would start recording. The video footage was time-stamped.

VANELLI: What time did the suspect leave?

MARTINEZ: She exited the front door about 2045, so around 8:45 p.m.

VANELLI: And she left alone?

MARTINEZ: That's right.

VANELLI: Were there also security cameras inside the home?

MARTINEZ: Unfortunately, no. The doorbell camera was the only one.

VANELLI: And you said, after talking to someone

at the grocery store where the victim's truck was located, you went to the front-desk clerk of the Super 8 motel?

MARTINEZ: That's right. The clerk made a positive ID based on the photo I showed him. Said he thought the suspect's name was Ruby. He didn't know her last name, and we learned she was staying in room 6A. Apparently, she had been staying there a few months with a man who was renting rooms 6A and 7A. They were adjoining rooms.

VANELLI: So after learning the suspect was in room 6A, what did you do next, Detective?

MARTINEZ: After knocking and announcing, we entered room 6A to find the suspect alone.

VANELLI: And do you see the person you found at the Super 8 motel, room 6A, in this courtroom today?

MARTINEZ: [Nods]

THE COURT: Detective, you need to answer aloud for the record.

MARTINEZ: Oh, sorry. Yes.

VANELLI: Could you point her out to the Court and identify what she's wearing?

MARTINEZ: She's over there at that table next to the guy wearing the red tie with the penguins on it. And she has on a—what is it?—a dark green shirt and navy skirt. Looks a lot more sober now than when I found her, I can tell you that much.

TATE: Your Honor?

THE COURT: All right. Move on, please.

VANELLI: May the record reflect that the detective has identified the Defendant?

THE COURT: So reflected.

VANELLI: Okay, Detective, did you notice any injuries on the Defendant?

MARTINEZ: No, she seemed perfectly fine.

VANELLI: No cuts?

MARTINEZ: No cuts, no bruises. Nothing.

VANELLI: So you found the Defendant in room 6A. Did you find anything else?

MARTINEZ: There was drug paraphernalia, a bong, and a plastic cup with purple drank residue.

VANELLI: And what is purple drank?

MARTINEZ: It's a recreational drug. Illegal.

VANELLI: And what is it, exactly?

MARTINEZ: It's a combination of prescription-grade cough syrup and soda. It's sometimes mixed with some kind of hard candy to make it taste sweeter.

VANELLI: I see, and did you have the Defendant tested for intoxicants?

MARTINEZ: Yes, once we got to the station, we did a blood draw on her.

VANELLI: And what did you find?

MARTINEZ: The suspect's blood was positive for opioids.

VANELLI: And would that be consistent with consumption of purple drank?

MARTINEZ: Yes, drank typically contains codeine.

VANELLI: And can you tell by the test when a person last ingested purple drank?

MARTINEZ: Not precisely. It depends on too many factors. How big a person is. Whether they are repeatedly using. Stuff like that. But usually, a positive blood draw means the person ingested the drug in the last twenty-four to forty-eight hours.

VANELLI: So the test tells you that, in the day or two before testing, the Defendant had ingested opioids?

MARTINEZ: That's correct.

VANELLI: Okay. What else did you find in room 6A?

MARTINEZ: The victim's wallet was found on the bed next to her. There was no money inside, which family members indicated was strange since the victim usually carried at least a few hundred dollars in cash.

TATE: Objection, hearsay.

THE COURT: Sustained.

MARTINEZ: She probably stole the money and used it for drugs.

TATE: Your Honor, objection, speculation. And we also object on the basis of relevance since the witness is testifying when no question has been asked.

THE COURT: Sustained on both counts. Detective, I'll remind you to wait for a question before you answer. Continue, Mr. Vanelli.

VANELLI: And based on your twenty-six years of experience, what did you conclude based on your findings at the motel?

MARTINEZ: That the suspect had entered the victim's home in order to rob him. She killed him and then took off with his truck and wallet.

VANELLI: After you concluded the Defendant killed Mr. Hanson, what did you do next?

MARTINEZ: Since we had a shooting here, I bagged her hands.

VANELLI: And why would you do that?

MARTINEZ: To preserve evidence. Gunshot residue test.

VANELLI: You were confident you'd caught the person who had shot Mr. Hanson?

MARTINEZ: Yes.

VANELLI: And that person is the Defendant, who is sitting in this courtroom today?

MARTINEZ: That's correct.

VANELLI: So what did you do next?

MARTINEZ: I Mirandized the suspect, arrested her, and brought her in for questioning.

VANELLI: And did she answer your questions once you got to the police station?

MARTINEZ: Not really. She was pretty quiet, but that didn't matter. All of the evidence pointed to her.

HERE ENDS THE EXCERPT

FEBRUARY 20, 2023

Cadence taps the sealed letter Ruby just gave her against her hand. She examines the cat poster. Whoever decided to place a dangling cat with the words "Hang in There" in a women's jail has to be one sick son of a bitch.

Her client is on the other side of the table. They've switched places—the girl behind the table and farther away from the door. *To mix things up* is what Cadence told Ruby. But in actuality she was worried that jumpy guard might barge in again and cause Ruby more harm if she was within easy reach.

After all, Cadence spotted the scars when the girl's oversize shirt slipped off her shoulder at their meeting in juvie last November. She asked the jail's physician about them, and he confirmed there are many. She sees the bruises on the girl's wrists, the crescent moons caused by digging fingernails into the flesh of her hands. Not to mention the dark circles under anxious eyes that are always scanning for danger.

She's been told of the sheets and pillow removed from her cell *just in case.*

Cadence steps away from the wall and places Ruby's letter inside her messenger bag. "I've been wondering about your mother. Does she know you're here?" She lowers herself into the chair across from Ruby and slides her long legs under the table.

The darting eyes find her. "No, and I want to keep it that way."

"You don't think she's worried?"

Ruby lets out a harsh laugh. "It's not like in the movies where she's going to make me some cocoa and tell me everything bad in my life will sort itself out."

Cadence tilts her head. "I could try to reach out to her."

Ruby's expression hardens. "I don't want to talk about my mom." Cadence is debating whether she should press harder when she hears the soft beg in the girl's voice. "Please."

She considers her young client before picking up her notepad and pen. "We haven't talked about your dad yet."

Ruby's hands find the back of her neck and then the hair above her ears. She tugs the ends, like she's still not used to how short it is. "What do you want to know?"

Cadence flips through the pages until she finds one that's blank. "Tell me the first thing that comes to mind."

"He left."

She nods. "Anything else?" The girl doesn't answer immediately, and Cadence decides it may be time to let silence do the work. She rests her notepad on her lap, allowing the absence of sound to fill the room.

Ruby has a far-off look in her eyes. "There is one thing," she says after a while. "I'm not sure if it's real or not."

"That's okay," Cadence says.

"He worked the night shift at this office building." Ruby's eyebrows scrunch together. "I think he would sometimes bring me there with him when he worked. Maybe when Mom was . . ." She doesn't finish her thought. "I don't remember much, but I have this memory of waking up in this strange room with red chairs. I was screaming, scared."

"Why were you scared?"

"I didn't know where I was." Ruby shifts uncomfortably. "I cried so hard, snot was running into my mouth."

"And your dad was there?" Cadence asks.

Ruby nods. "He came flying in like Superman or something and got me a Twix out of the vending machine to help calm me down." Her stomach gurgles.

The sound unsettles Cadence. "Are you still not getting enough to eat? Maybe I should talk to the guard."

"No," Ruby says, pinching the skin between her thumb and forefinger. "Dad said I'd had a bad dream and sang to me until I stopped crying."

"Do you remember what he sang?"

A slight smile tugs at Ruby's mouth, and Cadence can't help but catch a glimpse of the child beneath the mask. "No. But Mom said I got my singing voice from him."

"That must've made you proud."

The child vanishes as quickly as she came. "Not really. That's why she never wanted me singing around her."

"And how old were you—when he left?"

"Four, maybe?" Ruby shakes her head. "It was my fault."

Cadence opens her mouth to reassure Ruby that couldn't have been the case—that it was never the case—but then reminds herself: *Just let her talk.*

After a brief silence, Ruby shrugs. "I think he figured I was always going to be needing something from him and it was too much."

"But of course kids need things." Cadence lowers her pen. "Food and shelter. Love and comfort. That's normal."

Ruby flinches. "So is it *normal* I kept singing that stupid song every night, thinking it might bring him back? Is it *normal* my mom cried when I sang, but I kept doing it anyway until her boyfriend finally told me to shut the fuck up?"

Cadence wills her face to remain neutral, reminded of her own mother and the hungover men who yelled at her time after time after time to shut the fuck up before they slept it off.

"Mom said it wasn't going to bring him back, and I needed to stop."

Cadence squeezes her pen, puts her own memories out of her mind. "You said 'that song.' So you do recall what he sang to you."

Ruby crosses her arms over her chest.

"Okay," Cadence says, deciding not to push. "Did you hear from him again after he left?"

"Once." Ruby's arms loosen. "There was a ring he sent for my sixth birthday—like, a silver band with a turquoise heart? I'd been missing him really bad, and it appeared like magic."

Cadence nods. "Sounds pretty."

Ruby looks at her right hand as if imagining. "I thought it was perfect, even though it was too big at first and would only stay on my thumb. I was still wearing it when the cops picked me up. It pinched like hell, but I didn't care." She brushes a finger across the spot where the ring once resided. "I never took it off until they arrested me."

"And you wore it there on your right pinkie?"

"Every day." Ruby presses her lips together and then sighs. "They had to cut it off."

Cadence scribbles a note about the ring. "That must've been hard."

"They put it in this envelope, said I'll get it back if I ever get out of here. Do you really think I have a chance of getting out?"

Cadence stops writing and looks up. There she is again: the child.

Yes. No. Maybe, if you tell the truth. Maybe, if you lie.

Cadence knows avoidance is a form of lying. She knows Ruby knows this. But for reasons she can't explain, Cadence can't bear the thought of hurting Ruby with the truth, even if Ruby knows it already: How easy it will be for the prosecutor to paint her as the girl looking for trouble, the addict who was so desperate for her next hit that she'd go so far as killing someone for the money to get it. And how hard it will be to convince anyone otherwise, no matter what they learn about Ruby and Eric Hanson and the day he died.

"You know what?" Cadence says, returning her notepad to her bag. "I think I saw a Twix in the vending machine earlier. Want one?"

Ruby doesn't answer.

"My treat," Cadence says.

"Yeah, sure," Ruby says, the child disappearing once more.

THE COURT: All right, the Court agrees that Dr. Quincy has met the requirements of an expert witness in forensic science and will be recognized as such.

VANELLI: Thank you, Your Honor.

THE COURT: Any objection, Counselor?

TATE: No, Your Honor.

THE COURT: Then let's continue.

After being duly sworn, **DR. DELL QUINCY** testified as follows:

VANELLI: Since the jury has already heard your qualifications, Dr. Quincy, let's get to your report, marked as State's Exhibit 5. Do you have that in front of you?

QUINCY: Yes.

VANELLI: Can you tell me generally what Exhibit S-5 contains?

QUINCY: It's the report I created that lists my findings based on the evidence in this case. Primarily testing blood samples, skin-cell samples, things like that.

VANELLI: Testing for what?

QUINCY: Mostly DNA. I received DNA samples from both the victim and the Defendant and then compared them to the evidence collected by DPD. In other words, I compared samples of blood found on the items submitted for testing by DPD to DNA samples provided by the Defendant and the victim in this case.

VANELLI: And by "DPD," you're referring to the Dallas Police Department?

QUINCY: That's right.

VANELLI: Okay, moving down your report to Sample Q-35, what did you test there?

QUINCY: What I've tagged as Sample Q-35 is the towel taken from room 6A in the Super 8 motel.

TATE: Are we talking about State's Exhibit 16?

VANELLI: My apologies. Yes, that's right. Exhibit 16.

TATE: Thank you.

VANELLI: So on what's now marked State's Exhibit 16, what did you determine from the blood sample?

QUINCY: That the DNA markers from the sample matched those of the victim in this case.

VANELLI: Anything else?

QUINCY: Yes, we also found skin cells belonging to the Defendant on the towel mixed with the victim's blood cells, and it was a bit unusual.

VANELLI: Why was it unusual?

QUINCY: You have to scrub pretty hard to get the number of skin cells we found on the towel.

VANELLI: So, based on those findings, is it reasonable to conclude the Defendant used the towel to wipe off the victim's blood from her skin?

QUINCY: That's correct.

VANELLI: And moving to Line Item Q-13 in your report, you also tested samples taken from beneath the Defendant's fingernails?

QUINCY: That's right. Scrapings from beneath the Defendant's fingernails show the DNA markings match those of the victim, both blood and skin.

VANELLI: So the victim's blood and his skin cells were found beneath her fingernails?

TATE: Objection, leading the witness.

THE COURT: Sustained. Rephrase, Counselor.

VANELLI: So what did that lead you to believe?

QUINCY: That both the blood and skin cells beneath the Defendant's fingernails belonged to the victim.

VANELLI: Now, there was a gunshot residue test here?

QUINCY: That's right. But no residue was found on the Defendant's hands.

VANELLI: Is it common to not have gun residue even if someone has shot a gun?

QUINCY: If the person washes her hands thoroughly, that can also wash away any residue.

VANELLI: But still leave DNA under the fingernails?

QUINCY: Absolutely. Most people do a very superficial washing of their hands. So while the residue can be washed from the skin, DNA from blood or skin can still remain under the nails.

VANELLI: Thank you. And Exhibits 21 and 22? I believe those are Q-3 and Q-4 in your report.

QUINCY: Let me just flip to that. Ah, yes. That was a skirt and T-shirt that I tested. There were blood flecks with DNA markers consistent with the victim's blood on both items.

VANELLI: So the victim's blood was on both the Defendant's skirt and T-shirt found in the motel room?

QUINCY: Yes.

VANELLI: Now, if you could please look to your findings on State's Exhibit 25—the bullet lodged in the wall of the master bedroom. Was that item tested for DNA?

QUINCY: It was. But we found none. And we also found none on State's Exhibit 28, the bullet located outside the glass door.

VANELLI: And State's Exhibit 26?

QUINCY: That was a slug found out on the pool coping, the southeast corner of the pool.

VANELLI: And did you find any DNA on that bullet?

QUINCY: There were traces of both blood and brain matter that matched the victim's DNA markers in this case.

VANELLI: Now, State's Exhibit 27 is the bullet that was extracted from Mr. Hanson's lung?

QUINCY: Yes, I believe that's correct. Yes, yes, that's right.

VANELLI: Did you test that?

QUINCY: No. Since it was found inside the victim, there was no need for DNA testing.

VANELLI: I have nothing further, Your Honor.

HERE ENDS THE EXCERPT

FEBRUARY 22, 2023

Dear Maya,

I'm eating cheese! I know that's a weird way to start a letter, but I'm so excited to have something to eat besides the crappy meat glop and dry bread they serve us in the cafeteria.

I'll tell you more about the cheese in a second, but first I wanted to tell you I made a friend today. Poppy is one of the inmates and her job is to help with the cooking. Since I mop the cafeteria floor after dinner now, she started randomly talking to me. She really isn't supposed to, but Harrison doesn't give a shit so long as we keep doing our work. I think Harrison gets that I'm kind of missing being around people.

Anyway, Harrison was telling us about this inmate over in Cell Block G named Ally. She said it was okay if I told you about it since it's all over the news. I can't remember her last name, but maybe you've heard of her? Ally has been on trial and is waiting for her verdict. The word is the jury was trying to decide whether she was guilty or not when the judge shut them down and shipped them off to some hotel for the night even though they hadn't decided whether Ally was guilty or not. I didn't even know a judge could pull that kind of shit.

Apparently she microwaved her baby. That seems pretty fucked up, right? The weird thing is, from all I've been told Ally is really sweet. Even Harrison said so. I guess everyone has a breaking point.

I keep thinking about Ally even though I don't know her. It would totally suck to have to wait like that. Knowing this is it. Poppy is in the same block as her and said everyone's trying to think good thoughts, saying it's a good sign it's taking so long. That's what Poppy told me. She said Ally has been on trial almost 2 weeks. The jury's deciding if she's guilty of capital murder (same as me), but since she's an adult, Ally can get the death penalty. She's 19. That's only 4 years older than me. Next thing I know, I started crying right there in the middle of the cafeteria. I don't know what happened, but I couldn't stop. Then I started worrying somebody would hear, and that only made me cry more.

Harrison pretty much ignored me since I was still mopping through it. But Poppy stepped out of the kitchen to try to talk me down even though she didn't have to.

Turns out Poppy is from our neighborhood. Maybe you know her. Poppy Williams? She's probably 23 or 24, so older than us. Anyway, she said my crying reminded her of her kid when he gets all worked up and she has to remind him to breathe or whatever.

I finally stopped crying when Poppy said she'd get me some cheese from the kitchen if I'd quit blubbering. She already got me a slice that I put down my pants to bring back to my cell. I think Harrison saw, but she didn't say anything. I'm trying to eat real slow to make it last while I write to you.

The cheese is awesome, but I can't let myself cry in here again. Not ever. I don't know what made me do that.

It's nice to have a friend again who sneaks me food kind of like you used to do. You'd like Poppy if you met her. I already told *her she reminded me of you. Don't worry, I didn't tell her anything about you or the stuff that happened to you. But is it okay if I ask Harrison where your grandpa got locked up? I think the guards can find that kind of thing out. I'm so happy he'll die in there and you'll never have to see him again.*

Better finish my cheese!

Your friend,
Ruby

FEBRUARY 27, 2023

Ruby's head is throbbing. She can't make herself still, though she keeps trying to sit on her hands to stop them from shaking. It almost feels as if she's going through withdrawal again. She wonders what the hell the jail's doctor, the one who told her just to call him "Doc," gave her.

"That's quite a knot on your forehead," Cadence observes.

It's still fucking February. Cadence complained how it's that wet-cold outside and her throat is covered in a heavy checked scarf, so Ruby wonders why this tiny room is so thick with heat. She pulls at the undershirt that's stuck to her back with sweat.

"Can you tell me how you got that?" Cadence asks, gesturing in the general direction of Ruby's face.

Ruby is not in the mood. She glares at the scarf around Cadence's throat, wondering how the hell she can stand to wear that thing in this heat. She wants to rip it from her neck.

"Did you get into a fight?"

Ruby rolls her eyes.

"You look angry."

No shit. "Don't you ever get pissed?"

"Sure, I get upset," Cadence says, pointing to Ruby's face again, "but that doesn't usually result in a head injury."

"It's that fucking preacher's fault."

"Preacher?"

"Yeah," Ruby says, impatiently thumbing toward the door. "You know, the one who comes in here a few times a week."

Cadence's eyes widen. "*He* did that to you?"

"No," Ruby says, shaking her head. "He made me do it."

"I'm not following."

Ruby huffs her annoyance. "I was out walking in the yard by myself since they only let me go out when no one else is out there." She checks to make sure Cadence is with her. When she nods, Ruby continues. "I was out there and singing real quiet so the guard couldn't hear when this preacher guy comes up to me and hands me a booklet."

"What kind of booklet?"

"One of those with a question on the front: *Are you saved?*"

"That upset you?" Cadence asks, her voice edged with judgment.

"Yeah, and then the asshole had the nerve to smile at me." Ruby scoffs. "Here I was just singing and getting the sun on my face, and he hands me that bullshit? I ripped it up right in front of him."

"Why did that upset you?"

Because Maya was convinced God wouldn't save her after what she did, and if he wouldn't save Maya, there certainly wasn't any hope for me. "I'd like to stand." When Cadence nods, Ruby rises from her chair and begins to pace. "I was thinking about this lady, Ally. One of the guards in here told me about her. She was on trial for capital murder, same as me, and she got the death penalty. She wasn't saved." She stops in front of the cat poster, wanting to rip it off the wall. Wanting to rip everything clean. She comes to a stop right next to Cadence, every muscle tight. "And I sure as hell don't see God in here helping me out."

Cadence quickly rises from her chair, and now she's the one looking down on Ruby. "Do you believe in a god like that—one who goes around saving people?"

"How the hell should I know?"

"No judgment either way," Cadence says, hands turned outward.

Ruby shakes her head. "All I'm saying is that judgy bullshit isn't helping anyone in here."

"So you were worried about what's going to happen at your trial."

"Of course I'm worried." Ruby begins to pace again, moving away from Cadence into the far corner of the room. "I told the guard to take me back to my cell. Dickhead didn't care. He was happy to have more time for a smoke break."

"Dickhead?"

Ruby thrusts a finger toward the door. "The guard that brings me in here."

Cadence releases a bark of a laugh before clearing her throat. "I still don't understand how you got that knot and bruise on your forehead."

Ruby returns to the other side of the table and grips the back of her chair so hard, her knuckles turn white. "When I was walking to my cell, I got even angrier at that preacher. He took up like half my time outside with his shit. What if they won't let me go out again?"

"I'm sure that won't happen," Cadence says, not sounding sure.

"I was so pissed, I wanted to tear something from the wall in my cell."

With the table between them again, Cadence lowers herself into her chair, picks up her pad, and starts scratching out notes.

"I couldn't get the damned sink-toilet combo to pull away, which made me even madder. I kind of blanked. All I remember is screaming, and at some point I must have slammed my head against the wall."

Cadence looks up. "So you injured yourself?"

Ruby drops into her chair. "Yeah, Dickhead took me to see Doc to make sure I didn't have a concussion. I don't, but my head is fucking killing me."

"Why do you think the preacher upset you so much?"

"Because he's full of shit, and they let him in here anyway?" Cadence's eyes aren't judgmental, aren't fighting with her the way Ruby feels like she's been fighting with herself. She sighs. "I don't know, I guess the stress is starting to fuck with my head. I mean, what if I end up getting life?"

Cadence stops writing. "I know that it's a lot. But we can only take this one day at a time, remember? Brian is working hard for you, and—"

"Yeah, I know, the more I can tell you about what happened before I was arrested, blah, blah, blah." Ruby presses her fingernails into her hands, finding the tiny crescent-moon scars. "Prison is supposed to be even harder than this. And what am I going to do when I turn eighteen and they put me in one of those cells with someone else?"

Cadence shakes her head. "Listen to me. We're doing everything we can to prevent that from happening. You know that, right? I promised."

Ruby nods, but she knows everyone lies.

THE COURT: Mr. Vanelli, am I remembering correctly that the State intends to call its ballistics expert next?

VANELLI: That's correct, Your Honor.

THE COURT: And no objections to Dr. Roth as an expert in ballistics, Mr. Tate?

TATE: No, Your Honor. We have agreed that Dr. Roth is an expert in that area and also in fingerprint analysis.

THE COURT: That's right. I remember now. Sorry, I was confusing this case with another pretrial hearing late yesterday. Also a fingerprint-analysis expert. Okay, now that the Court is on the same page, please proceed with your expert.

VANELLI: Thank you, Your Honor.

After being duly sworn, **DR. GRETA ROTH** testified as follows:

VANELLI: Dr. Roth, you ran the ballistics testing in this case?

ROTH: That's correct.

VANELLI: And can you explain to the jury the purpose of ballistics testing?

ROTH: Yes. Forensic ballistics is the science of matching a bullet to a particular firearm.

VANELLI: How do you go about doing that?

ROTH: It's primarily accomplished by comparison-microscope techniques in which a test bullet from the suspect weapon is compared to the bullet or bullets from the scene of a crime. The micro-machining marks on the barrel's rifling are unique to each particular gun. At least for a period of time.

VANELLI: What about fired cases, can you test those as well?

ROTH: Yes, firing-pin indentations in the primer will also show distinctive machine markings, which are invisible to the naked eye.

VANELLI: Can you detect fingerprints on bullets?

ROTH: Usually not on the bullets themselves. If we're lucky, the person who loaded the weapon will have left fingerprints on the cartridge cases.

VANELLI: Okay, I'm going to have you turn your attention to State's Exhibit 25. That's Q-13 in your report. Can you find that, please?

ROTH: Found it.

VANELLI: And State's Exhibit 25 was the bullet DPD found lodged in the wall of the master bedroom?

ROTH: Yes, it was the slug, that's right. Nine-millimeter.

VANELLI: Moving to State's Exhibit 26. What did you learn about that bullet?

ROTH: I identified it as a nine-millimeter as well.

VANELLI: So was the bullet extracted from the

victim's lung, State's Exhibit 27, also nine-millimeter?

TATE: Objection. He's leading his own witness.

THE COURT: Sustained. Remember you're on direct, Counselor.

VANELLI: Yes, Your Honor. Dr. Roth, what did you learn about the bullet extracted from the victim's lung?

ROTH: That the slug was also nine-millimeter.

VANELLI: Were you able to determine whether the bullets you tested were all fired from the same weapon?

ROTH: Yes.

VANELLI: And how do you know that?

ROTH: Like I mentioned, there were micromachining marks left on the fired bullets that match it to the gun in question. Let me see—the gun marked as State's Exhibit 12.

VANELLI: And State's Exhibit 12 was the gun found inside the purse located at the Super 8 motel?

ROTH: I believe that's correct, yes.

VANELLI: And what type of gun is State's Exhibit 12?

ROTH: It is a SIG Sauer P320 nine-millimeter handgun.

VANELLI: And both the bullet that was extracted from the victim's chest and the bullet that passed through the victim's skull, what caliber were they?

ROTH: Both were nine-millimeter.

VANELLI: Moving to fingerprints, you dusted a plastic cup for fingerprints? Now looking at Exhibit 17.

ROTH: Yes, there was a plastic cup found in the room at the Super 8. There was a purple residue inside the cup.

VANELLI: I see. And did you test that residue?

ROTH: No, my understanding is DPD tested the substance.

VANELLI: Okay, did you find anything on the cup itself?

ROTH: Yes, I found a smeared thumbprint and a clear index finger that matched the Defendant's prints, along with the prints of someone by the name of—let me find it—Joe Shandler.

VANELLI: How did you obtain the prints of Mr. Shandler?

ROTH: Law enforcement maintains a database of anyone who has been previously booked in the Dallas County jail, and there was a match there.

VANELLI: Thank you. Now, did you perform any fingerprint testing on the weapons?

ROTH: Yes, that's, uh, that's on page two here. I tested for prints on three guns, one found in a chest of drawers or nightstand, one found beneath a mattress, and one found inside a purse. All located by DPD at the Super 8 motel.

VANELLI: And what were your findings?

ROTH: All three guns had the Defendant's prints and the prints of Joe Shandler.

VANELLI: And were the victim's prints on any of the guns?

ROTH: Yes, we found a few smeared prints at the tip and the handle that matched the victim's fingerprints. Those prints were on the handgun located inside the purse by DPD.

VANELLI: And were the Defendant's prints also on the handle?

ROTH: Yes, we were able to lift one clean set. Most of the prints on the handle and tip were smeared.

VANELLI: And that indicates a struggle for the gun?

TATE: Objection, speculation.

THE COURT: I'll allow it.

VANELLI: You can answer the question.

ROTH: Yes, smeared prints like we had here from both the victim and the Defendant could indicate a struggle for control of the gun.

VANELLI: So, based on your findings, is it reasonable to conclude that the gun found in the Defendant's purse is the one that was used to kill the victim?

ROTH: In all likelihood, yes.

HERE ENDS THE EXCERPT

Gun in purse

Sexual
Ruby shuts dow
Problem

FEBRUARY 28, 2023

Dear Maya,

I've been thinking about the first time I saw you. I never told you this—I know you probably remember us first meeting at Sonic. But I'd seen you before that. It was the end of my eighth-grade year, and my class was visiting the high school to learn about all the "exciting opportunities waiting for us." Classes, sports, school dances, all that. But all I wanted to do was hide.

It was hot as fuck that day, but you were wearing a long-sleeved hoodie with your shorts. Your curls were longer then, pulled back with a headband and touching your shoulders. When you got to the bathroom, you must've thought nobody else was there, because you took off your hoodie to splash cold water across your face. But I was there, peeking through the crack in the door in the bathroom stall. Your hands shook as you turned off the faucet. You were leaning over the sink, and I saw the bruises on your arm. The kind that fingers make, pressed into skin. And there was a scar—pinkish and round on your brown skin—on your right wrist. The size of a cigar. Right then, I knew we had something in common.

It wasn't until a few weeks later when I got the nerve to talk to you. I found your account on Instagram and saw you were Maya Olimpia Jones. I thought that was a powerful name for someone with such shaky hands. You didn't post much, but someone tagged you. That's how I figured you worked at the Sonic. I came and said hi to you, and you told me I should try the cookies 'n cream milkshake. "It's like heaven on earth," you said. Remember?

You were going to be a junior, and I was just going to be a freshman, but you must have seen it in me, too, because you acted like you wanted to be my friend right away, and it was almost like I felt protected.

I remember when you taught me to count. "It keeps your mind busy, and it's like you leave," you said while you were adding extra cherries to my milkshake. "It's like a superpower to leave your body like that, so he really can't hurt you anymore."

Did you really believe what you were telling me when you said that? Because I tried. Again and again. I'm still trying to count my way through, but I can never completely leave. Maybe I'm not as powerful as you.

I know I was a bitch the last time we saw each other and I should've been there for you when you were dealing with all of that shit, but I really thought you would have written back by now. How long are you going to stay mad at me?

Your friend,
Ruby

MARCH 2, 2023

Cadence silently studies her client from across the table. Other than handing over the most recent letter she's written to Maya, Ruby hasn't said a word since she entered the interview room. She appears greasy, her short hair sticking out in all directions. Cadence was told Ruby has been prone to outbursts lately, so the guards haven't taken her to the shower in a couple of days. *For her own safety*, they claimed. It's all Cadence can do to keep from covering her nose from the smell that has filled the small room: stale sweat and vaginal stench.

She clears her throat instead. "How's your head?"

Ruby's jaw tightens, the veins in her neck bulging.

Cadence worries her scarf, knowing every bit of trouble the girl causes in jail is potential fuel for the prosecutor. "You seem angry," she says.

Ruby's gaze catches just below Cadence's jaw. "What's with the fucking scarves?"

Cadence stiffens, and for the briefest moment, she wonders if removing the handcuffs wasn't a good idea this time. She's been alone with clients who have suddenly turned violent before; Ruby hadn't seemed the type. Yet. "You don't like this one?"

The girl reaches.

Cadence jerks back, protecting the base of her throat with both hands. "What do you think you're doing?"

Pink floods Ruby's cheeks as she seems to notice her outstretched fingers, bent like claws. She drops back in her chair, folding her arms over her chest. "Nothing. You just wear them all the time. Like in that horror story where the lady wears the green ribbon around her neck until her husband unties it and her head falls off? It's creepy as shit."

Cadence wills her heart to slow as her fingers quickly work the fabric, adjusting, tightening, but her pulse is still pounding by the time she finishes. Her scarf hasn't slipped that much in front of a client, not for a while. She has to be more careful.

"Sure. Cover it up," Ruby huffs. "You expect me to be a goddamn open book, but I ask you about one scar . . ."

I'm not the one on trial for murder, Cadence wants to say but doesn't. She reaches into her bag for her pen and then leans back in her chair. "Why don't you tell me what's really bothering you?"

The girl snorts.

"I don't think you expect me to believe that my scarf is suddenly a problem for you," she says. "So tell me what's going on."

Ruby shakes her head. "I hate this fucking place, that's what's *going on*."

Cadence catches the tremor in Ruby's hands. "I . . . I know how difficult it can be in here. But I don't think it could have been easy for you out there, either."

"Stop with the bullshit," Ruby says, slapping the table. "You said talking to you would help, but it's only making things worse."

"Look, I know you don't believe what I've been telling you, but I've done this before. And I know it will get easier if we keep going." Despite what just happened, Cadence wants to stretch across the table, to touch Ruby's arm. But she doesn't. "These things take time, but I know you can do this. You have to trust me."

"Bullshit," Ruby says, louder. "You don't even know me."

"*I know that*, Ruby." Cadence props the notepad on her lap like a shield. "So help me. Tell me something I don't know about you. Start small, if you'd like."

Ruby sneers.

"Do you have any hobbies?"

"Are you serious right now?"

"Some of the women keep a hobby," Cadence says, crossing and uncrossing her long legs under the table. "Like pottery or drawing."

"Where do you think I am? Some fucking summer camp? No, I don't have any *hobbies*."

Cadence eyes the guard's profile on the other side of the window. *Sure, he comes in when things are calm. But when things actually get dicey . . . He really is a dickhead.*

"I can't sing in here either," Ruby continues, "so don't start on that again."

Cadence returns her focus to Ruby. It's not the first time the girl has mentioned singing. "Would you like to sing?"

"Stop trying to help, okay? This place sucks."

"All right, then. Tell me about that."

"You want to know what I hate about jail?" Ruby pushes back in her chair—metal scraping concrete. "Fine. I hate the taste of orange glop they call food. Last night's dinner is still coating my tongue even after I brushed my teeth with their stupid rubber toothbrush. Too hot in your cell? Too bad. You can't have a fan because they think you'll take it apart and make a weapon."

"Ruby," Cadence says, keeping her voice steady.

107

"Want to talk to someone? You can't. You're all alone in your cell. Want to go outside? Tough shit. It's not on the schedule today. And how about the underwear? These paper panties rub my ass raw."

"*Ruby*," Cadence says, louder.

"Want to sleep? Too bad. Your cell reeks of shit because the toilet is only a foot from your bed. And on top of that, someone on your block is either crying or . . . or moaning."

"Moaning?"

Ruby slaps the table with the flat of her hand. "Because they're fucking masturbating, okay?"

"Ruby," Cadence says one more time, willing herself to remain calm, to remain seated, even as Ruby is standing now. "I know how awful it is here, I do. And you know how unfair I think it is that you—"

"Where's Redd?"

"Redd?"

"Stop with the questions for one fucking second. You know who I'm talking about. I saw you write like a billion notes when I told you about him. He was supposed to be here. We promised we'd take care of each other if either of us ever got in trouble. So where the fuck is he?"

Cadence's eyebrows pull together. There's outrage in the girl's voice, but there's also something more—a deep sadness surrounding Redd. Cadence's expression softens as she realizes why: Ruby loves him.

"And stop looking at me like that." Ruby lifts her chair an inch off the floor and slams it back down, making it clatter against the concrete. It's the same old mask. Ruby isn't angry; she's hurting.

The door flies open. "What's going on?" Dickhead asks.

Oh, sure. Now he comes in. Cadence stands, too. "We're fine. She got a little excited, that's all."

But the guard's focus is on Ruby. "Stupid bitch." He snatches her arm.

Ruby instantly turns wild, grunting and thrashing in his grasp.

A familiar panic seizes Cadence. "Please," she begs as she steps gingerly toward them.

"Stay the fuck away, lady," he says, breath heavy. He yanks Ruby sideways. Cadence backs up, her hands splayed against the light green paint.

Ruby tries to twist free, but his nails rip her skin. "Get your fucking hands off me!"

"So that's how you want it!" he screams, throwing her face-first against the wall.

Cadence suddenly feels helpless, frozen. For a split second, she's under the bed again, dust tickling her throat with rapid breaths as her tiny hands clench at her sides. The vein in his right arm bulges as he throws her mother face-first against the wall. She comes back to herself. "Officer, please," she says, her voice thin.

The handcuffs click—one wrist, two.

Ruby is still grunting and flailing. She kicks but misses. Somehow her lip is bleeding.

"Stop. Kicking," Dickhead huffs as he hits Ruby's hip with the chain before twisting it around her waist.

She buckles, like a fish on a line. There's a smudge of crimson on the wall.

"Ruby," Cadence whispers.

The girl looks, but her eyes have gone black. She thrashes again, and for the first time, Cadence envisions the Ruby that the prosecutor sees: Something dangerous. Something deserving of a cage.

Cadence wraps her arms around herself with a shudder, breath held as the guard drags Ruby away.

MARCH 3, 2023

Dear Maya,

How did you know what my mom's boyfriend was doing to me when I didn't say anything about it? Clay didn't give me bruises on the outside like you had. I didn't have anything to show on the outside. Not then.

I guess I'm thinking about all this because Cadence and I kind of had a fight. She's always pushing me about what I've been through, and all this shit is getting mixed up inside my head. Sometimes I think it would be okay to tell her, but then, when I'm in the room, I can't. Thinking about it only makes it worse. I just want to forget.

Remember that guard Steve I was telling you about? He squeezed my shoulder before lights-out tonight. I almost elbowed him in the balls for touching me. Maybe he knew what I was thinking because he smiled like he knew I couldn't fight back without going on lockdown. Prick.

Steve reminds me of Clay. My stomach hurts just thinking about it. Every time I see him it's like I'm reliving that bullshit when Clay would wake me up and smack my face and it was like a million light bulbs exploding in my eyes. The jagged smile before he pushed my head down so hard, I thought he was going to break my neck. The way his dick bent to the left. The memory makes me gag.

111

Even counting isn't helping anymore. I keep counting the days until my trial, and all it does is make me crazy. I ripped down Mr. Tate's calendar, and I'm staring at the cross behind it. Someone scraped it into the paint above my bed with names inside. Jennifer. Anna. LaToya. I have no idea who they are. Did they get convicted and sent to prison? Or are they back on the outside? Or are they dead?

I added my name to the cross tonight. I etched RUBY in the center of that fucking cross. You once said God meets us where we are. Do you think that's true, even in a shithole like this?

Your friend,
Ruby

THE COURT: Ladies and gentlemen, the Court recognizes Dr. Yuan as an expert witness, and you will weigh her testimony as such.

VANELLI: Thank you, Your Honor.

After being duly sworn, **DR. LUCY YUAN** testified as follows:

VANELLI: Could you please state your name and employer for the record?

YUAN: Sure. Dr. Lucy Yuan. And I'm with the Dallas County Medical Examiner's Office.

VANELLI: I know we went through this during voir dire, but could you please tell us again how long you've been with the Dallas County Medical Examiner's Office?

YUAN: Three years.

VANELLI: And, in short, what duties do you primarily perform as part of the functions of your job?

YUAN: I perform medical exams on deceased individuals. Mostly those who die a sudden, unnatural death.

VANELLI: So, autopsies?

YUAN: That's right.

VANELLI: Getting to this case, you are the medical examiner who performed the autopsy on the victim; is that correct?

YUAN: Yes, I examined Mr. Eric Hanson, aged thirty-two at the time of death.

VANELLI: And you are the person who created the report now marked as State's Exhibit 31?

YUAN: Yes.

VANELLI: Thank you. First of all, did your tests reveal anything, any intoxicants, in Mr. Hanson's bloodstream?

YUAN: Yes, the victim had a BAC, uh, blood-alcohol content, of 0.08.

VANELLI: And would a BAC of 0.08 be considered intoxicated?

YUAN: In the state of Texas, a BAC of 0.08 or more is considered intoxicated, yes.

VANELLI: And is it possible to get an accurate blood-alcohol content after someone has died?

YUAN: Yes. Although there can be some postmortem fermentation, BAC readings up to forty-eight hours after death are typically found to be valid if all protocols are met.

VANELLI: Was the BAC for Mr. Hanson taken within forty-eight hours?

YUAN: Yes, I examined him on January 8, the day after death.

VANELLI: And were all protocols followed?

YUAN: Yes, Mr. Hanson's body was stored in a cool, dry place, and blood was drawn from the femoral veins.

VANELLI: But in Texas, you can be intoxicated in your own home?

TATE: Objection, Your Honor. Dr. Yuan is an expert in cause of death, not the law.

THE COURT: I'll allow it but briefly. Keep it moving, Counselor.

VANELLI: Thank you. You can answer.

YUAN: My understanding is that you cannot drive while intoxicated.

VANELLI: But was Mr. Hanson driving at the time of his death?

TATE: Objection.

THE COURT: Overruled. You can answer, Dr. Yuan.

YUAN: Not to my knowledge, no.

VANELLI: And we've already heard there were multiple lacerations across Mr. Hanson's body. Is that correct?

YUAN: Yes, Mr. Hanson had several lacerations across the right side of his face. His neck. And both arms. I also found a few small pieces of glass still stuck in wounds at his neck and in both arms.

VANELLI: And would you say those wounds are consistent with falling through a glass door?

YUAN: I would. By the time I examined Mr. Hanson, bruises had formed along the right side of his body—his face, arm, right hip—also indicative of a hard fall.

VANELLI: All right, and if you could pick up

State's Exhibit 31. Got it? Okay, please read your conclusion as to the cause of Mr. Hanson's death to the jury.

YUAN: "Homicide caused by multiple gunshot wounds."

VANELLI: So drinking was not the cause of death here?

YUAN: No.

VANELLI: And falling through a glass door was not the cause of death?

YUAN: No.

VANELLI: So what did cause Mr. Hanson's death?

TATE: Objection, asked and answered.

THE COURT: I'll allow it.

VANELLI: Dr. Yuan, what was the cause of Mr. Hanson's death?

YUAN: Multiple gunshot wounds.

VANELLI: Thank you, Dr. Yuan. Now, how many gunshot wounds did Mr. Hanson suffer?

YUAN: I found two and labeled them as such in my autopsy report.

VANELLI: Could you please describe the nature of the wounds to the jury?

YUAN: For the first, a bullet entered the front of the victim's chest cavity, just under the heart, and lodged in the victim's lung. So it was a penetrating wound since there was only an entrance wound.

VANELLI: And the second?

YUAN: The second appears to have entered through the back of the victim's head and exited above the left ear. So a perforating wound with both entrance and exit wounds.

VANELLI: When examining the victim, can you tell how close the shooter was to the victim at the time of the shooting?

YUAN: I can approximate based on the entry sites.

VANELLI: How?

YUAN: Well, with number one, the stippling and soot around the wound at the chest is indicative of close range.

VANELLI: Were both of the wounds inflicted from close range?

YUAN: No, it appears the wound to the head was more from an intermediate range based on the lack of stippling.

VANELLI: Dr. Yuan, was the wound to the chest fatal?

YUAN: If left untreated, yes. It would be fatal, yes.

VANELLI: Was the chest wound his first injury or second?

YUAN: It was his first.

VANELLI: And how do you know that?

YUAN: The shot to the chest, individually, would have been life-threatening. It may have killed him eventually. But with the shot to the head, death would have been instantaneous.

VANELLI: Looking at the evidence, then, the defendant shot Mr. Hanson up close—

TATE: Your Honor.

VANELLI: —and then chased the victim shooting him in the back of the head—

TATE: Your Honor.

VANELLI: —is that correct?

TATE: Objection.

YUAN: It's possible.

THE COURT: Hold on, please. State your objection, Mr. Tate.

TATE: Your Honor, Mr. Vanelli's question fails to lay a proper foundation, is speculative, and is more prejudicial than probative.

THE COURT: Response, Mr. Vanelli?

VANELLI: The expert has already testified that one of the shots was from close range and the other from a distance. I'm merely trying to establish the possibility of order here.

TATE: With all due respect, Your Honor, now he's testifying for the witness.

THE COURT: I tend to agree with Mr. Tate. Restate your question, Mr. Vanelli.

VANELLI: Is it possible the Defendant shot Mr. Hanson at close range and then pursued him when shooting him in the head?

TATE: Objection, speculation.

THE COURT: Overruled. She's an expert, so I'll allow a little leeway.

VANELLI: You can answer, Dr. Yuan.

YUAN: The victim had already been shot by the time he moved outside through the glass door. And that first shot could not have been the shot to the head.

VANELLI: Is it reasonable then to conclude Mr. Hanson was running away from the shooter by the time he received the fatal shot to the head?

YUAN: Yes. It would have been impossible for Mr. Hanson to have received the shot to the head and then run outside.

HERE ENDS THE EXCERPT

MARCH 4, 2023

Cadence hovers as close to the locked door as the armed attendant will allow, while surveying the lobby of the Dallas County jail. The frenetic atmosphere is palpable as families attempt to adhere to the strict visitation policies.

Babies cling to grandmas and aunts. Toddlers cry and scream and dangle from their uncles' legs while teens simply ignore their families altogether. In the chaos of the overcrowded waiting area, Cadence can't help but think of something she read recently: visiting a loved one in jail can make family members feel like "quasi inmates," controlled by intimidation through long waiting times and little advance warning about changes in the rules, and when they finally do make it to the visitation room, they are prohibited from touching their loved one. It's especially hard on the kids.

Cadence shakes her head. If that's what it is like for a child who visits, how does it feel to be a kid locked inside?

The security guards' continuous confiscation of umbrellas, cameras, and pocketknives, followed by the screams of the offenders who brought them, along with the heat and smell of too many bodies, too much despair, makes Cadence's stomach turn. She feels the glares of the adults around her and clutches her credentials tight in her fist in case anybody asks why she's been spared the degradation of being frisked by the guards.

There's the electrical buzz of the lock releasing before the door opens.

"Dr. Ware," the guard calls as he steps into the lobby. It's the one with ears too big for his head. He gives Cadence a nod of recognition before she adjusts the bag over her shoulder, sliding her credentials into the pocket, and follows him inside.

The door latches with a finality behind her as she follows the guard. What's his name again? It starts with a *P*—Paul? Peter? When they've traversed the length of the cinder-block hallway, he gestures to the left.

She stops and points to the right. "The elevators to the meeting rooms are that way."

He shakes his head. "You aren't on the schedule today. You'll have to wait here."

"Here" being the room they sometimes use for art classes. Completely open with three sides surrounded by glass. No privacy. Anybody walking by could see and hear her conversation with Ruby.

Cadence tries a polite smile. "I'll need a room with more privacy, please. I know I neglected to schedule a time today, but there's an emergency in my client's case."

It's a lie. There's no emergency. More like a feeling in the pit of her stomach she hasn't been able to shake since Dickhead dragged Ruby away two days ago. A feeling Ruby might come undone at any second and ruin everything they've been working toward.

"It's never been an issue before," she adds.

"It is today," the guard responds, glancing over his shoulder like he has far better things to do. "You want the room or not?"

Her false smile fades as she thinks of a good name for him. One Ruby might appreciate: *Prick*. It even starts with a *P*.

She nods stiffly.

"Then wait here."

When he's gone, she drops her bag on one of the four octagonal tables bolted to the floor. Taped around the room are the inmates' colorful artwork, mostly sloppy watercolors or paint-by-numbers, until her gaze lands on a pencil sketch in the corner of the room.

Cadence wipes her hands on her blazer as she steps closer to examine the sketch. Two figures are embracing. One of them is a young girl with her eyes closed in comfort. The other is a man—at least, she thinks it's a man. In the place of his face is a skull. He has a knife in his hand.

Phantom pain shimmies along Cadence's throat, and she's fifteen again.

Where is she? he'd yelled at them. The bruises he'd left, purpling the last glimpses she'd had of her mother. His yellow smile and the hawk tattooed across his chest, it's bladelike feathers spread wide from one shoulder to the other. Her grandmother's apron trimmed in pink lace. The glint of silver as Cadence reached. The red stain.

"Are you all right?" It's a deep voice behind her. "I've been calling your name."

Cadence turns now, her hand falling from her scarf, but she can still feel her pulse in her head. She takes a deep breath as she recognizes the face of the balding Black man in the doorway and wonders how long he's been standing there.

"Fred. I'm sorry. You didn't have to come all the way down here," she says. Fred is the assistant deputy chief of detention.

Prick must have complained about her. It wouldn't be the first time one of the guards called her difficult, or more likely a bitch, to those in charge.

Fred shrugs. "It's no problem. I'm sure you've heard about our staff shortages. Things are a little crazy around here." He smiles. "Besides, it's been a while. It's good to see you."

"You too." She shakes his outstretched hand. The pressure from his squeeze is enough to let her know he takes her seriously.

"How's the family?"

"Ian is good. He's in preschool now, and Jack is still teaching art history at SMU and still loving it." She shakes her head. "Look, I'm actually here to see one of my clients."

Fred laughs. "And I'm doing good, too. Thanks for asking."

"I'm sorry," she says for the second time, and smiles warmly. "It's Ruby Monroe, the minor. I've just been really worried about her since our last meeting, which didn't end well, and with her being considered high-risk . . ."

"It's nice to know that some things never change. Still taking work home, I see."

Cadence nods, knowing this is her reputation in the building. Her colleagues are convinced it will lead to her eventual burnout. "I suppose you could say that." They may be right, but she refuses to expunge her client's troubles when she leaves, only to pick them back up when she returns to the office, especially when she's often the only person who *is* thinking about them.

He shrugs. "I wished you'd called first, because I'm afraid you've wasted a trip. You can't see her today. That's what I came to tell you."

Cadence's eyes narrow. She wasn't expecting to be stonewalled today, especially not by Fred. "You know as well as I do that I have the right—"

He puts up a hand. "Ordinarily, I'd agree with you. But your girl has been put on lockdown."

"She what?" She couldn't have heard him right.

"No visitors."

Cadence feels as though she's had the air knocked out of her. *Fuck.* "For how long?"

"Depends," Fred says, crossing his arms over his badge. "She got into it with another inmate."

Cadence stiffens with alarm. Those arrogant, reckless guards. They're supposed to be watching out for Ruby, *guarding her*, not throwing her to the wolves. "I didn't think the other inmates were permitted anywhere near her."

"Except when she's working in the cafeteria." His arms fall to his sides. "Against my specific instructions, she's been friendly with one of the inmates who works with her there. The guard has been reprimanded for allowing the contact in the first place, but it seems as though they got into an argument of some kind and your girl struck the woman. Sent her to the infirmary. She's still there."

Shit, shit, shit. She can already see the shit-eating smile on Vanelli's face as he adds yet another feather to Ruby's alleged violent-offender cap. There will likely be an investigation, with the results turned over to the DA's office. She wonders if Ruby has already been interviewed. "Has Ruby said anything about the incident?"

"No, she said she'd only talk to you and Brian Tate, which of course she can't do so long as she's on lockdown." The corner of Fred's mouth lifts. "You two have taught her well."

124

Cadence breathes a little. Maybe there's still time to run interference on this. She'll have to contact Brian as soon as she walks out of here—more fuel for her workaholic reputation, but there's too much at stake. They'll have to convince Vanelli it was actually the guard's failure to abide by the judge's instructions to keep her away from the other inmates that forced Ruby to act in self-defense. It has to be the only explanation. He can't blame her for that.

Poor Ruby. She must be terrified. Cadence walks over to her bag on the table. "Can you give her something for me?"

Fred raises a suspicious eyebrow.

She pushes aside the bag of M&M's, knowing there's no way they'd allow Ruby to have them in lockdown, and pulls out the set of stationery she'd brought. She offers the stack of paper and envelopes to Fred. "It's part of her counseling."

Fred shifts his weight between his feet.

"Please," Cadence says. "I drove all the way down here. And I really don't want her to slide backward."

"Seems like she can't go much further back."

"I know. That's why this is important."

Fred sighs. "Fine. But don't expect me to give her anything else. It's up to her to get out of lockdown."

She strains to think of anything else she can give Ruby besides the paper, something to let Ruby know she's thinking of her. "Also, can you tell her I said to hang in there?"

If Cadence is right, Ruby thinks that cat poster in the interview room is as ridiculous as she does.

"I'll see what I can do."

Cadence pats his arm. "It really is good to see you, Fred."

"Now, get out of here," he says with a wink before gesturing toward the lobby. "Go spend time with that beautiful family of yours." Thankfully, he stops short of warning her about burnout.

She shoulders her bag with a smile and steps into the hallway. "Give my love to Linda and the kids."

"Hey," he calls. "Try not to worry. We've got an eye on her. The kid isn't going anywhere."

Cadence bites her lip and nods. That's exactly what she's afraid of.

MARCH 6, 2023

Dear Maya,

I'm on fucking lockdown in my cell.

They won't let me work in the cafeteria or go outside or do anything. It's my third day in here. They won't let me see Cadence even though one of the wardens told me she came by. She brought some real paper for me. That's why this letter looks so nice. I guess I'll give it to her when I see her. IF I see her.

I can't even go to the showers now. The guards bring me a gray rag and some soap to get clean. But the soap dries me out so bad, I have a rash of red bumps under my arms that I can't stop itching. Their dry shampoo leaves my hair like straw and smelling of medicine. The only good thing is the women don't call me Sugar or Baby anymore. Now they call me Smack.

What do you think? I kind of like it.

You're probably wondering what I did to get on lockdown. Remember Poppy from the cafeteria? It's really not my fault, but we got in a fight. I know you weren't ever really into fighting, but Poppy deserved what she got. I swear. She was giving me another slice of cheese, and when I reached out to take it, she ran her finger down my throat like she thought she was going to get some. I guess she thought because she'd given me a couple of slices of cheese, I'd let her go down on me in the storage closet. Or I would go down on her. Who the hell knows?

But when she touched me, it was like something snapped inside. My mind went blank. Next thing I know I was swinging a tray against her ugly face. There was a loud smack (which is why they call me Smack), and blood gushed from her nose. It was all over the place. On her apron. Some even got on me. She called me a fucking tease. I think I broke her nose. Harrison dragged me away before I could find out. Harrison is definitely stronger than she looks, but she still had to get another guard to help shove me back into my cell.

When they told me I was going on lockdown for fighting, I put up my calendar again so I don't lose track of the days. It's getting hard to know if it's day or night without a window.

I miss the sky. Funny how you can miss something like that when you never really thought that much about it before. I miss a lot of things like that. The smell of grass. The feel of fuzzy socks and the fuzz they leave between your toes. The taste of milkshakes. I even miss the way your laughter would crack right before you bent over and could hardly breathe when you thought something was really funny.

I hope you don't think it's weird for me to bring that up. It only happened a couple of times, but when you laughed like that, it felt like the world was going to be okay. I miss feeling like that.

I miss seeing day turn into night and then day break away from night again. There's safety in knowing you can count on things like that. Day. Night. Day. Night. But now I can't.

The only way I've been able to keep track of time is by the trays they bring me from the cafeteria and the sound of the women coming and going from their cells and when they try to talk to me at night. "Hey, Smack, how you holding up?" "Smack, I wanna talk to you about some business when you get out of lockdown." "Now I know why you're here, Smack." "Hey, Smack, don't you talk?"

But mostly, I hear Cadence's voice in my head telling me to "hang in there." That's what the warden told me she said. It sounds stupid, but it's kind of this inside joke from our meetings. I really think I scared her last time I saw her. I got mad about some stuff she was saying, and Dickhead didn't understand, so he came running in and grabbed me. It really pissed me off, so I exploded again. I didn't mean to. But everything happened so fast, and I'm worried Cadence won't want to see me anymore. I'd never seen her look at me like that. She was scared. I hate that I did that.

I only wish she'd stop trying to make me talk about all the shit I was going through before I got here. She keeps saying it matters, but why would it matter to a judge, or a jury, when it's literally never mattered to anyone ever? Besides Redd, and you, maybe. Anyway, it all seems like a load of shit. But the thing is, I think she really believes it when she says it to me.

Would you trust her if you were me? Do you think she'd actually listen? Do you think she'd look at me the same if she knew the truth?

Actually, don't answer that.

Your friend,
Smack

THE COURT: It's getting toward the end of the day, Counselor. Should we break for the weekend?

VANELLI: Your Honor, this next witness had to miss a day of classes already to be here, and I was hoping he wouldn't have to come back on Monday and miss another. His testimony shouldn't take very long.

THE COURT: Okay, I want to be mindful of the jury's time, but if you think this one is quick—

VANELLI: I do, Your Honor.

THE COURT: All right, let's be attentive to the clock. Mr. Tate, any objection to us pushing ahead with the next witness?

TATE: No, Your Honor.

THE COURT: Let's knock this one out, then. Proceed.

VANELLI: The State calls Darnell Johnson.

After being duly sworn, **DARNELL JOHNSON** testified as follows:

VANELLI: Mr. Johnson, if you could please state your name for the record?

JOHNSON: Darnell Michael Johnson.

VANELLI: And how old are you, Mr. Johnson?

JOHNSON: I'm twenty years old.

VANELLI: What is your current occupation?

JOHNSON: I'm a student at SMU. Premed.

VANELLI: You knew the victim in this case; is that correct?

JOHNSON: Yes, he was my mentor through the Big Brothers program here in Dallas.

VANELLI: How old were you when he became your mentor?

JOHNSON: Thirteen or fourteen? Something like that. It was after my mom was arrested, so I guess I was fourteen.

VANELLI: And how did you become a part of the Big Brothers program?

JOHNSON: My auntie heard something about it at church. And since I was staying with her by then, she made me go.

VANELLI: Made you go? So it wasn't something you wanted to do?

JOHNSON: No, not at first. I was a pretty angry kid back then. Thought the world owed me something.

VANELLI: And when did that change?

JOHNSON: It was slow at first. But I'd say Eric really played a big part in that.

VANELLI: And by "Eric," you're talking about Eric Hanson, the victim in this case?

JOHNSON: That's right.

VANELLI: Now, Mr. Johnson, did you ever know Mr. Hanson to pick up prostitutes?

TATE: Objection. Counsel is mischaracterizing the evidence.

VANELLI: How?

THE COURT: All right, gentlemen. I'm going to allow it.

VANELLI: Thank you, Your Honor. Mr. Johnson, did you ever know Mr. Hanson to pick up prostitutes?

JOHNSON: Never. He wouldn't disrespect his wife like that.

VANELLI: Why do you say that?

JOHNSON: Well, he always spoke really highly about his wife. And one time there was this kid next to us at a restaurant who made a comment about the waitress's body. Eric gave that dude a tongue-lashing. Made him apologize to the waitress and everything.

VANELLI: So, when the Defense argues that Mr. Hanson picked up the Defendant to have sex with her, what do you think?

JOHNSON: That they're lying. Or, at least, that the girl misunderstood what he was trying to do. The only reason Eric would pick up a kid is to help her. He was a good person like that.

VANELLI: Mr. Johnson, were you and Mr. Hanson still in communication at the time he died?

JOHNSON: Oh, yes, sir. I aged out of the program a couple of years ago, but he'd check up on me every now and then. See how my studies were going. Make sure I had everything I needed. Stuff like that.

VANELLI: And would you say that Mr. Hanson is the reason you are in college?

JOHNSON: Absolutely. He was a true mentor. When I was a kid, we went to eat every Thursday. And if I tried to get out of it, he'd come get me at my auntie's house. But I was always glad when I went with him.

VANELLI: And what did you two talk about during these meals?

JOHNSON: Lots of things. He'd talk a lot about God and putting my trust in Him. That I had to put in the work to receive His favor. Eric really valued hard work. We'd talk about a plan for me—education, finding direction. And if I didn't have a plan, Eric made sure I was working on it. Yeah, he was a godsend for me.

VANELLI: How do you mean?

JOHNSON: Well, I'd probably have ended up on the streets and selling drugs if Eric hadn't stayed on me. I was already on my way, I can tell you that much, considering the crew I was running with. At first, I wasn't sure if Eric was genuine or not, but he was the real deal. I stopped hanging out with those guys pretty soon after we started talking.

VANELLI: And did Mr. Hanson help pay for your college expenses?

JOHNSON: Yes, he was a generous person. Like I said, he always made sure I had what I needed. The only catch was I had to work hard and have a plan.

VANELLI: And how are you planning to pay for school now?

JOHNSON: I've applied for some loans to help cover expenses.

VANELLI: I would guess Mr. Hanson's death has been pretty hard on you, then?

JOHNSON: Yeah, but not because of the money. I mean, that was nice and all. But I really looked up to him. Like a big brother. I miss talking to him.

VANELLI: Anything else you'd like to add, Mr. Johnson?

JOHNSON: Just that I miss him every day.

HERE ENDS THE EXCERPT

Self

Defense

MARCH 15, 2023

Dear Maya,

You think you're better than me. That's why you're not writing back, right?

It seems like everyone has something to say about me. The guards. The prosecutor. Mr. Tate and Cadence. Before I got on lockdown, I heard what those reporters were saying about me on the news. I bet you think I'm a monster too.

If that's what you're thinking, fuck you. Who are you to judge? I'm in jail, probably for the rest of my life, and you're out there, living your stupid life. How's that fair?

You know what? I'm glad you didn't write back or come to see me. Because then I'd have to hear all over again how I shouldn't have gone with Redd. How you knew that he wasn't good for me and all the reasons you weren't there for me when I needed you most.

You knew all along it wasn't really me he wanted. I don't need you telling me what I already know, so fuck off!

Ruby

Ruby almost can't believe it when she sees Cadence sitting in her usual spot, right next to that stupid cat poster.

"You're here," she says, breathless. When the guard told her it was time to see Cadence, she practically ran.

Dickhead unlocks her handcuffs. "This one couldn't wait to get here," he says. "I thought I was going to have to throw down a barricade to get her to slow down."

Ruby does her best to stay still so he can remove the belly chain.

"There," he says, freeing her from the restraint. "Behave yourself this time." He looks to Cadence. "I'll be outside."

Ruby digs her fingernails into her arm to make sure she's not dreaming.

The door clicks shut; Cadence tilts her head. "Why do you look so surprised to see me?"

"I just thought—" Ruby stops herself, her hand dropping to her side. She can't admit she was worried Cadence had given up on her, too. She nods toward the poster. "Hang in there. Funny."

Cadence smirks. "I thought you might like that."

"I didn't mean to lose it with you."

She waves her pale hand in front of her face. "You think I've never been yelled at by a client before?"

Ruby blinks. *A client. That's all I am to her. A fucking*

client? She tries to breathe, worried if she loses it again—and she probably will—Cadence may never come back. "I shouldn't have done that."

"It's fine," Cadence says. "I mean it. You were upset. I would be, too, if I were where you are." She gestures toward the empty chair. "Would you like to sit down?"

Ruby nods.

"Better?"

"It's okay."

"So, I have to ask . . ."

Ruby was hoping they could keep to the meaningless chatter a little longer. The kind that doesn't make her shut down or feel like she's going to lose it. She holds her breath, bracing for the inevitable question: *Why can't you control yourself?*

Cadence leans her notepad against the table. "Were you still thinking about our last meeting when you got into the fight with Poppy?"

Air escapes between her lips. Her first instinct is to say no, but— "Maybe."

"I'm sorry we didn't end well last time. I'll try to be more sensitive to your boundaries in the future." Cadence laughs to herself. "I know I can push a bit too hard, just because I'm conscious of how few meetings we have before the trial. But I'd be grateful if you let me know when you need more space. That's my fault, okay?" Cadence's smile fades. "Were you hurt in the fight?"

Ruby shakes her head, wondering what the hell is happening. *She* is the one who should be apologizing.

"Was the person you hit hurt?"

"I broke her nose," Ruby says uneasily.

Cadence scribbles something onto her notepad. "Did she threaten you?"

"Kind of." Ruby moves her hands under the weight of her thighs, pressing, to keep herself together, to keep from unraveling.

"Was it something she said to you?"

Ruby shakes her head, keeps her hands pinned. "She tried to touch me."

"And you hadn't given her permission to do that." It's not a question. Cadence makes another note. "Did you try to talk to her? Or tell a guard?"

"No," Ruby says, pushing her full weight into her hands, crushing them. "I don't really remember. I just grabbed a tray and smacked her as hard as I could." She takes another breath and eases up on her aching fingers before asking, "Would that piss you off?"

"Absolutely," she says without hesitation. "But I probably would have told her not to touch me first, if I felt it was safe to do so."

"Yeah," Ruby says. It didn't even cross her mind. She just reacted, and by the time she realized what was happening, it was too late.

"Hey." Cadence leans down to catch her eye. "That doesn't mean this was your fault. Nobody has the right to touch you without your consent. Nobody." Cadence writes something else. "It's just, maybe next time, try taking a deep breath first to clear your head." The pen scratches against the notepad with quick strikes.

"A deep breath?" Ruby repeats.

When she stops writing, Cadence looks up from her notes. "I know you think it sounds silly, but sometimes it's helpful to take a step back."

"That won't work," Ruby says automatically. She frees her

hands from beneath her legs before shaking them out.

"How do you know?"

"Because in here, hesitating makes you look weak. You can't back down or they'll come after you."

"Who will?"

"Everybody." Ruby counts off on her fingers. "The other inmates. The guards."

"The guards?"

"Yeah."

Concern creases Cadence's forehead. "If the guards are coming after you, we should—"

"No," Ruby interrupts. "Don't say anything. That will only make it worse."

"But if you're being harassed by the people who are supposed to protect you, you have to let someone know."

"That may work for you. But in here, there's nobody to protect me but me." Cadence opens her mouth to speak, but Ruby continues, "You told me to tell you when you're pushing too hard, and I'm telling you."

After a moment, Cadence nods. "Okay." She smiles to herself and makes another note.

"What?"

"I didn't say anything," she says. "I heard you, and I'm backing off."

Ruby shifts in her chair. "The thing is, I don't know why I get pissed so fast. I just do. It's like something sets me off, and my mind goes blank. I wish I knew how to stop."

She continues writing. "I know how you feel."

Ruby isn't sure whether she heard her correctly. "You do?"

Cadence taps the top of her pen against the table, like she's considering what to say, so Ruby waits. "I'd get like that when I was younger." She lets out a sad laugh. "A lot, actually. So angry, I couldn't focus on anything else. I couldn't eat. Sleep."

Ruby tries to picture Cadence angry, but she just can't see it.

Cadence flips the page on her notepad and clears her throat. "You received the stationery I got for you, I take it?"

"Yeah," Ruby says, caught a bit off guard with the sudden change of subject. "Uh, thanks."

"I'd brought something else, but I knew they wouldn't let you have it while you were on lockdown." Cadence reaches into her bag, pulling out a large unopened sack of peanut M&M's, and gives a conspiratorial wink. Ruby swallows hard as Cadence tears open the bag. The woman places a few into her mouth before sliding the M&M's across the table. "By the way, I don't know if he told you," Cadence says between chews, "but the guard gave me your latest letter while you were still on lockdown."

Ruby's cheeks flush with regret as she recalls what she'd written. How she told Maya to fuck off again. Even though she didn't mean it *again*. "Is it . . . Is it too late to get that one back?"

"Sorry," Cadence says, shaking her head. "Why?"

Ruby shrugs. "I kind of screwed that up, too."

"How do you mean?"

"I said some shit to Maya that I shouldn't have." She fishes a green M&M from the sack.

Cadence quietly twists the earring at the top of her earlobe. "Could you apologize?"

"I said some pretty bad shit," she mumbles through chewing. The chocolate suddenly makes her thirsty.

"Water?" Cadence asks, as if she can read her mind, and pulls out two plastic bottles.

Ruby would rather have a Coke, but she thanks Cadence anyway as she takes one of the bottles and swallows half in a single gulp. "I'm thinking I should stop writing to her."

"Why? I thought the letters were helping you process your situation."

"They are, kinda," Ruby says with a weak shrug. "But she hasn't written me back, and I'm starting to feel stupid."

Cadence twists her mouth, as if considering. "Perhaps Maya just doesn't know what to say. You haven't had any of your letters returned, have you?"

"No."

"Then I wouldn't give up yet." Cadence smiles gently. "Perhaps you're overthinking it."

Ruby nods. "There's too much time to think in here."

"What have you been thinking about?"

Ruby doesn't want to discuss every bad thought she has every single day. Instead, she crunches M&M's, one after the other until she realizes she's almost eaten the entire sack in the silence. "Want some?"

"I'm good," Cadence says. She waits another minute, probably to see if Ruby will say more. When she doesn't, Cadence hesitantly reaches inside her messenger bag. "There is something else."

Ruby stops chewing. Something about the tone of Cadence's voice. "What?" she asks.

"You asked me about Redd a while back, and . . . I did some digging."

Ruby manages a breath. She *knew* it. She knew Cadence would be able to find him.

Cadence pulls out a small stack of paper. She removes a paper-clip from the top. "Honestly, I'm not sure if I'm doing the right thing here. Sometimes it's easier not to know, but I also don't think it's fair to keep this from you either." After a moment more of seeming reluctance, she offers the top page to Ruby. "I made a copy of the article so you could see. I knew it might be hard to believe if you couldn't see it for yourself."

Ruby wipes her mouth with the back of her hand and reads the headline:

Accused Drug Dealer Found Dead Inside Car

She doesn't understand why Cadence would give this to her.

"A few months ago," Cadence adds softly.

Then Ruby reads it again. *No.*

"I'm so sorry, Ruby."

She doesn't allow herself to read past the headline, too afraid of what it says. Terrified of her reaction. She can't lose control again. Not in front of Cadence. She can't.

"I was going to tell you sooner," Cadence says, "but I didn't want a guard to deliver this news to you while you were on lock-down. In case you wanted to talk about it."

The room tilts. The M&M's are churning in Ruby's stomach. She's going to be sick.

"Ruby?"

She folds the page in half with shaky hands and tells herself, *I will not explode. I will not explode.* "I'm not feeling so good right now." Ruby stumbles from her chair.

"Careful—" Cadence comes around the table and reaches out—to catch her, maybe—but then pulls back, straightening. And Ruby knows why.

In this moment, she *hates* that Cadence won't touch her. She knows it's her fault, but—

She looks up to Cadence's concerned eyes and wills her to see that she won't hurt her. That she can't bear the thought of hurting her. And that's the reason Ruby's backing away now, turning toward the door.

"I think I ate too fast," she finally chokes out.

"Would you like to talk about this?"

She shakes her head too many times. "I need to go." She slips the folded paper beneath her waistband and covers it with her shirt.

"But—"

"Yes?" Cadence says.

Ruby can't read the social worker's expression, but she can't afford to worry about that now. "Will you come back? Not tomorrow, but maybe in a few days?"

Ruby reaches for the doorknob, but Cadence moves to grasp it first. "I need to do it. Or he might get the wrong idea." She nods, and the social worker opens the door to the guard. "Ruby is ready to return to her cell now."

Dickhead pulls out his phone and looks at the time, but he doesn't say anything. He just shrugs, then retrieves the chain and handcuffs.

Ruby offers her wrists to him without being told. "You will come back, right?" she asks Cadence one more time as he secures the cuffs to the belly chain.

"You let the guards know when you're ready, and I'll be here," she says, and then touches her lightly on the shoulder.

Ruby can't help but notice it's only after she's been restrained.

Accused Drug Dealer Found Dead Inside Car

BY LAURA CONSUELA
Staff Writer

A man who was charged last month with possession and attempt to distribute narcotics was found dead inside his car outside a Super 8 motel in Northwest Dallas on Wednesday.

Dallas Police Department spokesperson Alicia Williams said the death of twenty-five-year-old Joe Shandler, also known as "Redd Dogg," is being investigated as a homicide.

"We suspect this was a drug deal gone bad," Williams stated. "Mr. Shandler had a history of drug-related crimes. We are still investigating, but we believe this may have something to do with his involvement in the Crown Alliance."

The Crown Alliance is a growing drug-and-prostitution ring in North Texas.

On December 19, Shandler was released from jail after posting bond. He leaves behind a wife and four children.

THE COURT: I hope everyone had a good weekend. Typical Monday, we're already running a bit behind schedule, so let's go ahead and call your next witness, Counselor.

VANELLI: Yes, Your Honor. The State calls Charlotte Hanson to the stand.

After being duly sworn, **CHARLOTTE HANSON** testified as follows:

VANELLI: Good morning, Mrs. Hanson. Please state your name for the jury.

HANSON: My name is Charlotte Victoria Hanson.

VANELLI: And how did you know the victim?

HANSON: He was my ex-husband.

VANELLI: How long were you married to Mr. Hanson?

HANSON: By the time I filed for divorce, we had been married about eight years.

VANELLI: When was your divorce granted?

HANSON: Our hearings kept getting rescheduled, and the mediation. But everything was finalized maybe three or four months before Eric was killed.

VANELLI: When you say "Eric," you're referring to the victim in this case?

HANSON: [Inaudible]

VANELLI: It's okay, Mrs. Hanson. Take your time.

HANSON: Yes, Eric Hanson was my husband and is the victim here.

VANELLI: Can you tell the jury how you met Mr. Hanson?

HANSON: We met in college. We were both juniors at TCU. And we met in the spring of that year at a party hosted by his fraternity. He was a Beta. And I was a Tri Delt.

VANELLI: I see. And did you know pretty quickly that you were going to marry Mr. Hanson?

HANSON: Well, we were just kids then, but I fell pretty hard for him very quickly. He wasn't like any guy I'd dated before.

VANELLI: How do you mean?

HANSON: I guess he always thought of other people first. Even back then, he was volunteering for Habitat for Humanity, Big Brothers. He had a big heart.

VANELLI: And did the two of you have any children?

HANSON: A few years before the divorce, I had a miscarriage. We were finally ready to have kids, and it was probably the happiest we'd ever been. But after I lost the baby, things changed.

VANELLI: What changed, Mrs. Hanson?

HANSON: Eric was a workaholic even before the miscarriage, but after, I don't know, losing the baby deeply affected him. He became more distant, threw himself even deeper into his work. In the last year we were married, he poured every bit of himself into his company. And his volunteer efforts.

VANELLI: What did Mr. Hanson do for a living?

HANSON: He ran a construction company. His father's. His father died unexpectedly when we'd only been married about a year or so, and his mother asked him to take over the company. So he did. We'd been thinking of having kids back then.

VANELLI: What is the name of the company he took over?

HANSON: It's Hanson Commercial Construction. Eric worked on a lot of buildings in the Victory Park area—new hotels, restaurants. His company led the recent renovation on the art museum.

VANELLI: I don't mean to be crass, but it sounds like with that kind of business, Mr. Hanson was probably a wealthy man.

HANSON: He was. We were. The company was very successful, even before he took it over. Before his father died, Eric was thinking of going into law. But he couldn't score high enough on that darn test. The LSAT?

VANELLI: I can certainly understand the struggle there.

THE COURT: And here I thought you aced the LSAT, Mr. Vanelli.

VANELLI: Thank you for that, but I'm afraid not, Your Honor. Mrs. Hanson, you mentioned Mr.

Hanson's volunteer efforts. What did he do?

HANSON: Before he was killed, Eric served on our country club's board, the board of Big Brothers Big Sisters, and his church's finance committee.

VANELLI: Did Mr. Hanson attend church?

HANSON: Oh, yes. Didn't miss a Sunday unless he was out of town for work or on vacation. He'd been going to First Baptist downtown since he was a little kid. His faith was very important to him.

VANELLI: Do you find it unusual, the Defense's story, that Mr. Hanson met the Defendant at a Taco Bell and chose to leave with her?

HANSON: Not at all. Eric believed it was his duty to help the less fortunate, and he had a real passion for kids in need. He was always helping through Big Brothers Big Sisters. Eric would reach out to them. Take them out for a meal. Give them a ride wherever they needed to go. He would ensure they had clothes that fit for school. I'm sure that's why Eric picked this girl up. He was trying to help her.

VANELLI: Can we go back to what you said earlier, that his volunteer efforts and work got in the way of your marriage?

HANSON: I know it sounds selfish, but I wanted a family of my own. If we weren't going to have kids naturally, I wanted to look into in vitro or adoption. He said he would explore it with me, but then he'd get too busy with—well, with other people's kids. We barely saw each other in that last year and a half. It was like we weren't married anymore. It wasn't a life.

VANELLI: So you filed for divorce?

HANSON: I did.

VANELLI: When you filed, you made some allegations against your husband about the manner in which you were being treated toward the end of your marriage. Is that right?

HANSON: Yes. I was very upset at the time.

VANELLI: Did you and Mr. Hanson ever fight?

HANSON: Well, sure. We were married, after all. One of the worst times was right after I filed for divorce. Eric didn't like the things I'd said in my filing. I was so hurt and angry then. In hindsight, I probably should have been more discreet.

VANELLI: More cognizant of how your filing could be perceived?

HANSON: That's right. I suppose I wanted to hurt him then, and there is a lot I should have let go. But in the end, it was an amicable separation. We agreed a divorce was the best thing for both of us.

HERE ENDS THE EXCERPT

Intense → Arrogant

MARCH 29, 2023

Dear Maya,

I'm really sorry for what I said in my last letter. I was pissed I hadn't heard from you, but really, I think I was even more pissed about other things. It's just a lot, being in here. But I shouldn't have taken it out on you. You don't deserve that.

Remember when you asked me if I thought you were a murderer when you got the abortion? You felt so guilty because you thought you let God down and were terrified He'd never forgive you. I keep thinking how I didn't say anything and that probably only made it worse for you. Like you probably thought you'd let me down, too, and that's maybe why I turned my back on you. And yeah, I was pissed then, at you and at a lot of things, but you need to know, I don't think you're a murderer. I was wrong to let you think that. You are smart and honest and nice and beautiful.

I am nothing like you. I'm stupid and mean and ugly. I lie.

I'm glad you made that choice. Really. I'm glad you can live your life now. You tried to talk to me. You needed a friend, and I just left you to deal with all that alone. I was too wrapped up in my own bullshit to see everything you were going through.

I just found out Redd is dead. Maybe that's why you haven't been writing? Did you know he had a wife and 4 kids?? He said he loved me, and I know he did. But he never told me he had a *fucking family. I was so stupid. I just wanted to believe him so bad. And I didn't want to believe you, so I left. For what? I thought things would be different with him. That Redd was different. That we could be different. But if he was married, and he didn't even tell me, there was no way he was going to stay with me.*

Why couldn't he just tell me? Would he have ever told me? What's wrong with me?

I guess I wanted to write one more time to tell you that I didn't deserve you. I know that. I still don't, but please don't be mad. It's okay if you don't write back, but I just can't have you mad at me. I'm so, so sorry. For everything.

Your friend (I hope),
Ruby

THE COURT: Would the Defense like to cross-examine the witness, Mr. Tate?

TATE: We would, Your Honor.

THE COURT: Please proceed.

TATE: Mrs. Hanson, am I correct in saying that, after Mr. Hanson died, you inherited his share of the company and all of his possessions?

HANSON: Yes, except for an old grandfather clock that had been in his family for generations. His father had given it to us for our wedding, and his mother wanted that back. So of course I gave it back to her.

TATE: Thank you. You're engaged now, though; isn't that correct?

HANSON: Yes.

TATE: That's pretty quick after your husband's death, isn't it?

VANELLI: Objection, Your Honor. Badgering. I think Counsel needs to remember this witness's ex-husband was brutally killed.

TATE: Your Honor?

THE COURT: I'll allow it, though briefly. Please answer the question, Mrs. Hanson, unless you need it repeated?

HANSON: No, I think I've got it. Eric was my ex-husband when he was killed, and I'm engaged to a man we both knew for years before Eric's death. Kyle actually worked for Eric at the company.

TATE: I see. You should have Defendant's Exhibit 18 in front of you. Do you see that?

HANSON: Yes.

TATE: Could you please explain to the jury what that is?

HANSON: It's the Petition for Divorce that I filed.

TATE: And this is the Petition for Divorce you filed in order to legally end your marriage to Mr. Hanson?

HANSON: Yes.

TATE: You mentioned that you and Mr. Hanson sometimes fought?

HANSON: Don't all couples?

TATE: But you said the divorce was amicable?

HANSON: It was.

TATE: Thank you. Flipping to page three of the Petition for Divorce, could you please read Item Four: Reasons for Filing?

HANSON: "Petitioner does not feel safe in her home."

TATE: Did you not feel safe around Mr. Hanson?

HANSON: Oh, I was just mad, and my lawyer said I should list as many reasons as I could think of as to why I wanted to obtain a divorce.

TATE: Now, can you tell me what Defendant's

Exhibit 19 is? It should be up there as well.

HANSON: This one?

TATE: Yes, could you please tell the jury what that is?

HANSON: It's a Petition for Protective Order.

TATE: Did you request a protective order to be issued against Mr. Hanson?

HANSON: Yes. Again, my lawyer recommended it. It was all part of the divorce papers. I was angry with Eric for ignoring me for so long, and I wanted him to pay for it. I didn't really want to see him once I filed for divorce.

TATE: While you were married, did Mr. Hanson keep pornographic materials in the house?

HANSON: You've got to be kidding. Do I really have to answer that?

VANELLI: Objection, relevance.

THE COURT: Overruled. Please answer the question.

HANSON: Eric kept some videos and magazines around the house. But I'm not really sure what that has to do with anything.

TATE: And Mr. Hanson asked you to watch the pornographic videos with him; is that correct?

HANSON: What does any of this have to do with Eric's murder?

TATE: Your Honor?

THE COURT: Please just answer the question.

HANSON: I don't understand any of this. What's the question?

TATE: Did Mr. Hanson ask you to watch pornographic videos with him?

VANELLI: Objection, hearsay.

THE COURT: Overruled.

TATE: Do you need me to repeat the question?

HANSON: Fine. Yes, okay? He asked me.

TATE: And did you watch those films with him?

HANSON: A couple of times, but I— They made me uncomfortable.

TATE: Why did they make you uncomfortable?

HANSON: [Inaudible]

TATE: Mrs. Hanson?

HANSON: Because they were violent.

TATE: How were they violent?

HANSON: They weren't violent. They were—

TATE: But you just said they were violent.

VANELLI: Objection. Counsel is badgering the witness.

THE COURT: Mrs. Hanson, please listen carefully to the question before you answer.

VANELLI: Can I have a ruling on my objection, Your Honor?

THE COURT: Overruled. Do you need Mr. Tate to repeat his question?

HANSON: No. The videos, they—they showed men violating women. Hitting and tying the women up. It was hard to watch.

TATE: I can understand that. What do you mean by "violating"?

THE COURT: Sit down, Mr. Vanelli. I know it's uncomfortable, but please answer the question, Mrs. Hanson.

HANSON: Sticking objects in the woman's vagina and—anus.

TATE: Did Mr. Hanson want to engage in those sorts of acts with you?

HANSON: [Inaudible]

COURT REPORTER: I'm sorry, I didn't hear the answer.

THE COURT: Could you please repeat your answer?

HANSON: I didn't know I'd have to— No, he didn't ask me.

TATE: Even though you state in your written divorce affidavit that Mr. Hanson, quote, "asked me to participate in dangerous fetish sex like that in the videos"?

VANELLI: Objection.

HANSON: How did you get that?

THE COURT: Hold on, Mr. Tate. Mrs. Hanson, I know this can be a bit overwhelming, but I'm sure the prosecutor told you that you could be charged with perjury if you don't tell the truth here today?

VANELLI: Yes, we did speak about that, Your Honor.

HANSON: I'm sorry. This is—

THE COURT: There's a box of tissues right there if you need one.

HANSON: I'm just trying to move past all this. I didn't think—

VANELLI: Mrs. Hanson, please wait for a question before you speak.

HANSON: Oh, I'm—I'm sorry.

THE COURT: Mr. Tate, I want you to ask your last question again. Please listen carefully before you answer, Mrs. Hanson.

TATE: Did Mr. Hanson want you to engage in the same sorts of acts that you witnessed in the pornographic films?

HANSON: He wanted me to do that kind of thing with him, but I refused.

TATE: Did he ask you more than once?

HANSON: Two or three times, maybe.

TATE: And did he get angry when you refused?

HANSON: He was upset.

TATE: In those videos that Mr. Hanson wanted you to watch with him, was the violence always directed toward women?

HANSON: Yes.

TATE: Did Mr. Hanson's videos make you feel unsafe?

HANSON: No. Maybe.

TATE: Which is it, Mrs. Hanson?

HANSON: Sometimes.

TATE: Did his requests make you feel unsafe in your own home?

HANSON: Not all the time, but sometimes.

TATE: Mrs. Hanson, did Mr. Hanson ever hit you?

HANSON: I— How much longer do I have to sit up here?

THE COURT: Until you're dismissed.

TATE: Your Honor, I think I'm about to wrap it up. Would the witness like a glass of water?

HANSON: I could use a drink.

THE COURT: Mr. Vanelli, could you get your witness a cup of water? Use the cups in front of you. There should be some water in the pitcher on your table.

VANELLI: Yes, Your Honor. May I approach?

THE COURT: Just give it to the bailiff. He'll give it to her. Better?

HANSON: A little.

THE COURT: Good. Let's continue. Repeat your last question, Mr. Tate.

TATE: Did Mr. Hanson ever hit you?

HANSON: After he'd been drinking at a party we went to, but he apologized profusely the next day. He'd never done it before, so I forgave him.

TATE: Did he hit you more than once?

HANSON: He— No, I don't think so.

TATE: Did he ever violate you sexually?

VANELLI: Objection, Your Honor. How is this relevant?

THE COURT: Overruled.

TATE: Mrs. Hanson, did Mr. Hanson ever violate you sexually?

HANSON: We were married, so . . .

TATE: Did Mr. Hanson ever have sex with you without having your full consent?

HANSON: [Inaudible]

THE COURT: Ma'am, you need to speak up.

HANSON: Yes.

TATE: And did that make you feel unsafe?

HANSON: What do you think?

TATE: Your Honor?

THE COURT: Mrs. Hanson, please just answer Counsel's question.

HANSON: Yes, of course it made me feel unsafe.

TATE: And because you felt unsafe with Mr. Hanson, is that the real reason you filed for divorce?

HANSON: It was a reason.

TATE: Was it the main reason you filed?

HANSON: It was a long time ago. It's hard to—

TATE: I understand, but please try to remember: When you filed for divorce, was the fact that you felt unsafe with Mr. Hanson the primary reason you filed for divorce?

HANSON: At the time?

TATE: Yes, ma'am.

HANSON: Probably.

TATE: Thank you. No more questions.

HERE ENDS THE EXCERPT

is that?

long?   Trafficked?

APRIL 6, 2023

Ruby had asked the guards to call Cadence, but now that she's here, the girl doesn't know where to begin.

"Are you all right?" Cadence sits on the other side of the table while Ruby paces.

All of her senses are heightened from whatever Doc gave her. Ruby pinches her nose against the harsh odor of cleanser laced with something bitter. "Do you smell that?"

Cadence blinks, sniffs. "Smell?"

"You don't smell it?" Ruby's heart races. It's as if tiny bugs are crawling around inside her.

"If you keep scratching, you're going to hurt yourself."

For the first time, Ruby notices the inflamed skin on her arms. "Doc gave me some shit that was supposed to help calm me, but he must've fucked something up."

"Maybe try to sit?"

"Yeah, okay." Ruby sits.

Cadence takes a deep breath. Ruby instinctively takes one as well and wonders if that was Cadence's intention.

"Better?"

Ruby shrugs. "You really don't smell that?"

"What am I supposed to be smelling?"

"That, like, burnt-garlic smell." Ruby pinches her nostrils closed so hard that her eyes begin to water.

"I'm sorry, I don't." Cadence seems to consider her for a moment. "Maybe try putting your hands on the table. It's something solid to hold on to."

The girl complies, the metal table cool against her sweating palms. Lines of red welts run up and down her arms.

"Why don't you tell me what's going on?"

"That bitch burned the garlic." Ruby presses her palms to her eyes, preventing more tears. "I was mopping the cafeteria, and then I started freaking out. They said they'd call you."

Cadence nods. "I came as fast as I could."

"Okay," she says, reassuring herself. "I hate how it just set me off, you know?"

"I can see—"

"They took me back to my cell," Ruby interrupts. "It was Harrison who was there when it happened. In the cafeteria. She's the only nice guard around here. She let me come back to my cell to splash cold water on my face."

Cadence makes a note. "And did that help?"

"About as much as that deep breath did." The crawling feeling under her skin resumes. She scratches. "Is it okay with you if I walk around a little?"

Cadence glances at Ruby's arms and then nods. "Of course. Whatever makes you comfortable."

Her chair scrapes the concrete; she paces a line again, wall to wall. "I don't—"

"It's okay. I'm here." Cadence readies her pen, nodding reassuringly.

Ruby takes a long, deep breath and rubs her eyes, round and round and round.

"This doesn't have . . ." the social worker begins. "Does this have anything to do with your mom?"

The rubbing stops; her hands drop. Harrison must have heard her mumbling. And told Cadence. She must have.

"You haven't really told me about her yet."

"That's because I don't want to talk about her."

"You called me here." Cadence taps the table. "You must want to talk about something."

She did, but now she doesn't know where to begin. "This sucks," Ruby says, swiping the end of her nose.

"I know," Cadence says. "One day at a time, remember?"

"Why do people say that? Like it's even possible to take more than one day at a time."

Cadence laughs. "Good point."

Ruby presses her shoulders against the opposite wall and squeezes her elbows. "We used to make spaghetti sauce from scratch." She steps away from the wall and resumes her pacing.

"You and your mom?"

"Yeah."

Cadence writes something down. "Did your mom teach you how to make it?"

Ruby nods, then shakes her head, her feet still moving. "Mom would chop the tomatoes and onions and garlic with the big knife. I'd add the pinch of sugar." Ruby stops for a second. "That was my favorite part. It was our secret about the sugar." She starts moving again, remembering how her mother would whisper in her ear, *It's time.* That was the moment Ruby would add the sugar. Her mom smiled. At least she thought her mom smiled. Maybe it's mixed up and Mom only smiled in Ruby's head.

"How old were you when you started cooking together?"

"Seven or eight. I don't really remember." Ruby scratches her arms. "Richie lived with us."

"Your mother's boyfriend?"

"One of them."

"So you and your mom would cook . . ."

"Yeah, she'd start browning the garlic and onion in a little bit of olive oil. I would stand there with my jar of sugar. And this one time, Richie came up behind us and slapped Mom on the ass." Ruby tries to ignore the burning in her eyes. "I jumped."

"Ruby?" Cadence asks, her voice low. "What happened?"

"She told him not to do that shit in front of me." Ruby takes a sharp breath as she paces. "He got real pissed real fast. He jerked her head back by her hair." Her footsteps slow as she notices how quiet it is. Too quiet.

Ruby is seven years old again. She can see Mom's wide eyes, her pale skin, the vein bulging in her forehead. Her body shrinking against the wall. And then her bare feet scrambling like an insect's against the wood floor as he dragged her to the bedroom. "I was yelling for him to stop. Mom was crying. He told me to shut the fuck up or he'd kill me. I put my hands over my mouth so tight, I could barely breathe." She brings her fingers to her lips and presses.

The overhead vent suddenly rattles; she shivers from the instant chill down her neck. Her fingers come off her mouth. "Mom told me to stay in the kitchen. Not to open the door—no matter what— but I could still hear her screaming. I couldn't stop shaking." Ruby places a jittery hand against the wall to steady herself, smears a tear from her cheek. "The garlic was burning. That bitter smell filled our apartment for days. We couldn't get rid of that fucking smell."

166

Cadence slowly shifts in her chair. "Did you talk with your mom about it after?"

She starts pacing again, and the tightness in her chest starts to ease. "I could tell she was scared I'd ask, so I didn't." A sad laugh escapes from somewhere deep inside. "Mom was pissed we didn't have any more garlic to start the sauce again. She ordered a pizza. Pepperoni and black olive. That was Richie's favorite."

"So what happened next?" Cadence asks gently.

Ruby tries to think back, strains to grasp anything more from that time when Richie was around, but she remembers nothing. She shrugs and shuffles toward the center of the room. "All I remember is pretty soon after that, he left. I was so happy he was gone, but Mom—" Ruby shakes her head. "She was really sad."

"Did she tell you she was sad?"

"No, she just started using again," she says flatly and drops into her chair.

Cadence nods. "So why do you think she was sad when he left?"

Ruby contemplates the question for a second. "I used to think Mom was sad because of what he did to her."

"And what do you think now?"

Ruby sighs. "Now I think she was sad because she loved him."

APRIL 12, 2023

Dear Maya,

It's the middle of the night, and there's this new lady a few cells away who won't stop crying. It's the third night in a row and it's gotten really bad. The inmates cry a lot, and I can usually tune it out after a while. But this is the kind of crying that gets under your skin and you just have to do something. That's why I'm writing to you now.

The last couple nights, I've heard the other women laughing at her and planning. They're going to hold her down in the shower and beat her ass and use the electric razor to shave off her pubes and do God knows what else. I wish she'd just shut up and maybe they'll leave her alone. Probably not, though. They already know she's weak.

It's gotten around how I gave Poppy a beatdown, so they're asking me to be in on it. I don't know how the hell they expect me to do that when the guards take me to the shower at a different time than everybody else. I'm just glad that gives me an out. I don't want any part of that life. I only hope they don't think I'm being soft or making excuses. But I can't get on lockdown again. Not when I have all this trial stuff coming up. I need to be able to talk to Mr. Tate and Cadence.

There's another thing. I've been waking up on my side with my

168

arms crossed tight in front of me and my hands squeezing the tops of my shoulders. I'm squeezing so hard, my fingers are all cramped when I wake up in the morning. I've been doing it more and more lately, and when I asked Cadence about it, she said, "You're under a lot of stress. You're probably sleeping like that because your brain is working overtime to protect you when you're asleep. Your brain wants to keep you safe."

I didn't tell her when I wake up like that, I can feel the scars through my shirt. My brain should already know it's too late.

God, I hope that woman stops crying. I know she's sad, but I don't want them to hurt her when the whole reason she's crying is because she misses her kids.

Do you think Mom ever misses me?

Your friend,
Ruby

THE COURT: Is the Defense ready to call its first witness, Mr. Tate?

TATE: Ready, Your Honor. The Defense calls Jennifer Monroe to the stand.

After being duly sworn, **JENNIFER MONROE** testified as follows:

TATE: Please state your name for the record.

MONROE: Jennifer Monroe.

TATE: And how do you know Ruby?

MONROE: I'm her mother.

TATE: Are you currently incarcerated in the Dallas County jail?

MONROE: I'm not wearing this green-striped shit for my health.

TATE: Is that a yes, Ms. Monroe?

MONROE: Yeah.

TATE: You are currently awaiting trial?

MONROE: That's right.

TATE: For charges of fraudulent possession of a controlled substance?

MONROE: Yeah.

TATE: And you are testifying today of your own free will; is that right?

MONROE: No one is forcing me, if that's what you mean.

TATE: And neither the Defense nor the State has promised anything to you, like a lighter sentence, in exchange for your testimony?

MONROE: Nope.

TATE: Why did you decide to testify today?

MONROE: I guess 'cause I've had a pretty fucked-up time with Ruby's dad leaving and all the shit that's happened. I did what I could, you know?

THE COURT: Ma'am, could you please sit still?

MONROE: Huh?

THE COURT: It's hard for the reporter to hear you with your chair squeaking constantly.

TATE: Ms. Monroe, do you need a drink of water?

MONROE: What?

TATE: Water?

MONROE: What were you asking me again?

TATE: How old are you, Ms. Monroe?

MONROE: Thirty-three.

TATE: And how old were you when you had Ruby?

MONROE: I was eighteen.

TATE: Ms. Monroe, how long have you been using drugs?

MONROE: Shit, I guess I started when I was about eleven, drinking and smoking pot.

TATE: And what kind of drugs have you used over the years?

MONROE: Heroin, meth. Scrips, when I can get my hands on them.

TATE: That's what landed you in jail this time?

You allegedly wrote a fake prescription for Xanax?

MONROE: That's what they're saying.

TATE: When you were pregnant with Ruby, did you stop using?

MONROE: I drank some, smoked some weed. Oh, sorry. It's still squeaking.

TATE: What did you drink during your pregnancy, Ms. Monroe?

MONROE: Vodka, rum, cooking sherry. Whatever I could get my hands on.

TATE: How often did you smoke or drink during your pregnancy?

MONROE: Every day, I think. I really don't remember.

TATE: And why did you choose to drink during your pregnancy?

MONROE: Because my life was shit, that's why. At first, I didn't even know who got me pregnant. I didn't think I could deal with a baby.

TATE: And what about when she was born?

MONROE: Things were better at first. Her dad was helping more by then, paying some of the bills and changing her diapers, feeding her, that sort of thing. And she was so cute when she was a baby. I'd dress her up in dresses that my cousin's baby wore. My mom let us live with her. But pretty quick, she started putting down all these rules. We had to move out, and after her dad left, Ruby started showing her true colors.

TATE: Ms. Monroe?

MONROE: What?

TATE: The chair?

MONROE: Oh. Sorry.

TATE: What do you mean by "true colors"?

MONROE: The girl has an attitude problem. Singing all loud and shit and always trying to get attention. Got to be so bad, I couldn't take it.

TATE: Now, at any point when Ruby was living with you, did you stop using drugs?

MONROE: I guess when she was younger. I'd be clean when she was really little. I—I always went back to it.

TATE: Oh, I should've already asked you, did Ruby have any siblings?

MONROE: I couldn't have kids after her.

TATE: I'm sorry. There are tissues—

MONROE: [Inaudible]

TATE: I promise I'll move on soon. But why did you choose not to have any more children?

MONROE: I just couldn't have any more.

TATE: Okay. Was Ruby ever removed from your home due to your drug use?

MONROE: CPS took her a few times, but I usually cleaned up so I could get her back. Ruby didn't like it when they took her from me.

TATE: "They" being Child Protective Services?

MONROE: Yeah.

TATE: How did you know she didn't like it?

MONROE: I don't know. She'd get all clingy and shit. Be on her best behavior. It never lasted, though.

TATE: Did Ruby ever drink while she was living with you?

MONROE: She's a teenager. What do you think?

TATE: Is that a yes?

MONROE: Yeah, she drank.

TATE: Did you provide her with alcohol?

MONROE: I didn't give it to her, if that's what you mean. But I knew she was stealing it from me.

TATE: Is that why you eventually kicked Ruby out of your house?

MONROE: Is that what she told you? Hell no. She was flirting with my boyfriend. That's why I kicked her out. We were living in his apartment.

TATE: How old was Ruby at the time?

MONROE: Uh, it was the end of the summer. That would've been two years ago, I guess. Maybe a little less. So she was thirteen, almost fourteen. Her birthday is August 1.

TATE: So she was thirteen years old when you kicked her out?

MONROE: Yeah, she was messing around with my boyfriend, Clay.

TATE: How old was Clay at the time?

MONROE: I don't know. Thirty-four. No, thirty-five, I think. Hell, I don't know.

TATE: What do you mean by Ruby was "messing around" with Clay?

MONROE: Acting all flirty and shit. She would sing these songs from the radio all the time, like I was saying. I couldn't get her to shut up, but he'd practically fall all over her. I think there was something going on there.

TATE: Like what?

MONROE: She was letting Clay put his hand up her shirt to get beer and cigarettes from him.

TATE: What makes you say that?

MONROE: Because one time when I saw she had a six-pack of beer, I asked where she got it, and she told me Clay gave it to her as a present.

VANELLI: Objection, hearsay.

THE COURT: Sustained.

TATE: And did his attention on Ruby continue?

MONROE: Pretty soon she came up with some story and was crying, but I knew she was faking. That girl was always lying about something. She'd been walking around the house in this short skirt or cutoffs for a week and giggled every time he made some comment about her ass or boobs.

TATE: So you kicked her out?

MONROE: I did. She knew exactly what she was doing. That attitude just got old. I couldn't take it no more.

TATE: Did you see her at all after that?

MONROE: Here and there at first. She would come around, asking for a place to crash for a few hours, but I think she really just wanted to pinch a few beers from my fridge.

TATE: Did you ever ask Ruby to come back home?

MONROE: I told her if she was ready to start acting like a daughter should, I'd think about it. She'd take off when I said that.

TATE: Do you know where she went?

MONROE: I think she went to my mom's at first, but she ain't no motherly type, so she turned her away. Probably at a friend's house for a while. I'm not sure. Then I guess she ended up living with that asshole boyfriend of hers up at the Super 8.

TATE: Do you know the name of her boyfriend?

MONROE: Yeah, Redd Dogg.

TATE: And do you know Redd Dogg's real name?

MONROE: Shit, it's like Joey something. Joey?

TATE: Joe Shandler?

MONROE: That's it.

TATE: Did you know Joe Shandler?

MONROE: No, I more knew of him. You should really get this chair fixed.

TATE: How did you know him, Ms. Monroe?

MONROE: I'd seen him at a few parties. He was usually pretty strung out, but he always had these girls around him. He was a real good-looking guy, and he knew it, too. He acted like he owned those girls or something.

TATE: I see. And when you learned Ruby was dating Mr. Shandler, did you say anything?

MONROE: Like what?

TATE: Did you think to warn her about him?

MONROE: Look, I had enough problems of my own. I didn't know anything about him except what I'd seen. And we've all dated a few dickheads, right?

TATE: Thank you, Ms. Monroe. No further questions.

HERE ENDS THE EXCERPT

Millionaire Arrested Following Public Outburst

BY CHASTITY BELL
Staff Writer

Eric Hanson, president and CEO of Hanson Commercial Construction, was arrested for public intoxication and destruction of property early Saturday morning. Hanson was attending a charity fundraiser for Puppies for People at The Adolphus Hotel in downtown Dallas Friday evening when he allegedly got into an argument with Harold Krucheck, the coordinator of the silent auction.

Hanson had donated a weekend getaway to his home in Aspen for the auction. "Mr. Hanson was upset that his gift also bore the name of his wife, Charlotte," Krucheck said. "I tried to explain that I didn't know, but he insisted I fix it right then and there, and when I couldn't to his satisfaction, he pushed over the table and started throwing things."

A source close to the Hanson family who wished to remain anonymous stated, "Eric has been devastated since Charlotte filed for divorce." According to public divorce papers filed in Dallas County on June 10, 2020, Mrs. Hanson claims "irreconcilable differences" between the couple and seeks well over half the value of the business started by Hanson's late father, James Hanson.

Hanson was released on $5,000 bond early Saturday morning.

According to Krucheck, Mr. Hanson has already apologized to the parties involved and paid for the damage to The Adolphus Hotel and made an additional donation to Puppies for People. When asked if charges will be filed, Krucheck added, "It was a simple misunderstanding. No charges will be filed."

APRIL 25, 2023

As the guard leaves the room, Cadence takes the last of the files out of the box and places it on the table, just out of Ruby's reach.

"Hey," Ruby says. She eyes the box beside Cadence's chair; Cadence can tell from her look that she recognizes it. "Is that the box you had at our first meeting?"

"Have a seat." When Ruby complies, Cadence places a hand on one of the files. "Yes, these are the same ones. Court files. Files from your school counselors. Notes from Child Protective Services."

Ruby pales. "What— Why did you bring them?"

Cadence had been hoping she wouldn't have to do this. But the trial is only a little over two months away. She takes a breath. "Would you like to read what they have to say?"

The girl shakes her head.

"I've read all of them," Cadence continues. "Brian has read them, and the prosecutor has, too. There's a lot here, Ruby, and they give us a pretty good idea of what you've been through, of who you are." Cadence pushes the files aside. "Of who *other people* think you are, anyway."

Ruby lowers her chin to her chest. "They're going to use that shit against me. At the trial."

"You're right," Cadence says with a nod. "The prosecutor is going to drag this stuff out to show what a so-called delinquent you were. To show the jury where you came from, to show them that you're the sort of girl who goes looking for trouble. Who gets high and sleeps around with guys and lies and steals, because that's all she knows."

"Yeah, I get it, okay?" Ruby says without lifting her head. But the words are quiet, not angry, not defiant.

"Hey," Cadence says, and after a moment, Ruby looks at her with tired eyes. "The thing is, I don't believe these files are the full picture."

"What does it matter?" Ruby stares at her hands again. "It doesn't change what I did. And they aren't going to believe what I say happened anyway."

"You don't know that. I know I've been telling you this for a while, but I think talking about your past honestly—filling in the gaps of what these files leave out—could give the jury some insight into what led you to make the choices you made."

Ruby sucks in her cheeks.

"Can you tell me when your mom started using?"

"I know what you're trying to do," Ruby says, her whole body tight.

Cadence leans back. "You're angry."

"No shit, I'm angry. I don't want to talk about this. You think I'm proud of the things I've done? Of everything my mom did, or her fucking boyfriends? Everything I did before she kicked me out? And after? Don't sit there and pretend that any of that shit is actually going to help my case."

"We're not going to know until you talk to me," Cadence says calmly.

Ruby runs her hands through her hair, tugs. "Why are you doing this?"

She pulls a notepad and pen from her messenger bag. "Because we're running out of time, and I'm guessing I know what's underneath all of that anger." Cadence sighs. "It hurts to be angry with her, doesn't it?"

"Fuck off," Ruby says as she springs from her chair, catching it before it clatters to the floor.

"I can't." *I won't*, Cadence thinks as she gives a rough shake of her head. "This is too important."

Ruby steps back, distancing herself. "You're really pissing me off right now."

Cadence smiles. "Good."

"Good?"

"Yeah. Because if you're still feeling anger about what's in these files, that means you can feel other things too." Cadence opens the nearest file and begins to read from the CPS worker's notes. "Child, age six, removed from home due to endangerment. Mother's drug use presumed."

Ruby flinches. "Shut up."

She lowers it and grabs the next file. "Child, age nine, removed from home due to abandonment. Child shows signs of malnutrition and lack of proper hygiene. Continuous neglect evident."

Ruby swats the file from her hand. "I said stop."

Cadence ignores the dropped file and picks up another. "I can go on."

"I already told you my mom was a user." Ruby plops into her chair. "So what? Her life wasn't easy, and I didn't make it any easier."

"How?"

"She was on her own. Dad just left us. And I was a needy kid.

Got into trouble a lot." Ruby scrubs a hand across her face. "She couldn't handle it. It was hard for her. *I* was hard for her."

Cadence shakes her head.

"Why can't you just let me feel bad about this?"

"You need to stop punishing yourself for being a normal child who needed a mother." Cadence stacks the files and pushes them aside before lowering her voice. "It was scary being taken from her, wasn't it?"

The color rises in Ruby's cheeks. "What do you know about it?"

Cadence is ready for this. If she wants the girl's mask to come off, she's going to have to take hers down a bit, too.

"I know it was scary for me," she says. "The string of strangers telling me everything was going to be okay. The strange houses. The kids of the foster parents, the way they looked at me, like they felt bad for me and at the same time didn't trust me. All I wanted was to be back home. At least that was a horrible I already knew."

Ruby clenches and unclenches her fists. "Why didn't you say something before?"

"I'm saying something now." Cadence points to herself. "I was angry and sad and hurt, all of the things I know you're feeling, because I knew if I was just *better*, if I just didn't upset her, next time she wouldn't use, and they wouldn't have to take me away again—"

"But she did use."

Cadence nods.

"She's dead," Ruby says. "Right?"

It's Cadence who looks away now, just for a moment. She picks up her notepad. "I think it's time we talk about you."

Ruby rubs her arms. "Why am I the one who always has to answer the fucking questions?"

Cadence looks Ruby straight in the eye to make sure she hears. "You know, that rage you're feeling isn't a bad thing."

Ruby huffs a laugh. "Tell that to the guards."

"The only thing damaging about anger is how it sometimes gets communicated." She gives a firm nod. "Physical or verbal abuse is harmful, but communicating your frustration in a nonviolent way can help repair relationships and lead to healing."

Ruby smirks. "Okay, Dr. Ware."

"I'm serious. Your mom was probably more upset with herself than anyone."

"Could have fooled me."

Cadence snaps her fingers. "Exactly. It's probably one of the reasons she self-medicated. She was holding in all of her anger and pain. She used alcohol and drugs to cope."

"She used because shit was *hard*. Because I made things hard. And don't tell me I'm making that up because that's what she said." Ruby swipes at her eyes. "It was like she was jealous or something. I didn't ask for any of that shit. She could keep her fucking boyfriends. I didn't want them."

"Of course you didn't," Cadence says, her voice soft. "I don't know if she was jealous or not, but even if she was, maybe it wasn't for the reason you think."

"Why else would she have been jealous?"

"Because you were stronger than her."

Ruby scoffs. "Yeah, right."

Cadence scoops up Ruby's history and drops the files into the box one by one. When she finishes, she gestures to the full box.

"Look at everything you've been through, and yet here you are. Still standing."

Ruby swallows. "That doesn't mean anything."

"It means you're a survivor." Cadence's gaze shifts away from the box. "And to survive this, we need to start thinking about your testimony. You'll need to go over and over it in your mind—have it down backward and forward—so you're ready by the time trial comes around."

"Already?" Ruby asks.

"Sometimes even the truth is hard to remember. I want you to feel confident in telling your story." Cadence taps the top of the box. "But I think there's still more we need to cover."

"Like what?"

"I've heard the things you've told me about Redd and Maya, and I can read between the lines. There's more there, but I can't truly know what took place unless you tell me."

"I don't know what you're talking about."

"Like what happened when you left with Redd?"

Ruby sucks in her cheeks.

Cadence can sense she's already losing the girl, but she also knows that getting Ruby to talk about it may be the only way to start breaking down other people's assumptions about her. "Ruby, I need to know what happened in those months that led up to when you met Eric Hanson."

The girl goes rigid. "What does that have to do with anything?"

"I know this is difficult—"

"Time's up." Ruby jumps from her chair.

"Please don't run away from me," Cadence says as she stumbles from the table. "Let's talk about this."

185

The girl stops and leans her forehead against the door; she takes a shuddering breath.

For a second, Cadence thinks she may have her, but then the guard pushes the door open. He must have seen them through the window. "Finished?"

Cadence shakes her head, but Ruby nods and silently allows the guard to restrain her before he escorts her from the interview room.

MAY 3, 2023

Dear Maya,

We're about two months out from my trial, and it feels like someone is sticking a bunch of needles in my brain. Each one is something new for me to worry about.

Cadence wants me to start going over my testimony in my head for practice. She wants me to "feel confident telling the jury my story." But just when I feel like I've got my story down, I get nervous about all the shit they're going to ask me. She also brought in these files she had to convince me to start talking to her. It was notes from social workers and school counselors and judges and shit. Stuff that goes way back. She asked if I wanted to read them so I could know what everybody was saying about me.

I told her no. I told her that because I already know what they're saying, because I've been hearing it my whole life. Troublemaker. Liar. Thief. Druggie. Worthless. Bitch. Whore.

Lately, I've been thinking a lot about the whole "presumed innocent until proven guilty" thing. Mr. Tate said the jury is supposed to start the trial thinking I'm innocent, and the prosecutor has to prove I'm not. But I don't think that's how it works for real. I'm the one on trial, so I'm betting they think I did something to end up here. And they're not wrong. Why would they believe me after hearing the shit I've done? If I have to tell them my own mom kicked me out, that I was living in the Super 8 and getting high and that other shit, do you really think they'll presume I'm innocent?

I know Cadence is only trying to help, but I don't want to go over the testimony in my head. It's too scary. I'll probably tell her I'm doing it just to keep her off my back.

My brain is aching, and I'm already feeling sick just thinking about it. What if I screw up? What if the jury doesn't believe me? Would you?

Your friend,
Ruby

TRANSCRIPT EXCERPT, JULY 12, 2023

THE COURT: Ready to call your next witness?

TATE: The Defense calls Ruby Monroe.

THE COURT: Miss Monroe, before you approach the witness stand, I must ask if your attorney has advised you of your Fifth Amendment right to remain silent.

MONROE: [Nods]

THE COURT: I'm going to need a verbal response, please.

MONROE: Uh, yeah. I mean yes, sir.

THE COURT: And you realize you have the right to not incriminate yourself?

MONROE: Yes.

THE COURT: But even knowing this, you still want to testify on your behalf?

MONROE: Yes, sir.

THE COURT: All right, then. Please proceed.

After being duly sworn, **RUBY MONROE** testified as follows:

TATE: Hi, Ruby. I know we know each other, but could you please state your full name for the record?

MONROE: Ruby Danielle Monroe.

TATE: And how old are you?

MONROE: Fifteen.

TATE: I'm going to back up a few years before you met Mr. Hanson and ask you about your home life; is that okay?

MONROE: Okay.

TATE: Was your mom a drug user?

MONROE: Yeah.

TATE: What kind of drugs did she use?

MONROE: Pretty much anything she could get her hands on. Before she kicked me out, it was mostly prescription stuff that she'd buy off people with whatever money we had. Sometimes meth.

TATE: Did your mom drink?

MONROE: Yeah.

TATE: And how long had your mom been using drugs and drinking, Ruby?

MONROE: Pretty much as long as I can remember. She used to try to hide it from me, you know, when I was little. She'd send me outside to play. But then I guess she decided I was old enough and did it in front of me. I was six, maybe, the first time I saw her smoking crank.

TATE: And crank is methamphetamine?

MONROE: Yeah.

TATE: Child Protective Services removed you from your home a few times; is that right?

MONROE: [Nods]

TATE: Is that a yes, Ruby?

190

MONROE: Uh, yeah, sorry. Yes.

TATE: How many times were you removed from your home?

MONROE: Three.

TATE: And how old were you the first time?

MONROE: Probably like six or seven.

TATE: Why were you removed from your home?

MONROE: Mom's boyfriend was cooking meth in the microwave and caught our apartment on fire.

TATE: So CPS took you away?

MONROE: Yeah, and I had to stay with this foster family. They had lots of kids.

TATE: How long did you stay with that family?

MONROE: It felt like a real long time. But it was probably only a few months.

TATE: And the second time CPS removed you, how old were you?

MONROE: Nine.

TATE: How did that come about?

MONROE: Neighbor ratted me out.

TATE: How do you mean?

MONROE: My mom was gone for a few days, and I guess I forgot to bring in the mail because our neighbor came over to complain that our mailbox was overflowing, and she saw I was staying by myself, so she called the cops.

TATE: Did you know where your mom was?

MONROE: No.

TATE: Did your mom leave you with another adult?

MONROE: I was old enough to take care of myself by then.

TATE: But CPS felt differently, didn't they?

MONROE: I guess they did because I ended up with another foster family.

TATE: And how was that?

MONROE: It was okay. Those people made sure I ate. I had my own room, and they bought me some new clothes since I'd outgrown my old ones.

TATE: But you went back to your mom eventually?

MONROE: Yeah, she promised she'd take care of me better. Same old story, so CPS sent me back.

TATE: And the third time CPS took you from your home, how old were you?

MONROE: I—

TATE: Ruby? Do you need to take a break?

MONROE: I'm fine. About eleven?

TATE: Okay, you just let me know if we need to stop for a second, okay?

MONROE: [Nods]

TATE: Do you need to take a break, Ruby?

MONROE: Um, I'm not sure.

HERE ENDS THE EXCERPT

Ask Brian

self-defense

assault

en aske

MAY 11, 2023

Cadence waits for Ruby in the interview room and rubs her eyes, unable to escape the weight of exhaustion. Last night was the first time in a long time that she'd had one of the nightmares. The hawk tattoo. The blade. Even though her mother wasn't actually there, she was in the dream, smiling as her grandmother bled out on the front porch.

Cadence had awakened screaming, shaking. Her husband held her, whispering to her—*you're safe, you're safe, you're safe.* She finally pretended to nod off so he could get back to sleep.

She knew what Jack said was true. She knows it to be true even now as she sits in the small interview room. She's safe. She'll be able to walk out of here and go home. Play with her son, Ian. Have dinner with her family.

But what about Ruby?

Cadence knows why she had the nightmare again: Ruby's trial. The possibility of her short life being cut even shorter if she's sent to prison. Even if the girl has agreed to start talking—which is what the guards told her when she got the call to come over—Cadence has no idea if anything she learns in the short amount of time they have left will be enough. What she does know is how quickly Ruby can shut down, so she has to be careful, creative, to get the information Brian needs. Otherwise all of this could have been for nothing.

The door pops open, startling her.

"Hey," Ruby says with that cocky head lift she's recently adopted. Cadence doesn't like to see it, the girl assuming the false confidence of the other prisoners. Another mask.

The guard releases Ruby from her handcuffs, followed by the belly chain. "I'll be outside if you need me," he says in that bored way most of them do after a few years on the job. He's already pulling out his phone before he closes the door behind him.

"What happened to you?" Ruby asks, examining Cadence's face. "You look like hell."

Cadence laughs at Ruby's honesty. She unlatches her messenger bag. "Didn't sleep well. But good news: today is National Eat Whatever the Hell You Want Day."

Ruby eagerly falls into her chair. "Sounds made up to me."

"Probably. But just in case, I brought these." Cadence places a package of Oreos, followed by a sleeve of Saltine crackers, on the table between them.

Ruby automatically reaches for the Oreos.

Cadence puts a hand on top of them. "I want to ask you something first."

Ruby's face pinches. "Seriously?"

"During my morning walk, I was thinking about something. You know how men sometimes talk about girls, how they call them 'sweet' or 'salty'? Women, too. Like we're meant for their consumption."

"Don't forget spicy," Ruby says.

Cadence sighs. "And spicy. But for the purpose of this, let's just stick to the two."

Ruby shrugs, her attention back on the food.

She touches the Oreo package. "If a girl is sweet, she's kind, friendly, passive." And then she moves her hand to the crackers. "But if a girl is salty, she's tough and assertive."

"You aren't seriously using these to teach me a lesson, are you?"

Cadence smiles at the girl's perceptiveness. "Let's just say it's a metaphor. A bad one. But bear with me."

"Fine." Ruby shakes her head.

"Which one do you think you are with me mostly?"

A wry smile crosses Ruby's face as she taps the Saltines.

Cadence leans back. "Brian has said his experience is different from mine."

Ruby shrugs. "No one likes a bitch."

"And which one is the bitch here?"

"The salty one." She nods toward the cookies. "Can I have one now?"

"You told me you didn't like Oreos when you were in juvie." Cadence opens the sleeve and offers Ruby a cracker instead.

She frowns. "I lied, okay?"

"Yeah, I know," Cadence says with a smirk.

"Whatever. You gonna punish me because I lied about some cookies?"

"I'm not, but I am wondering why you think you have to be different with Brian than you are with me. Who is the real Ruby?"

"I don't know." Ruby shrugs. "Both. Everyone is different with different people."

"Sure, but why can't a girl be both with a guy? Sweet, salty, sour, bitter, *and* spicy. Everything."

"Guys don't like bitchy girls," she says again.

"Don't tell that to my husband," Cadence says before catching herself.

"Wait, you're married? You didn't tell me you were married."

"You didn't ask." It's too late for her to berate herself now, so she doesn't.

"That's because you never tell me anything when I ask about you."

Cadence clears her throat. "Did your mother teach you girls should only be sweet around guys?"

Ruby rolls her eyes.

Cadence lifts an eyebrow. "How about Redd?"

"This is stupid," Ruby says, crossing her arms over her chest. "Are you going to let me have an Oreo or not?"

"Was he your first boyfriend?"

Ruby releases a heavy sigh and glances at the package of cookies. "If I answer, will you let me have one?"

Cadence opens the Oreos and slides them toward her.

Ruby yanks one from the package and shoves the whole thing into her mouth before mumbling, "There was one guy before. I'd just turned thirteen and he was in high school."

Always older. "Who was he?" She pulls out her notepad and pen.

"Nathan. He was a junior. My friend Jade introduced us. Said it was about time I got with someone so maybe my mom's boyfriends would leave me alone."

The hairs on the back of Cadence's neck lift. "Your mom's boyfriends were coming on to you?"

"Sure," Ruby says, snatching another Oreo.

Cadence tries to breathe. First the nightmare, now this.

"Hey," Ruby says between chews, "you okay?"

Cadence swallows hard. "Tell me about Nathan."

Ruby shrugs. "He lived in the same apartment building, and

197

we hung out a few times—hooked up once or twice—then he got pissed."

"What happened?"

She shoves another cookie into her mouth. "I saw him hugging on another girl and asked him about it. He said I was making something out of nothing." Ruby picks up the sleeve of crackers and shakes them. "Too salty, see?" She drops the sleeve on the table. "He said we weren't *together*, so he didn't know why I was making such a big deal out of it."

"Did you agree you weren't together?"

Ruby shrugs.

"So you had sex with Nathan, but you weren't together?"

"Look, I don't need you judging me, all right?" She twists an Oreo, separating the halves. "We were just having fun."

"So you wanted to have sex with him."

Ruby pushes one of the halves into her mouth and chews slowly.

"You didn't," Cadence guesses as she spots the slurry of cookies smeared across Ruby's front teeth. "Here." She retrieves a sealed bottle of water from her bag and hands it over.

After taking a sip and swishing the water around her mouth, Ruby swallows. "So I have a thing for assholes. So what?"

"I think people are naturally inclined to seek out relationships that feel familiar, even when they're harmful."

"Because I have 'daddy issues' or something?" Ruby says, making quotes with her fingers.

Cadence presses her lips into a thin line, both impressed and saddened once again by Ruby's quick wit. "Well, what do you think? Do you think you might have chosen to date older guys because you have a subconscious desire to be with someone who can protect you, since your dad didn't?"

"That's what a guy is supposed to do, right?" Ruby asks, like it's obvious. "Protect you?"

"Is that why you were with Redd? Did he protect you?"

The vein in Ruby's forehead pulses.

Cadence tilts her head. "What were you doing before January of last year, Ruby?"

"I'm not doing this."

"Why?" Cadence says, her frustration threatening to surface. "It's been months, and every time we start to get somewhere, you shut me down." She draws in a breath and slowly releases it, trying to remain calm. She takes another. "Look, I know talking about this is hard and probably hurts like hell, but I need you to take some responsibility here."

"Nobody's going to believe me anyway, so what's the point?"

"You don't know that. Please, Ruby, talk to me."

The girl crosses her arms over her chest. "And after I do, you'll be gone, right?"

Is that what this is about? She thinks Cadence is going to abandon her once she gets what she needs from her? "So long as you want me here, I'm not going anywhere. I'll keep showing up. You need to trust me."

"*Trust* you?" Ruby asks, her voice rising before she checks the door. The guard is too busy with his phone to notice.

Cadence gestures between them. "It's just the two of us. You have the power to determine how this goes."

Ruby kneads her hands. "You told me I wouldn't have to do this."

"I never said that," Cadence says, shaking her head. "Look, I can understand why you find it hard trusting people. Believe me, I do. And maybe you don't think I deserve your trust. But if you're going to save yourself here, it's the only way."

Ruby scoffs. "There you go again."

"I'm serious," Cadence says, desperate to make her understand. "If you can't even tell *me* the truth, how are you ever going to get a jury to believe you?"

MAY 14, 2023

Dear Maya,

Each day we're getting closer to trial, and I keep shutting down. It's like my body goes numb and my brain goes blank. It's getting too hard.

Cadence says I need to trust her, and talking will help, but it just brings up all this bullshit. Even when I think about you, I can't get past all that shit between us. Like how did you know about Redd when I couldn't even see it?

I guess I loved him so much, and that love was like a dye that spread through my veins and colored my whole world. At first it was beautiful—all that color. But too much color eventually turns black.

I was blinded by him. I'd do anything for his love. I did everything. I blamed you, not him.

Anyway, this will be my last letter. It's just getting too hard.

Ruby

TATE: Ruby, you ready to keep going?

MONROE: Yeah, sorry.

TATE: No problem. You just let me know if you need to stop and take a break for a second.

MONROE: Okay.

TATE: Now, I believe you said CPS removed you a third time from your home?

MONROE: Yeah.

TATE: Why did they remove you the third time?

MONROE: Um, so I'd told this guidance counselor at my school about some problems I was having with my mom's boyfriend, Jonathan.

TATE: What kind of problems?

MONROE: Uh, he was kind of touching me and stuff.

TATE: Touching you where?

MONROE: I was just getting my boobs, and he'd push on them and say how cute they were.

TATE: And you told your guidance counselor?

MONROE: Yeah, I guess I was acting weird about it. I couldn't really concentrate in class, and she called the cops even though I told her not to. They made me meet with this social worker, but I didn't want to talk to her.

TATE: Did they remove you from your home again?

MONROE: Yeah, but that was only for a day. I didn't want to go to another foster home, so I told them I was making that stuff up about him so they'd send me back to my mom's.

TATE: Were you making up that stuff, Ruby?

MONROE: No, but Mom got pissed that I'd made such a big deal out of it. Jonathan moved out. He didn't talk to us after that.

TATE: I'm going to fast-forward a few years. Is that okay with you, Ruby?

MONROE: Okay.

TATE: When did you leave home?

MONROE: Um, about two years ago.

TATE: So July 2021?

MONROE: That's right.

TATE: And did you want to leave home in July of 2021?

MONROE: Um, no, Mom kicked me out.

TATE: Did you know where your dad was living at the time?

MONROE: He'd left when I was about four. I didn't know where he was.

TATE: How old were you when your mom asked you to leave the house?

MONROE: Thirteen.

TATE: Why did she ask you to leave?

MONROE: Because she didn't like that her boyfriend was paying more attention to me than her. Even though I told her I didn't like him like that.

TATE: Was this the same boyfriend who touched and commented on your breasts?

MONROE: No, that was Jonathan. We were living at Clay's apartment then.

TATE: Clay Jenner?

MONROE: [Nods]

TATE: Is that a yes?

MONROE: Yes. Sorry.

TATE: How old was Mr. Jenner at the time?

MONROE: In his thirties. Maybe thirty-five.

TATE: And you were thirteen?

MONROE: Yeah.

TATE: And why was your mother jealous?

VANELLI: Objection, calls for speculation.

THE COURT: I'll allow it.

TATE: Ruby, why would your mom be jealous?

MONROE: Because he would always make little comments like, "Why can't your ass be more like hers?" You know, and he'd be pointing to me and compare me to some real famous singers and talk about how my body was like their body and stuff like that. I don't know. I think she caught him staring at me when he thought she wasn't looking.

TATE: Did Mr. Jenner ever hug you?

MONROE: Yeah.

TATE: Did he hug you often?

MONROE: Mm-hmm. He'd come up on me and give me a hug, and I just let him until it was over.

TATE: Did Mr. Jenner ever kiss you?

MONROE: Maybe once. Wait, twice.

TATE: On the mouth?

MONROE: The first time was on the cheek. The other was on the back of my neck.

VANELLI: Your Honor, objection. Is there a point to this line of questioning? Mr. Jenner is not on trial here.

THE COURT: I'm starting to agree. Mr. Tate, let's get this moving.

TATE: Yes, Your Honor. Ruby, did Mr. Jenner ever touch you inappropriately?

MONROE: [Nods]

TATE: Is that a—

MONROE: Yes.

TATE: How many times?

MONROE: Maybe eighteen, twenty times, I think.

TATE: Ruby, I know this is difficult, but where did Mr. Jenner touch you?

MONROE: In my bedroom. He'd wake me up and—

TATE: I'm sorry, I'll be clearer. Where on your body did he touch you?

MONROE: Oh, um, down there.

TATE: And by "down there," do you mean your vagina?

MONROE: Yes.

TATE: And did you touch him?

MONROE: Yeah, he'd grab my wrist and make me rub on him. Push my head down and— I—

TATE: That's okay, Ruby. I know this is diffi-cult. Did Mr. Jenner force you to give him oral sex?

MONROE: Yeah.

TATE: Was your mom aware of his inappropriate behavior?

MONROE: [Inaudible]

COURT REPORTER: I'm sorry, I didn't hear the answer.

TATE: Ruby, was your mom aware of Mr. Jenner's inappropriate behavior?

MONROE: Yeah.

TATE: How did you know she was aware?

MONROE: I asked her to make him stop.

TATE: How many times did you ask her, Ruby?

MONROE: I don't know. Three or four times, maybe.

TATE: Three or four?

MONROE: Maybe more than that, but I don't really remember.

TATE: And after you asked your mother to make Mr. Jenner stop, then what happened?

MONROE: The last time I asked her, she got real pissed. She called me trash and threw a trash bag at me. She said that guys can't help themselves, and I had it coming because of the way I dressed and flirted and sang all the time in front of people, trying to be all that. Then she kicked me out. I used the trash bag and put a few things in there—my toothbrush—and I left.

TATE: And that was two years ago?

VANELLI: Objection, asked and answered.

THE COURT: Sustained.

TATE: Where did you go when you left, Ruby?

MONROE: At first, I crashed at this girl's house, Jade. I knew her from the neighborhood, but her mom was weird about having people stay over. So Jade, she snuck me in after her mom was asleep, and I had to leave before everyone was up. But I overslept once, and that was the end of that.

TATE: During that time period when you were staying with Jade, were you going to school?

MONROE: It was summer when my mom kicked me out, and so we'd hang out at the park or over at the Sonic. School was out then.

TATE: And did you meet anyone that summer?

MONROE: That's when I met Redd.

HERE ENDS THE EXCERPT

MAY 31, 2023

Ruby overhears the echoes of two women fighting over a box of tampons—not the shitty kind the jail hands out, but the good ones. She tries to block out their screams and focus on the new guard in her cell. He gently clips Ruby's cuffs to the chain at her waist. Her heart beats a little faster. "Where's Dickhead?" she asks before realizing her slip.

Demarcus looks up from her wrists. He has green eyes. Smooth, tanned skin. Beautiful. "He had to take his wife to the doctor."

"He has a wife?" Ruby tries to picture the walking penis with a wife. She can't.

"I don't see it either." The guard's smile comes easily. Gleaming movie-star teeth.

Ruby can't help it: she smiles back.

Demarcus's gaze sweeps to her open mouth. "They said you were trouble." He puts a hand on her back, nudging slightly. "We should go."

"Already?" Ruby leans into his hand. She's been so lonely lately, longing for real human connection—not the romantic kind, necessarily, just for someone in here to see her as a person too. But could she really be flirting with him? In her jail cell. Inches from her bed. She suddenly realizes how long it's been; it's the only way she's certain to get his attention.

Still, her head tells her she shouldn't get with this guy. Ruby has heard stories of other women fucking the guards in closets, bathroom stalls, in interview rooms. It can mean worse than lock-down if they're caught, but then she allows her gaze to travel down his arm, the cut of the muscles from his shoulder to his hand clenching and unclenching at his side like he's fighting something deep inside. How easy would it be to fall back into this role?

"Sanders," another guard shouts, followed by the sound of pounding footsteps. The women have stopped screaming about the tampons. "You got that little bitch ready or not?"

Demarcus's face goes tight. His hand falls away from her waist; Ruby already misses the warmth of his touch. "Yes, sir," he says to his boss, who is now blocking the entrance to her cell with his military haircut and pinched expression. He gives Ruby the eye, like he knows she's hiding something. She smiles again.

The boss sneers. "Get her where she's going and don't let her out of your sight." He takes a step back.

"Yes, sir," Demarcus says with a firm nod. He yanks on the chain at her waist, making the metal cut into her skin. Ruby's eyes water from the sudden, unexpected pain. As they walk, the women toss lewd comments toward her, suggesting all the things the guard could do to her. With a sideways glance, she notices the hardness of Demarcus's jaw and, for the first time, wonders if he's really as nice as she thought.

She reminds herself to breathe like Cadence taught her. *It was nothing. He probably didn't mean to do it.*

When they reach the elevator, Demarcus presses the button for the ground floor, but Ruby usually meets Cadence on the second. The doors *whoosh* closed, trapping them inside, silencing the sounds of the jail. "Where are we going?" she asks, her pulse throbbing.

Demarcus doesn't answer, his eyes fixed forward until the elevator dings and the doors fly open. "Out," he grunts as he looks up at the security camera and pushes her, rougher than necessary.

Ruby stumbles forward as he maneuvers her to the right, down the long, doorless hallway, and with each thump of her heart, the fear of him replaces her desire.

She tries to breathe again, but it's getting harder. The nice ones are always the worst. She knows this. She should have seen it coming. Nice at first, and then . . .

Demarcus hustles toward the glaring exit sign and rams them both into the heavy door.

The filtered sunlight is startling, and Ruby tries to orient herself. She spots the dirt patches, where grass will never grow, the walking track, the fence topped by razor wire. It's the yard where she's allowed to walk outside once the other women have left. She's never entered from this direction; her usual door, on the other side of the expanse, is closed.

A sudden motion along the far edge catches her eye. On a bench under the shade of the guard tower, Cadence sits, her navy blazer draped over her messenger bag and a bright red scarf wound tight around her neck.

Before Ruby understands what's happening, the guard is removing the cuffs, followed by the belly chain. His fingers linger at her waist, and Ruby senses his gentleness return. "Sorry about being so hard on you just now," Demarcus whispers. "They've been riding my ass. Watching me." He nods toward the guard tower. "Forgive me?"

Looking into his pleading eyes, Ruby nods. Even though she knows his cruelty is within reach, she forgives.

His smile is back. "I'll be over here if you need anything."

She suddenly wishes it was only the two of them in the yard so they could make out under the racing clouds. But it's not just them. She's never really alone here. Ruby eyes his expectant lips a split second before turning toward Cadence.

With each step, she wonders how her ass looks. She can't believe she's thinking about it, wondering how yet another man sees her, but she is. She's pretty sure he could help her escape her own loneliness, if just for a little while.

She just wishes she had some makeup. Something to moisturize her lips. Especially when all she has to wear is this striped uniform, these graying socks, the scuffed Crocs on her feet. But she can still play the part. She still has that.

Cadence smiles as Ruby approaches.

"Hey," she says, stopping as she reaches the shade of the guard tower.

Cadence moves her jacket and bag to her other side and pats the bench. "Have a seat."

Ruby drops next to her and gestures to the empty yard. "What's going on?"

"I know you like being outside." Cadence smiles conspiringly. "The usual guard— *Dickhead*"—she raises an eyebrow—"he's out today, so I told this guy that we sometimes meet out here."

For the first time, Ruby stretches her neck and takes in the broad sky. Rain clouds gather on the horizon. The breeze plays on her skin, and she fills her lungs with the smell of the approaching storm.

"We can sit outside for a bit and then go inside to talk, if you prefer?"

Ruby shakes her head. "This is good." She figures Cadence is trying to butter her up by bringing her outside. She's going to want to talk about Maya and Redd, probably. But right now, Ruby doesn't care.

Cadence makes a not-so-subtle nod toward Demarcus. "Cute."

The comment surprises Ruby, and she glances over her shoulder at the guard looking back at them. He waves. She bites down a smile and turns toward Cadence with a shrug. "He's all right."

"I should advise you it's—"

"I know," Ruby says, cutting her off. "You didn't bring me out here to lecture me about Demarcus, did you?"

"Demarcus?"

"So I know his name. So what?"

Cadence pulls her notepad from her messenger bag before shouting at the guard, "Excuse me. Can you come here a moment?"

"Ma'am?" Demarcus asks and jogs toward them, the gravel crunching under his boots.

Ruby glances between Cadence and the approaching guard. "What are you doing?"

Cadence holds up a finger, shushing her. "Demarcus, is it?"

"Yes, ma'am," he says, squinting as he hovers over them.

"I know you just started working here." Cadence smiles, but Ruby knows it's not sincere. "How long has it been now?"

"Eight days," Demarcus answers, lifting his chin.

"And I'm sure you've seen what the inside of her cell looks like?"

He gives a slight smile. "Uh, yes, ma'am."

Cadence glares her disappointment at Ruby before looking back at him. "Not very appealing, right?"

The guard shifts between his feet. "Ma'am?"

Ruby rolls her eyes. It's not *her* fault he's been in her cell.

"How old are you, Demarcus?"

"Twenty-two."

Ruby heaves a sigh, looking up at his beautiful, confused face. "You've made your point, all right?"

"What's going on?" he asks.

"Demarcus, this girl is a minor," Cadence says, nodding toward Ruby. "Did you know that?"

He hesitates and then nods.

"Despite what you may have been told about her, that means if you touch her, I'll make sure my good friends at the DA's office throw your ass in jail for statutory rape."

"I thought you worked with the public defender."

Ruby's face heats. *Cute but stupid.* She shakes her head. *Still, could have been fun.*

"That's true," Cadence says, her smile taut, "but for you, I'll make an exception and take the elevator up a couple of extra floors. I bet we can even ensure you a tiny cell like Ruby's and a large, friendly roommate to share it with."

"Uh," Demarcus says before taking a few steps backward, practically tripping over himself. "Sorry, ma'am. Got it."

Ruby watches his ass as he retreats. "Could you *be* more embarrassing?"

"Yes," Cadence says, shaking her head. "You do know you couldn't possibly have a real relationship with him." She looks at her with the kind of sympathy that immediately bores under Ruby's skin.

"What do you know about it?"

"I know he's a guard. You're an inmate, and he's wanting to

take advantage of the situation."

She's starting to sound a little too much like Maya. That Redd was only wanting to take advantage of her. Heat blooms inside Ruby's chest. "Are you done?"

"For now," Cadence says with a nod. "I noticed you haven't written Maya in a while."

Ruby bristles. It's like Cadence is always reading her mind. "I don't want to talk about that."

"So what *do* you want to talk about, Ruby?" She gives a frustrated huff, and Ruby's face warms from the abrupt edge in Cadence's voice. "Your trial is a little over a month away, and there still seems to be some gaps in your memory. Maybe writing to Maya might help."

"She never writes me back, and I'm sick of trying."

"I think that's a mistake."

"Yeah, you already said that."

"Well? Why stop now?"

A sudden gust of wind kicks up the dirt around them. Ruby roughly wipes the grit from her eyes. "Because writing to her makes me feel like shit."

"Are you at least willing to talk about her?" Cadence taps her watch. "We're running out of time here."

"I don't know why you care so much about her. You already made me talk about my mom. Isn't that enough for you?" Ruby shifts on the bench, seeing the impatience on Cadence's face. "You're not going to let this go, are you? Even though you said you'd drop shit when I asked?"

"Nope." Cadence makes a note; her paper flaps in the breeze. "Not this time."

"Of course you want to talk about Maya. *Everybody* loves Maya."

Cadence's brow furrows. "Who's everybody?"

Out of the corner of her eye, Ruby spots Demarcus pacing. He refuses to look at her, and she can't help but wonder if he'll still be nice to her after what Cadence said to him.

"Can you focus, please, and stop looking at him?" Cadence shakes her head. "You do know he only wants one thing?"

Of course she does, and Ruby has no intention of giving it to him. All she really wanted was to feel not so alone anymore. But she doesn't say any of that, blurting instead, "What if I like fucking older men?"

"Oh, honey," Cadence says. Her voice is lined with sadness, and Ruby can't stand it.

"You think you're better than me, just like Maya did."

Cadence seems to consider Ruby for a second and then sighs. "Look, I get why you don't want to talk about any of this, okay? But I don't think you have an option not to trust me here. I'm doing everything in my power to show you that you can, and at some point, you have to decide. This is that point. And you know what? You need to earn my trust, too."

Ruby narrows her eyes but says nothing.

"Weren't expecting that, were you?" Cadence gestures between them. "Trust is a two-way street, and I'm sticking my neck out for you here." She collects her things.

"Wait," Ruby says, flustered. She can't just leave her like this. "Where are you going?"

"Guard!" Cadence calls. As Demarcus marches toward them, she rises from the bench. "Trust requires trust, Ruby. There's no way around it." She eases into her jacket. "I'm done wasting my time. Have them call me when you've figured it out."

The social worker turns on her heel and moves toward the exit without looking back. Right before the rain begins to fall.

~~JUNE 11, 2023~~

~~Dear Maya,~~

~~I'm sure you thought~~

~~JUNE 20, 2023~~

~~Dear Maya,~~

~~I don't know how~~

JUNE 29, 2023

It's been almost a month since Ruby last saw Cadence in the yard, and now that she's here with her in the interview room again, she feels foolish for ever letting so much time pass, especially since Ruby's nerves have only been getting worse—and the trial is less than a week away. She takes a ragged breath, hovering, uncertain.

Cadence gestures across the table. "Have a seat."

As Ruby takes her place in the chair on the other side of the table, she tries another half breath. "I think I'm ready to talk about Maya," she says.

Her voice is shakier than she'd like. She can't stop thinking of the last time she told someone about Maya. She told, even though she promised she wouldn't.

Cadence doesn't say anything or give her a smug look or anything like that. She just uncaps her pen and nods, and Ruby is relieved.

"Just try to breathe, Ruby. Maybe you could start with how you two met?"

Ruby inhales deeply. "Maya worked at the Sonic by our apartment, like I told you. I went looking for her. I knew her from school—I'd seen her around. I mean, she didn't know me. But when she saw me, she asked if she could get me something." The girl nervously taps the cold metal table with both hands. "I told her I didn't have any money. Maya brought me a milkshake anyway—cookies

219

'n cream—and—" She sighs, wondering for the hundredth time how Maya knew. She drags her palms, squeaking, against the table, before letting them drop to her lap. "I guess she saw it in me too."

"What?"

"The stuff that was happening to me. Because it was happening to her."

Cadence's pen scratches against the page. "Did you talk to her about it?"

"Not at first. But I came back the next day and then the next and pretty much every day after that. We just started talking about other stuff." She looks up at Cadence. "Maya's super smart, like you. She really likes to read and loves math. I mean, who loves math?"

"Not me," Cadence says, returning her smile.

"I know, right? She's also super religious. I wasn't sure about that at first. Like, goes-to-church-every-Sunday religious. I'd never been around anyone like that, but she was cool with me. She didn't really judge me even though she went to one of those really judgy kinds of churches—the kind where they say you have to repent or seek forgiveness for your sins or whatever."

"Did she talk about her beliefs with you?"

"A little. She always liked to say how church was the one place she felt like she had nothing to hide since God already knows everything about us anyway. She'd say God has a plan for our lives, doesn't give us anything we can't handle, that sort of thing."

"And what did you think about all of that?"

"I thought it was bullshit, especially since it wasn't even her fault." Ruby shakes her head, not wanting to talk about that yet. "Maya was into all kinds of weird stuff. She knits these little animals."

"Knits?" Cadence says, an eyebrow arched.

Ruby lets out a relieved laugh. "Yeah, I think her mom taught her or something. She always liked to talk about what she was going to do when she got out. Like maybe she'd become a doctor, or a nurse like her older sister."

"Got out of where?"

Ruby chews at the loose skin on her bottom lip, knowing Cadence will probably give up on her if she doesn't at least *try* to talk about it. "She was living with her grandpa. Their mom died of cancer a few years before, and her older sister had already moved out."

"So she wanted to get away from her grandfather?"

She bites too hard and flinches, tasting blood. Her fingers go to her lip, split and stinging.

"You need to stop for a second?"

Does she? Should she? She definitely should.

Cadence tilts her head, her voice gently nudging. "Ruby?"

Ruby covers her face with her hands. "I shouldn't be talking to you about this. It's not right." Her hands drop roughly. "You don't know. You have no idea."

"Then help me understand."

"I shouldn't be doing this."

"You can trust me."

She gasps for air. "Her grandpa got her pregnant."

Cadence's expression breaks for a split second. "Ruby, I'm—"

"He's in prison now," Ruby says in a rush, her chin trembling. She can't stand to hear whatever Cadence was going to say. She doesn't want to listen to her sympathy, her pity. Not when she just betrayed Maya again. She presses her sore lips together.

"What—" Cadence pauses for a moment, as if reconsidering what she was going to say. "What did you do when Maya told you?"

"She asked me what she should do about it—the baby." Ruby closes her eyes and tries another breath. "She asked what I thought about an abortion."

"Is that what she eventually decided to do?"

Ruby opens her eyes. "Yeah. It was right before they changed the law, and she wouldn't have been able to afford to go out of state, so she couldn't wait very long. She was really scared."

Cadence lowers her pen. "And I'm assuming the one place she felt safe no longer did?"

Ruby flinches, remembering how Maya cried because she thought God hated her for the choice she'd made.

"Did you two talk about it after?"

"Not really," Ruby answers, worry lining her voice. "After she told me what happened to her, everything that was going on with me seemed—" She gasps again.

"Hey. Your stuff was just as difficult," Cadence says. "Only different. I'm sorry that happened to your friend."

She thought she didn't want Cadence's sympathy, but something inside her unclenches, just for a moment.

"Ruby," Cadence says softly. "Did something else happen between you and Maya?"

She rubs her palms against her pants while recalling how she ruined everything. "Before she'd had the abortion, Redd started showing up at Sonic. Apparently, before we got together, he had tried to get with Maya. But she said no."

"Maya?" Cadence says, seeming surprised.

"Okay if I stand?" Ruby asks, too jittery to wait for permission.

"Maybe better to sit this time."

Ruby complies, her hands now trembling.

"Did Maya say anything to you about Redd?"

"We had a stupid fight. Not long after I met Redd, he asked me to move out of the neighborhood and move in with him to his place, up closer to LBJ."

"The interstate?"

Ruby nods. "He even offered to help take care of Maya and the baby." Ruby sniffs and swipes the heel of her hand against the tip of her nose. "I knew I shouldn't have told him about the baby. I really shouldn't even be telling you."

"I won't say a word to anyone."

"What about Mr. Tate?"

Cadence looks at her without blinking. "I promise."

"Okay," Ruby says, her voice uncertain.

Cadence's expression softens. "So what did Maya say when she found out you'd told Redd?"

"She was pissed." Ruby finds the crescent moons in her palms. Her fingers curl until she can feel the sharpness of her nails. "Maya kept telling me he was bad for me and asking why I was so stupid, trusting a guy like Redd. She said it was all a game for him. He didn't love me."

"And how did that make you feel?"

"Pissed. I mean, I love him." She shakes her head. "*Loved* him. Here was this nice guy, offering me a real chance. It was easy for her."

"What was?" Cadence asks, taking notes again.

"Everything."

"What makes you say that?"

"Guys really liked Maya." Ruby shrugs. "She's beautiful, and she didn't have to worry like the rest of us."

"Sounds like she had a lot to worry about."

"But why didn't she want to be with me? Redd was talking about getting me some auditions and helping Maya pay for college. We could have been together. Like a real family. We would have taken care of each other. Then none of this shit would have ever happened."

Cadence scribbles without looking up, like she can't get the words down fast enough.

"What are you writing?" Ruby asks defensively. "You said you wouldn't tell."

Cadence looks up from her notepad and shakes her head. "Open your hands."

Ruby loosens her fingers. She hadn't felt a thing, but there they are—tiny slashes of red across the crescents.

"Here." Cadence finds a tissue in her bag.

The room is suddenly too warm, suffocating. Ruby snatches the tissue and roughly presses it against her cuts while she tries to catch her breath.

"So you tried to convince Maya to go with you and Redd, to move in with you two?"

Ruby struggles for air. "I don't feel so good." She stops pressing, the tissue in shreds.

"We can stop for a second. Do you want some water or crackers?" Cadence reaches for her bag.

Ruby's stomach is churning. She wipes her forehead with the back of her hand. "I wanted Maya to come with me so bad."

"And she refused?"

"She was hurt that I'd told Redd about the baby—it was supposed to be between just us. But then I was so pissed she wouldn't go with us, and when she asked me if I thought she'd done something wrong when she got an abortion, if she was going to go to hell, I—I didn't say anything. I just let her think . . ." Ruby shakes her head. "Of course I didn't think she did something wrong. I was just so stupid. I was too wrapped up in my own shit. It was my fault she didn't want to come. I was a shitty fucking friend, and now—"

Cadence's hand comes away from her bag. "Maya's decision to stay had nothing to do with you. You know that, right?"

"Redd was just so—"

"Convincing," Cadence answers.

"I thought he loved me." Her cheeks warm with shame. "And I know what you're thinking."

Cadence takes up her notepad and pen again. "I'm thinking you were in a tough spot."

"She tried to warn me, but I wouldn't listen," Ruby says, her voice sounding far off. "I missed her after we left. I'd seen Maya every fucking day, and then—I didn't."

"It's hard to lose a friend, especially a good friend like that. They don't come around often."

Ruby shakes her head. "I don't know, maybe I only thought we were friends."

"Of course you were friends. Maya clearly trusted you. That's why she told you what was happening to her. And that's why she told you not to go with Redd. She was trying to protect you."

Ruby inhales Cadence's words. "I'd like to stand now, okay?"

Cadence glances toward the door, checking, before she nods.

Ruby begins to pace. "Redd told me to forget her after I went with him, but I couldn't let it go."

"I understand you didn't have much of a choice." Cadence presses the end of her pen into the paper, the ink pooling and spreading across the page. "But some may question why you decided to stay with Redd."

Ruby stops pacing as a familiar ache, black as Cadence's ink, saturates her chest: Because she loved him. Because he took care of her when no one else did. What would people not understand about that? "Redd set me up with some new clothes. A place to stay. Sure, he could be an asshole sometimes, but he was also really sweet." Her gaze slowly falls.

"But sometimes he wasn't sweet," Cadence guesses.

She looks up. "He took me on a date to this place not long after I moved in with him," Ruby says, her voice quiet. "Highland Park Village?"

Cadence lifts her pen and nods. "Pretty fancy."

Ruby wipes her forehead on her sleeve and starts moving again—faster—her fists pumping up and down at her sides. "Yeah, I'd never been before, and it made me really nervous being there. Redd had bought me some new clothes at the mall, but everyone there was dressed *super* nice. And I swear every car was a Mercedes or a Tesla. Even the kids were driving BMWs. Nothing like Redd's beat-up Ford pickup. Redd thought those cars were real sweet, especially this orange sports car with some Italian name. I can't remember."

"Can you slow down a little?" Cadence says.

Ruby swallows before speaking again. "I'd never seen anything like it. These women were walking around with these purses that probably cost more than our rent." She stops. "How does it even feel to live like that?"

"I don't know."

"Can you imagine?" Ruby can't help it; she almost smiles thinking about what it must be like. "You wouldn't have to worry about whether you'd still have a place to stay the next month or have to choose between food or electricity or steal tampons from the school bathroom."

"There's definitely security in having a regular paycheck," Cadence says, "but there's a difference between being able to afford necessities and paying thousands for something that's just meant to hold your keys. I have no idea what it feels like to live like that. Not sure I want to know."

"I wouldn't mind," Ruby says.

"Let's go back to your date," Cadence says.

"Redd said he wanted to show me off." Ruby slides a hand across her stomach. "That I was prettier than those rich bitches, and when they gave me dirty looks, that only meant they were jealous."

"Did that make you feel good?"

Ruby shakes her head. All she remembers is how badly she wanted to believe Redd thought she was pretty. "I was hungry. We didn't have any money for one of those nice restaurants, so we went to the Starbucks, and he bought me a vanilla drink that was kind of like a milkshake." She remembers the feel of the sun on her face, the slippery fabric of her new dress, the cold drink mixed with the warmth in her chest because she and Redd were out together, like boyfriend and girlfriend. "Then these other guys started giving me looks."

"Did you know them?"

"It was just these random guys sitting at a table close by." Ruby takes a breath. "We were sitting on the sidewalk, and Redd leaned over me and started licking the whipped cream from my lips. His hand slid up my leg . . ." Her heart begins to race like it did then—not with love, but with fear. By then, she knew better than to try to push him off, so she sat perfectly still until he finished. "That's the first time I counted, with Redd."

Cadence flips the page. "Counted?"

"It's this trick Maya taught me. She said to start counting, you know, in your head, when a guy does stuff you don't like, and it keeps your mind off it." Ruby lets out a dry laugh. "But you know what those other guys did?"

Cadence remains silent. She doesn't move.

"They gave Redd a thumbs-up when he finished. He gave them his card." Ruby returns to the table. "Nobody said a word that whole fucking time. None of those fancy people. Nobody walking by. Nobody said nothing." Ruby drops into her chair.

"Someone should have helped you."

Ruby shakes her head.

"I'm serious. That's not okay." Cadence lowers her pen. "You want to know how it would have made me feel if that were happening to me and no one was acknowledging it?"

"How?"

"Invisible."

"I guess," Ruby says, even though that's exactly how she felt then and every day that followed. "Pretty soon after, I got this." She tugs at the collar of her shirt, revealing the tattoo on her collarbone.

Cadence makes a note. "Did you want to get that tattoo?"

She shrugs. "Redd told me it showed everyone I was his girl.

It probably sounds stupid, but I thought he wanted me to get it because he loved me. I was actually proud of this." She covers her skin again with her shirt, her hand shaking. "But he didn't love me, did he?"

Cadence looks up from her notes. "I'm sorry, Ruby."

"I mean, he had a wife and four kids, right? How did I not see it? Fuck, Maya tried to tell me what he was . . . but I fell for the act. What does that say about me?" Her hands clench in her lap, her knuckles turning white. "Stupid."

"You weren't stupid. You were vulnerable, and that's exactly what pimps like Redd are looking for."

Her hands loosen slightly.

"He used you."

"I just really wanted to believe there was someone who could love me, you know?"

Cadence smiles sadly. "Of course I do."

JUNE 30, 2023

Dear Maya,

I know I said I was done writing, but I've been thinking about it, and you were right about Redd. I should have listened when you tried to warn me. I wouldn't be in this mess right now if I'd listened.

My trial starts next week, and it's like my fear has grown these fingers and they're closing around my throat. I can hardly breathe when I think about my case. But it's all I can think about.

Mr. Tate came to see me one last time before trial starts so we could go over my testimony. Cadence was right that he's got some pretty ugly ties. Today he was wearing a blue one with stormtroopers hidden in the paisley. When I asked if he was a Star Wars fan or something, he said his daughters gave it to him for Father's Day. I didn't say anything about how hideous it was since he seemed so proud.

I didn't want to be an ass, especially since he remembered I wasn't real happy that he didn't let me tell my story at the hearing and he's going to let me testify this time. He said, "Cadence thinks you're ready to testify, and I agree. The jury should hear it from you. They can only truly understand if they hear what happened to you in your own words."

Can you believe that?

I told him I've already gone over my story with Cadence, but he *still wanted to go over it with me. My heart is racing just thinking about it. I only hope Cadence is right that I'll remember everything I'm supposed to say and don't fuck it all up.*

Mr. Tate called going over my testimony "woodshedding." Did you know it was called that? I asked him why it was called that, but he said he didn't know. I've never known a guy who said when he didn't know something. Have you? Usually they act like I'm all stupid, but not Mr. Tate.

Then he started questioning me. Not only about what happened with Eric, but also about things before that, with my mom and with Redd. I didn't tell him everything, but thankfully he didn't push.

Mr. Tate told me to listen carefully and only answer the question I'm being asked. He even had these cards that had a picture of a traffic light on them. When I was answering his questions, he'd hold up the red light, which meant I should stop blabbing. If he liked my answer, he'd hold up the green.

At first I got a lot of red lights. He always liked my short answers better. He said, "You don't need to explain because it's the prosecutor's job to ask the right questions" and "You shouldn't make the prosecutor's job easy, because he's trying to put you away for life."

That fucked with my head, hearing Mr. Tate say it like that. I know what I'm facing, but hearing it out loud like that from him kind of freaked me out.

So I asked him if he thought we had a chance of winning. He didn't answer. Cadence never answers when I ask her that either. I think it's because they think we're going to lose and don't want to hurt my feelings when we've been working so hard.

He just said, "All you need to do is tell the truth. Listen carefully and answer the question you're asked, and try not to curse so much so the jury doesn't get distracted." He wants me to tell the truth, but I'm not even sure how the truth sounds. What if they don't believe me?

Now I'm shaky, thinking about the trial. I don't want Doc to give me any more shit, though. I need to be clear so I can answer the questions like we practiced.

I'll try to write again when trial starts. And since you always were the praying type, can you say one for me? Just in case.

Your friend,
Ruby

TATE: Now, Ruby, you indicated you met Mr. Shandler at Sonic?

MONROE: Yeah, I met him around the time Mom kicked me out. Except he told me his name was Redd Dogg. He was really sweet on me. He told me he wanted to take care of me.

TATE: And did you take him up on his offer?

MONROE: Not at first. Like I said, I met him around the time Mom kicked me out, and I was staying at Jade's at first, but when I had no place else to go, I said okay since we were already together by then anyway.

TATE: So what month and year was it that you moved in with him?

MONROE: September. I'd just started freshman year. That was in 2021.

TATE: How old were you at the time, Ruby?

MONROE: I'd just turned fourteen on August 1.

TATE: Okay, and how old was Mr. Shandler?

MONROE: Twenty-three, I think.

TATE: Did you think it was unusual that a twenty-three-year-old man was paying attention to a fourteen-year-old girl?

MONROE: Not really. I'd always gotten attention from older guys.

TATE: And did you and Mr. Shandler go on dates?

MONROE: At first we did.

TATE: Where did you go on these dates?

MONROE: Before I moved in with him?

TATE: Yes.

MONROE: Mostly we'd go eat or hang out. Like at the Sonic or Taco Cabana or something like that. One time we went to Highland Park Village. That was just after I moved in with him.

TATE: Would you say Mr. Shandler was your boy-friend?

MONROE: Yeah.

TATE: And were you intimate with him?

MONROE: Not at first.

TATE: When you and Mr. Shandler first started dating, were you holding down a job?

MONROE: Um, no. I tried, though.

TATE: You tried to get a job?

VANELLI: Objection, Your Honor. Asked and answered.

THE COURT: Overruled.

TATE: You tried to get a job, Ruby?

MONROE: Yeah, working the checkout line or babysitting. I applied at the Sonic to be a wait-ress. My friend tried to help me get a job there. But nobody would hire me. They said I was too young and should go back to school. That was August.

TATE: Did you return to school for your fresh-man year?

MONROE: At first, but then I stopped after I

moved in with Redd. It was only a few weeks into the school year.

TATE: Were you ever contacted by the school or anyone about your lack of attendance?

MONROE: No.

TATE: A truancy officer didn't reach out to you?

MONROE: No. If they tried, I wasn't living at home, so I never heard anything about it.

TATE: Did Mr. Shandler know you were trying to seek employment?

MONROE: Yeah.

TATE: Did he make any suggestions as to how you could make some money?

MONROE: Before I moved in with him, he said I had a good look and voice, so maybe I should just try being a singer. He knew how much I loved to sing.

TATE: And did Mr. Shandler have any suggestions for how you could become a professional singer?

MONROE: Redd said he had this friend who was a photographer who could hook me up on some modeling jobs. He also said he knew a talent scout and a producer friend that might be able to get me an audition for singing jobs, things like that.

TATE: Before you moved in with him, had Mr. Shandler bought you anything?

MONROE: Yeah, I didn't really have much stuff from home, so he bought me some clothes. Food. Normal boyfriend stuff.

TATE: Did he give you drugs?

MONROE: Not at first.

TATE: Was Mr. Shandler a drug user?

MONROE: I knew he smoked pot, and that's all he'd ever done before I moved in with him. Later, I saw him do other stuff.

TATE: Like what?

MONROE: Heroin. He'd smoke that black-tar stuff.

TATE: Did you smoke with him?

MONROE: Yeah, but just pot. After I moved in with him, he'd sometimes give me these pills to help me sleep, but I didn't like how those made me feel. He'd also give me some drank to keep me even.

TATE: And what's drank, Ruby?

MONROE: I don't know. Like this purple drink Redd gave me sometimes. It tastes like shit but makes you feel real good. Light.

TATE: And did you ever go out for one of those modeling jobs?

MONROE: No, Jade's mom kicked me out before I had the chance to try.

TATE: Is that when you moved in with Mr. Shandler?

MONROE: Yeah.

TATE: And where did you go?

MONROE: To the Super 8 motel.

TATE: Is that the Super 8 motel on Maxwell Boulevard in Northwest Dallas?

MONROE: That's right.

TATE: Mr. Shandler lived in a motel?

MONROE: He said he did.

TATE: I take it that was the first time you had been to his place, when you moved in with him?

MONROE: Yeah.

TATE: Before you moved in with him, had you been intimate with Mr. Shandler?

MONROE: No.

TATE: What about after?

MONROE: Yes.

TATE: Was the sex consensual, Ruby?

MONROE: I guess. I mean, I guess. He said that's what people do when they love each other. So, yeah.

TATE: Ruby, did you know Mr. Shandler was already married at the time you two were together at the Super 8 motel?

MONROE: No. I knew he'd had other girlfriends, but that's all.

TATE: So I take it you didn't know Mr. Shandler had children either?

MONROE: No.

TATE: Now, Ruby, after you moved in with him, did you learn Mr. Shandler was having some financial difficulties?

MONROE: Yes, he said he was waiting on a big payout. But there was this guy—I think he was a friend of Redd's or something—who was making threats about money he owed him.

TATE: What kind of threats?

MONROE: I'm not sure, but Redd was pretty upset.

TATE: Did Mr. Shandler ask you to help him take care of that situation?

MONROE: He—uh—

TATE: It's okay, Ruby. Take your time.

MONROE: I— Can you repeat the question?

TATE: Did Mr. Shandler ask you to help him take care of his debt?

MONROE: He asked me to help. I found out he still owed the guy after, though. I just kind of helped him put it off.

TATE: So you agreed to help him, then?

MONROE: Redd asked me, so—

TATE: How did Mr. Shandler propose you help?

MONROE: By giving—giving his friend a blow job.

TATE: And you did that?

MONROE: For Redd, yeah.

TATE: Do you remember the first time Mr. Shandler asked you to have sex with a stranger?

MONROE: It wasn't long after I moved into the Super 8.

TATE: And did you get paid for that sexual act?

MONROE: No. Like I said, Redd owed him money, so it was like a partial payback for that.

TATE: I see. And Mr. Shandler and the person you call "Redd" are the same person?

MONROE: Yeah.

TATE: Okay, so at what point did you realize Mr. Shandler was a pimp?

MONROE: I guess I kind of started to figure it out when I got this.

TATE: And for the record, you're pointing to the tattoo on your collarbone?

MONROE: Uh-huh.

TATE: Is that a yes, Ruby?

MONROE: Uh, yes.

TATE: And what is that tattooed on your collarbone?

MONROE: R. D.

TATE: What does R. D. stand for?

MONROE: Redd Dogg.

TATE: Is Redd Dogg Mr. Shandler's pimp name?

MONROE: I found that out later. I thought it was just a nickname, you know? But yeah, he made me get this to show everyone I belonged to him.

TATE: Like a slave?

VANELLI: Objection, Your Honor. Counsel is testifying.

THE COURT: Sustained.

TATE: Why would he do that?

MONROE: A lot of girls have them. I guess it's just something they do so other pimps don't try to get too close. So they know who you belong to and don't try to fu—mess with you.

TATE: What do you mean by "mess with you"?

MONROE: Try and steal you away, I guess. They don't like it when other guys try to steal their stuff.

TATE: And were you Redd's "stuff," as you say?

MONROE: Yeah.

TATE: I see. And did something change between you and Redd Dogg after you got that tattoo?

MONROE: Yeah, he said I needed to start making money.

TATE: And what did he propose you do?

MONROE: It— It wasn't singing.

TATE: What did he tell you to do, Ruby?

MONROE: He said the only thing I had that was worth anything was my ass and pussy, so I better start working it and make him his due. He said I already owed him for letting me stay with him.

TATE: And what was his due?

MONROE: He told me since he'd got me a place to stay, clothes, food, pot—those were loans. I had to pay him back.

TATE: Did he tell you that you were going to have to pay him back when he gave those things to you?

MONROE: No.

VANELLI: Objection, hearsay.

THE COURT: Sustained. The jury should disregard that last answer.

TATE: What did you do when he suggested you sell yourself for money?

MONROE: I told him no.

VANELLI: Objection, hearsay.

THE COURT: Overruled.

TATE: So you told Mr. Shandler that you didn't want to sell yourself to strange men; is that right?

MONROE: Yeah, that's right. I told him I wasn't interested in doing that shit. I wanted to get a job at the grocery store or something else.

TATE: Why didn't you just go home?

MONROE: My mom already kicked me out. And I—I loved him, and I didn't really have anywhere else to go. He was so mad, and I thought he'd stop being mad at me if I just did what he wanted. So I put some makeup on like he said. He picked out what I should wear and then drove me to the 7-Eleven on the corner. I was really nervous.

TATE: And did you sell yourself for money that night?

MONROE: Yeah.

TATE: How many people did you sleep with, Ruby?

MONROE: There were three guys that first night.

TATE: And how did that make you feel?

MONROE: [Inaudible]

TATE: Ruby?

MONROE: I don't know. Empty, I guess.

TATE: Did you keep the money?

MONROE: Redd took it.

TATE: Did he give you any of the money?

MONROE: No, he was pissed.

TATE: Why?

MONROE: He was mad I'd slept with those guys

even though he told me to do it. He was pretty lit by then. He said I smelled like other men. And that I needed to take a shower.

TATE: And so what happened next?

MONROE: He made me keep my clothes off after the shower. He wouldn't let me get dressed.

TATE: Why not?

MONROE: I guess he wanted to punish me, I don't know. He started saying shit about my body. Pointing out where I was too fat or skinny. Stuff like that.

TATE: Do you think he did that to keep you from running away?

VANELLI: Objection, calls for speculation.

THE COURT: I'll allow it.

TATE: You can answer.

MONROE: What was the question again?

TATE: Do you think Mr. Shandler didn't allow you to put your clothes on to keep you from running away?

MONROE: Yeah, partly. But then he slept with me. And I thought we were good, you know. I thought maybe it was all a mistake and he wouldn't ask me to do any of that stuff again.

TATE: Were you good, Ruby?

MONROE: No.

TATE: What happened next?

MONROE: Redd woke me up. He—

TATE: Ruby?

MONROE: Sorry. He did some stuff that woke me up.

TATE: Were you dressed or undressed when he awakened you?

MONROE: I didn't have clothes on. He didn't let me.

TATE: Why did he awaken you?

MONROE: He said I was lazy and needed to get back to work. That he needed money for some shit.

TATE: Did he mean drugs?

MONROE: Yeah.

TATE: And how did he look?

MONROE: All crazy. He was crashing pretty hard.

TATE: What made you think that?

MONROE: I'd seen my mom crashing enough times to know to get out of the way.

TATE: Did you get out of the way?

MONROE: I tried to leave, but he wouldn't let me.

TATE: Did he do anything to stop you?

MONROE: Yeah.

THE COURT: Mr. Tate, I'm going to stop you right there. It's almost five o'clock. If you are good with ending here for the day, we can resume with this witness in the morning.

TATE: Yes, Your Honor. Here is good.

THE COURT: Any objection to ending now, Mr. Vanelli?

VANELLI: No, Your Honor.

THE COURT: Very good, then. We'll resume with Miss Monroe's testimony in the morning. The jury is reminded not to discuss this case with anyone—not your spouse, no family members, no friends, not even the other jurors—until the end of trial. Okay, we'll stand in recess until 9:30 tomorrow morning.

BAILIFF: All rise.

[THE JURY EXITS THE COURTROOM]

HERE ENDS THE EXCERPT

n   wh

Ruby gets g

JULY 8, 2023

Dear Maya,

Sorry I haven't written sooner. It's the weekend after my trial started, and it's just been a lot being in that courtroom with everyone looking at me. I haven't testified yet, and I'm still really nervous.

It's early morning now and none of the women are up yet, but there's something I've been thinking about all night, and I couldn't wait to tell you.

Guys are a bunch of pricks.

I'm probably not telling you anything you don't know. The thing is, I just heard the news at lights-out about this guard I thought I liked. His name is Demarcus, but he got fired for fucking one of the other inmates down in the laundry. The woman got lockdown for two months, but I heard he got a new job working at some high school as a security guard.

Apparently, the warden found him midfuck on a pile of clean sheets. Thank goodness they still don't let me have any blankets or anything or I'd be stripping them off for sure right now.

I really think there's something wrong with me. You knew Redd was a prick and I didn't see that coming either. I mean, he had a wife and kids! How did I not see that?

Even though my trial has already started, there are some things I still need to tell you. All of these letters, they were supposed to

246

help me feel better, but all they've done is make me see how fucked up and lonely I really am.

I'm sorry I told Redd your secret. He was asking why you were so sad all the time, and I wanted him to understand, and I thought I could trust him. Even writing that now, it seems pretty stupid. I guess all I can say is I thought I was helping, but the truth is, I was just trying to get him to like me. I thought I needed your help since he already liked you, and I took it out on you when it wasn't even your fault. I'm really sorry.

There's something else you should know. Redd isn't the only one I told. I probably should've said something in my last letter, but I told Cadence too. I'd been telling her everything that led up to me leaving with Redd, and I just needed her to understand you and why you told me not to leave and what you and I had been through. I also had to tell her so she could know what a bad friend I was. How I got so mad at you when you wouldn't come with me and Redd, how I wanted to hurt you. The way I didn't answer when you asked me if you did the right thing getting an abortion and if God would forgive you.

I guess I just wanted her to know the truth about what kind of person I am. And I want you to know too.

I was so pissed after Mr. Tate wouldn't let me tell my side of the story at that hearing, but now I'm not so sure I want to tell anyone. I'm so fucking afraid all the time. Cadence seems to think that if I'm honest with her and with myself, and if I tell the jury my story, that's my only chance. But why would they believe me after they hear about the stupid things I've done? What if they lock me away for life?

Maybe Doc will give me something if I scream. Something to help me sleep even though it's morning.

By the way, you don't have to worry about Cadence telling any-
one your secret. That doesn't mean I don't feel like shit for telling
someone else, and I won't do it again. Please believe me.

The guard is coming. I'll try to write again soon.

Your friend,
Ruby

JULY 8, 2023

Cadence smiles as Ruby enters the interview room. She's pleased to see that, even though the girl appears tired, she's sober. Right before Ruby arrived, the jail's physician reported how she had asked a guard for something to help her sleep, but when Doc came to her cell, she told him to forget about it because she "needed to keep her head clear for trial."

"You look surprised to see me," Cadence says as soon as the door closes behind the guard.

"It's Saturday."

"With the trial, it's been hard to get a chance to talk in private, but I wanted to see how you're doing. I've been thinking about you."

A smile tugs at the girl's lips despite everything. "You have?"

Cadence nods. "It's hard enough to sit through all of that, and I'm not even the one accused. I can only imagine how difficult it has been for you." She gestures for Ruby to take her place at the table, and she does.

"Can I ask you something about that?"

"Of course. I might not have the answer, but I can try to find out, and Brian can let you know before everything resumes on Monday."

Ruby shifts in her chair. "That's just it. Why won't Mr. Tate let me talk to you or even look at you when we're in the courtroom? He says I can only talk to him."

"He's trying to protect you. Brian wants you to appear as though you're taking the process seriously," Cadence says, gesturing between them, "which of course *we* know you are. But it might not seem like it if you turn around, even just to say hello. I know it can be pretty nerve-racking with the judge and jury always watching."

Ruby mindlessly claws at her arm. "I'm pretty sure the jury already thinks I'm trash anyway, so—"

"You're not trash."

"Sure." Her hand falls to her lap. "I guess."

Cadence considers the girl for a second—slumped shoulders, eyes down, fight gone—and shakes her head.

It's as if Ruby can sense her gaze and looks up. "What?"

"You seem really down," Cadence says and immediately regrets it. *Down?* She's only living through something most adults would find terrifying. "I'm sorry. That was a stupid thing to say."

Ruby's eyes are rimmed in red, her expression unreadable.

Actually, "down" doesn't even begin to describe how Ruby appears right now. More like "devastated." When Cadence met Brian this morning over coffee, had he sensed the toll the trial had already taken on Ruby? *I think it's all going to come down to her testimony,* he'd said.

Cadence had known this from the first time she'd met the girl: it was always going to come down to Ruby's story.

But I still get the sense there's things she's not telling us, he'd added, and Cadence agrees.

Of course, they both understand how sympathy could serve as

a life raft for Ruby. "Ruby," she says softly.

The girl brings her feet up onto the chair and hugs her knees.

"The truth is, Brian asked me to come here today because he's concerned about your upcoming testimony."

"That makes more sense." She curls deeper into herself.

Cadence flinches. "No, that's not what I meant. I'm also here because I've been thinking about you, of course. We both have."

Ruby doesn't say anything.

"I'm not doing a very good job today, am I?" Cadence shakes her head, recalling the haggard look on Brian's face—the stubble across his chin, the stained T-shirt, the third cup of coffee. "I suppose with the way things are going, Brian has been losing sleep."

"He's not the only one."

No, he's not, Cadence thinks. "The good news is he feels we've had some small victories along the way. But in the end, he anticipates it will come down to your testimony."

"No pressure." Ruby pushes her chin into her knees.

"I thought you wanted to testi—" Cadence stops herself, too tired to waste any time rehashing things that have already been decided. Ruby *will* testify. "I agree with him, but to be completely honest, we're also concerned you might not appear sympathetic enough to the jury without a little more background."

Ruby's chin comes up. "I don't need their pity."

There's that fight. Cadence tries not to get ahead of herself, keeping her voice steady. "You said the jury already thinks you're trash. Why would you say that?"

The girl shrugs.

"Did Redd call you that?"

"Only when I did something to make him mad."

Okay, maybe. "It sounds like you blame yourself for the hurtful things he said."

Ruby's feet drop to the floor one by one. "It wasn't all bad, you know."

Cadence doesn't respond, hoping she will say more.

The girl glares. "He was good to me sometimes. Most of the time."

There it is. Cadence laces her fingers on the table, all too familiar with her own mother's trauma bonding. How she became addicted to the approval of abusive men. "Have you ever heard the phrase 'love bombing'?"

The girl's face pinches.

She continues, "It's when an abuser pretends you're everything they've ever been looking for and smothers you with affection. Like, well, a love bomb."

"Are you talking about Redd?"

Cadence nods. "He makes his victim believe the kind version is the 'real' him, but then he gets angry, sometimes even violent. She'll think it's her fault, so she stays to win back his affection."

Ruby leans back in her chair, her expression tight.

"I know this is difficult," Cadence says. After all, it's only been a little over a week since the girl started to come to terms with the truth about the person she thought she loved. "I know you don't want to talk about Redd, and I can't force you to talk about him or anything in your past, for that matter."

"You already know what he made me do."

"I do," Cadence says, hoping she doesn't cause Ruby to shut down altogether, not when they've come this far, "but I also sense there's more you haven't told me."

"Why would anyone care?" Ruby asks with an edge of skepticism. "Nobody's gonna believe me anyway. I stayed with him, even after everything. . . ."

"*I'll* believe you. And if we play this correctly, I believe that the more the jury hears of the whole truth about your life before you met Eric, the more likely they will be to believe you when you tell them what happened with Eric. The more likely they'll sympathize with what you were going through when you met him."

Ruby bristles. "I already told you: I don't want them feeling sorry for me."

"The objective is not to make them feel sorry for you"—*Though that certainly can't hurt*, she thinks—"but to help them understand why you made some of the choices you made."

Ruby's face flushes with defiance. "If you and Mr. Tate are so smart, tell me what you want me to say, and I'll say it."

"We're not—" She cuts herself off, grasping for a way to make her understand. "By now, I hope you realize that I wouldn't ask if we didn't think it was important. This piece of the story needs to be authentic; it needs to come from you. Understand?"

"I guess not," Ruby says, though Cadence suspects she does.

The woman takes a long breath, trying to calm herself, but it only makes her feel the press of exhaustion. "The whole reason you met Eric is because of Redd, right?"

She barely shrugs.

"So it makes sense that you would need to explain. The jury isn't simply going to understand the power Redd had over you. We have to give them an explanation. Did he threaten you?" Cadence asks. "Leaving your abuser can sometimes be the most dangerious part."

"You want to know if Redd 'love bombed' me or whatever?"

"You've hinted at some physical abuse," Cadence says, her pen hovering above the page.

Ruby's expression breaks for the slightest moment, like she can't believe Cadence said it out loud. She glances over to the door, checking, and then calmly rises from her chair.

Cadence looks up at her. "You can trust me, Ruby."

"You always say that."

"Because it's true."

She begins pacing. "I already told you, I did those things because I thought I loved Redd. It makes me fucking sick, all right?"

"And that's even more reason to tell the jury." Cadence counts off on her fingers. "They not only need to hear how he forced you to sell yourself, but did he threaten you? Or hurt you physically?"

She stops pacing.

"How often, Ruby?"

"I don't know what you think you know, but . . ." The girl tries to drop into her seat casually, but Cadence has been with her long enough now to see the cracks.

The air-conditioning vent rattles overhead as the air cycles on and off. Cadence rubs the sides of her head, silently scolding herself. Maybe her instincts are wrong; maybe Ruby isn't capable of giving them anything more.

Or maybe she simply doesn't trust her.

The girl's eyes remain trained on the scratches and dings along the surface of the metal table, her jaw set.

After what seems like forever, their combined breath eventually matches in rhythm. Cadence releases a long sigh as she recalls what she told Ruby that day outside in the yard: *Trust requires trust.* "I shouldn't be doing this."

Ruby looks up from the table.

With a shaky hand, Cadence tugs at the knot that holds her scarf in place and unwinds the delicate silk—

Exposing the angry, puckered scar that zigzags from the base of her throat up her long neck to her jaw.

She gently folds the scarf and places it on the table between them. "I got this when I was fifteen."

Ruby doesn't blink.

"Same age as you are now. My mother was hooked on heroin and turning tricks. She had me really young, and I never knew my dad. But she always seemed to have a boyfriend who stayed with us." She clenches her jaw for a moment, remembering the string of angry men that marched in and out of their lives. "I was so happy when CPS finally sent me to live with my grandma. And my grandma was happy too; she didn't even know she had a grandchild."

Ruby gestures toward Cadence's throat, her finger bobbing as if searching for the right words. "Her boyfriend?"

Cadence gives a slight nod. "Her pimp. When I was with my grandma, I let my guard down. I was naive enough to think my mother's boyfriends would never be able to hurt me again." She recedes into herself and closes her eyes, knowing Ruby doesn't deserve any of this. It's not her fault. Just like it wasn't hers. "They . . . threatened me if I ever said anything. Not that I had anyone I could tell at the time."

"I'm sorry," Ruby whispers, a sad recognition in her voice.

Cadence opens her eyes and takes in the girl sitting in front of her. Scared and caring, smart and vulnerable. Sweet and salty and bitter and sour and spicy. Her fingers brush the silk on the table. "I was finally adjusting to living in a somewhat normal home when my mother's pimp came looking for her. My mother was apparently missing—strung out somewhere, probably—and he was looking for her. When my grandma said she didn't know where she was, he called her a liar and pulled out a knife."

Ruby stills.

"I'd probably seen too many movies," Cadence says with a weak laugh. "I thought I could protect her. I tried to get the knife away from him. As you can see, that didn't work out so well." She drags a finger across the ridges of her scar, down her throat. "He cut me from here to here. My grandma jumped in front of me. I was told a neighbor found us."

"Was she okay?" Ruby asks. Though Cadence can tell she already knows the answer, she shakes her head.

"So that's how it happened. I went to live in a group home after that."

The vent rattles overhead again as Ruby seems to examine each bump and ridge along Cadence's neck. "Why didn't you tell me the first time I asked?"

"Because I'm not supposed to." Cadence grabs the edge of her scarf and squeezes, wadding it inside her fist before releasing the fabric. "It's unprofessional—me telling you all this. I shouldn't be using our time together to talk about my personal life. I'm supposed to be listening to you."

"But I wanted to know."

"Still," Cadence says. "I could get into trouble. For all of it."

"I won't tell."

The corner of Cadence's mouth lifts. "I know. That's why I told you." She sighs, smoothing the silk once more. "It's still hard. Even though it happened years ago, the fear and shame are still there." She nods toward Ruby. "But you should know, most of the time I'm okay. It took a lot of therapy and work, but now I don't even think about it most days." Cadence picks up the scarf and winds it around her neck.

"Do you think I could be okay, too?"

When Cadence finishes with the scarf, she looks directly at the girl. "Honestly?"

Ruby doesn't move.

"I don't know." She taps the table. "I can't even tell you one hundred percent that talking about all of the things that happened to you will help either. I just know talking with someone helped me. It made me feel not so alone in my pain and anger, when I finally started to share those dark things I'd been holding inside."

Ruby shifts in her chair. "So if I tell you, what then?"

"Then I'll have a conversation with Brian, and he'll decide what you two will tell the jury. You've already practiced your testimony with him?"

Ruby nods. "Last week."

"So I'm guessing he'll come talk to you again after you and I fill in the gaps so he can be prepared to walk you through everything with the jury—your past and how you grew up, your time with Redd—what happened with Eric."

"And what if I do and they still don't believe me?"

"That's why we're going to talk about it, and then you and Brian will practice until you feel confident telling your story, leaving no room for doubt."

Ruby rubs her hands on her pants as Cadence pulls another notepad from her messenger bag. "Brian did want me to ask you about a few things that have come up since your trial began." She chooses to ignore the nervous tapping of Ruby's Crocs against the concrete. "Should we start with those?"

"What kind of questions?"

"The reasons you decided to stay with Redd," Cadence says, bracing for Ruby's reaction, "even after you knew what he wanted you to do."

Her chin trembles as she whispers, "Anything else?"

Cadence flips the page, her heart aching for the girl. "Specifics about what happened between you and Eric the day he died."

Ruby presses her lips together and nods.

THE COURT: Welcome back, everyone. Miss Monroe, I'll remind you that, even though we took a break during your testimony yesterday, you are still under oath. Understand?

MONROE: Yes, Your Honor.

THE COURT: You may continue, Mr. Tate.

TATE: Thank you, Your Honor. Ruby, I believe yesterday when we left off, you were starting to tell the jury how Mr. Shandler wouldn't let you leave the Super 8. Do you recall that testimony?

MONROE: Yes.

TATE: Okay, I want to back up a bit to fill in some details before we get to that. Is that okay?

MONROE: I—

TATE: Ruby?

MONROE: Yeah, that's fine.

TATE: Okay, did you ever tell Mr. Shandler that you didn't want to sell yourself to strange men?

MONROE: Yeah, before the first time he told me to do it.

TATE: And what happened?

MONROE: I got a beating.

TATE: Who beat you?

MONROE: Redd.

TATE: Is that why you did what he told you?

MONROE: Uh-huh, partly. I was still crying when he told me to cover the bruise under my eye with some makeup and get dressed. He was so mad. But then after, he was mad again because I'd slept with those guys. I couldn't do anything right.

TATE: Did he hit you again?

MONROE: Not that night.

TATE: Okay, and you mentioned the next morning Redd did some stuff to wake you up. What did he do, Ruby?

MONROE: Um. He slapped me in the face. It startled me so much, I fell off the bed. He screamed at me to get up and kicked me in the stomach.

TATE: Were you dressed or undressed when he awakened you?

MONROE: I didn't have clothes on. He didn't let me.

TATE: Why was he hitting and kicking you?

MONROE: Like I said, he was saying how lazy I was and that he needed money because I was so expensive.

TATE: Okay. After you realized that he wanted you to go out and sell yourself again, did you try to leave the Super 8?

MONROE: I tried, but he wouldn't let me.

TATE: What did he do?

MONROE: [Inaudible]

TATE: Can you repeat that, Ruby?

MONROE: Pulled a gun on me.

TATE: He pointed a gun at you?

MONROE: He—held it to my face. Like right here.

He told me if I didn't get to work, he'd kill me.

TATE: What did you do?

MONROE: I got to work.

TATE: And by "work," you mean having sex with strange men?

MONROE: Yeah.

TATE: And how long did you work for Mr. Shandler?

MONROE: I don't know. A few months.

TATE: And over the course of that time, how many men did you sleep with?

MONROE: I don't know—

TATE: It's okay, Ruby. Take your time.

MONROE: Like fifty or sixty, maybe.

TATE: You had sex with fifty or sixty men you didn't know?

MONROE: Yeah.

TATE: And how many times did Mr. Shandler hit you or beat you up during that period?

MONROE: I don't know.

TATE: I know this is hard, Ruby. But was it more than once?

MONROE: Yeah.

TATE: More than twice?

MONROE: Uh-huh.

TATE: More than three times?

MONROE: Yeah. He—um—

VANELLI: Objection, Your Honor. I think we get the picture.

THE COURT: Let's keep moving, Counselor.

TATE: Yes, Your Honor. Okay, so I take it Mr. Shandler beat you several times?

MONROE: Yeah. One time was especially bad, so I had to take some time off, but yeah.

TATE: He beat you so bad, you had to stop working? Ruby?

MONROE: Yeah.

TATE: Okay, let's move to January 7, 2022. Are you okay with that?

MONROE: [Inaudible]

TATE: Did Mr. Shandler ask you to work that day?

MONROE: Yeah.

TATE: Did he drop you off at the 7-Eleven again?

MONROE: No, he was too strung out. So I put on my clothes, because he was still making me sleep naked, and then I started walking to Hines Boulevard.

TATE: Why would you walk to Hines Boulevard?

MONROE: That's where some girls go to find work.

TATE: And were you carrying anything unusual at the time?

MONROE: Redd was starting to put a gun in my purse by then.

TATE: Why would he do that?

MONROE: We'd heard about some girl getting killed, and Redd said some of the johns out there like to kill girls like me, so I needed protection.

TATE: And just for clarification, what is a john?

MONROE: A guy who pays for sex.

TATE: So you knew about a girl getting killed by a john?

MONROE: Yeah, and it really freaked me out.

TATE: How do you mean?

MONROE: I don't know. It freaked me out that the girl got killed not that far from where we were. I thought I'd even seen her once or twice. Anyway, I started shaking and saying I didn't think I could do it anymore.

TATE: Did Mr. Shandler do anything at that point?

MONROE: Yeah, he handed me a cup of drank. Said it would help calm me down.

TATE: So you consumed a cup of purple drank?

MONROE: Yeah, and then Redd said it was time to get going.

TATE: Did you find a john on January 7, Ruby?

MONROE: Not— Not at first. I'd been walking around for about an hour or so when I needed to go to the bathroom. I went into the Taco Bell.

TATE: The Taco Bell on Westover Parkway?

MONROE: Yeah.

TATE: And in order to work, you had to find a john—a man who pays for sex, correct?

MONROE: Yeah.

TATE: So while you were looking for a john on January 7, you stopped at the Taco Bell on Westover Parkway?

MONROE: Yes, to use the bathroom.

TATE: Is that where you met Eric Hanson?

MONROE: I was coming out of the bathroom. And he'd seen me walking in and decided to come inside the Taco Bell.

TATE: He followed you inside?

MONROE: That's what he told me. He said he thought I looked hungry and that he'd buy me something to eat if I wanted.

TATE: Did he buy you something to eat?

MONROE: Yeah, I hadn't eaten since breakfast the day before, and I guess I was pretty hungry. He let me order, and then he paid for it.

TATE: Did Mr. Hanson order anything for himself?

MONROE: No, which I thought was weird. But I just thought maybe he'd already eaten.

TATE: After you got your food, what happened?

MONROE: He asked to sit with me, and I was like, whatever, since he just bought my food. Anyway, he sat with me while I ate and started asking me questions.

TATE: Like what?

MONROE: Like where was I from. Where I went to school. Things like that.

TATE: And did you inform Mr. Hanson you were not in school at the time?

MONROE: I told him I was trying to become a singer.

TATE: Did he tell you anything about himself?

MONROE: Yeah, he said he was kind of a big deal.

Owned some construction business. At the time, I was thinking like a handyman kind of thing. I didn't know he meant a big company.

TATE: Did he tell you anything else?

MONROE: That he liked to help kids, volunteering.

TATE: Did he ask how old you were?

MONROE: Not until I was in his truck.

TATE: How did you end up in Mr. Hanson's truck, Ruby?

MONROE: He was telling me all about himself while I ate, and he asked me if I was up for some action.

TATE: And what did you take that to mean?

MONROE: That he wanted to have sex with me.

TATE: Did you agree?

MONROE: No, I just kept eating my burrito.

TATE: Did the subject come up again?

MONROE: Yeah, when I was almost finished, he asked me how much.

TATE: And you assumed he was still talking about sex?

MONROE: Yeah, I knew he was serious then. I really didn't want to, but I knew Redd would be pissed if I didn't come back with some money, so I told him two hundred dollars. It was a lot, but he had that business and all, and he was dressed real nice. He looked like he could afford it.

TATE: Did he agree to that amount?

MONROE: No, he said he'd already bought me lunch, so I should be willing to come down off my price. He offered me fifty dollars, I think.

TATE: Did you think that was a fair amount?

MONROE: No, but like I said, I knew Redd expected me to have money when I came back, so I told him one-fifty.

TATE: Is that one hundred fifty dollars?

MONROE: Yeah.

TATE: Is that what you settled on with Mr. Hanson?

MONROE: No, he said ninety was all he had, and he stood up like he was going to walk away. I knew I had to get some money, so I agreed.

TATE: So you got in his truck?

MONROE: Yeah, and I told him how to get to the Super 8.

TATE: And why did you direct him to the Super 8?

MONROE: 'Cause that's where I usually did that sort of thing. Redd had another room for that and was close if something went wrong.

TATE: And by something going wrong, what do you mean?

MONROE: I don't know. Some of these johns can be pretty crazy. Just because they're dressed nice or have a nice way about them, you just never know. I thought it'd be safer for me back at the motel.

TATE: And did you go to the motel?

MONROE: No, Eric was driving. And when we got

to the turn for the Super 8, he went a different direction.

TATE: Did you say anything to Mr. Hanson when he drove in the direction opposite to the Super 8 motel?

MONROE: Yeah, I told him he missed the turn, and that's when he told me we were going to his house. That was the first time he said anything about going anywhere different than the Super 8. I got pretty nervous.

TATE: Why were you nervous?

MONROE: Like I said, that girl had gotten killed. And Redd had put the gun in my purse, saying I needed protection. I don't know. I guess I was seeing the writing on the wall.

TATE: Did you tell him you didn't want to go to his house?

MONROE: No.

TATE: But I thought you said you were worried about your safety?

MONROE: I was, but he was a pretty big guy. I was in his truck. I didn't want to piss him off.

TATE: Did he say why he wanted to go to his house?

MONROE: He said he didn't want anyone to see us. He wanted us to have some privacy.

TATE: Was there anything during that ride that made you worry about your safety?

MONROE: Yeah, um, when we were at a stoplight,

he opened the glove box to get a pack of ciga-rettes. And I saw a gun in the glove box.

TATE: Did he pull out the gun?

MONROE: No, but he left the glove box open long enough to make sure I saw it.

VANELLI: Objection, speculation. The Defendant couldn't possibly have known Mr. Hanson's motiva-tion.

THE COURT: Sustained.

TATE: How long did it take you to get to Mr. Hanson's home?

MONROE: About twenty minutes.

TATE: And did you chat with him during the ride?

MONROE: Mostly he talked. He smoked a cigarette and told me about his divorce. He said his ex-wife was a greedy bitch.

TATE: Now, Ruby. You said Mr. Hanson had a gun in his glove compartment?

MONROE: That's right.

TATE: And you mentioned you were also carrying a gun?

MONROE: Yeah.

TATE: Why did you have a gun?

MONROE: Redd put it in my purse for my protec-tion.

TATE: And did that make sense to you?

MONROE: Yeah, Redd thought if that girl who was killed had a gun, she would've walked away.

TATE: So the gun wasn't yours?

MONROE: No.

TATE: Had you ever fired a gun before?

MONROE: Yeah, my mom had a couple of boyfriends who liked to shoot. I'd done, like, target practice. Shooting cans, stuff like that.

TATE: Did Mr. Hanson mention anything about guns or shooting?

MONROE: Yeah, he said he was a member of some fancy gun club. Said he'd earned his certificate and was almost as good as one of those sharpshooters in the marines.

TATE: And what did you think when he said that?

MONROE: It made me nervous, like maybe he was trying to scare me.

TATE: So, after about twenty minutes, you made it to Mr. Hanson's house?

MONROE: Yeah, and I was getting pretty nervous.

TATE: Why were you nervous?

MONROE: Nobody knew where I was. I mean, this guy could kill me, and nobody would ever know.

TATE: What happened when you arrived at Mr. Hanson's house?

MONROE: He gave me, like, a tour. Like he was showing off his house. He made himself a drink and asked if I wanted one.

TATE: Did you have a drink, Ruby?

MONROE: No, but at one point, I said something like, "You have all this, and you're only gonna pay me ninety bucks?" That pissed him off.

TATE: What do you mean?

MONROE: I don't know. His face got all red, and his voice changed.

TATE: So what happened next?

MONROE: I said I was sorry. I tried to explain that I was tired. By then, I hadn't really slept too good in a couple of days. I think the drank was starting to wear off.

TATE: And what did Mr. Hanson do?

MONROE: He seemed to calm down when I said I was sorry and said I could take a nap if I wanted. He said he was tired too. That's when he led me to the bedroom. I thought we'd nap, and I'd sneak out when he was asleep.

TATE: By this point, then, you'd already decided you were not going to have sex with Mr. Hanson?

MONROE: Yeah, he was just giving me this creepy vibe, you know?

TATE: Did you go to sleep?

MONROE: Yeah, I really hadn't been sleeping for a few days, so I was pretty tired. I think with the drank and because I'd just eaten, I guess I fell asleep pretty fast, even though I didn't mean to.

TATE: And did Mr. Hanson sleep with you?

MONROE: He lay on the bed next to me, but we both had our clothes on and stuff. I don't know how long he was there, though, because the second my head hit the pillow, I was out.

TATE: What happened next?

MONROE: I woke up to him hovering over me. I remember his eyes; they were wide. His face was all red, and he was shouting it was time for me to get what I deserved. His breath smelled like he'd been drinking.

TATE: How long had you been asleep?

MONROE: Maybe two or three hours.

TATE: And what did you think he meant when he said you were going to get what you deserved?

MONROE: I really thought, "This is it. He's going to kill me."

TATE: Ruby, what gave you the impression that Mr. Hanson wanted to kill you?

MONROE: He'd found the gun in my purse, and it really pissed him off.

TATE: He had gone through your purse while you were asleep?

MONROE: I guess.

TATE: What happened next?

MONROE: He slapped my face and pointed it at me.

TATE: And by "it," you mean the gun?

MONROE: That's right.

TATE: Did he slap you with the gun or his hand?

MONROE: The back of his hand. And then pointed Redd's gun at me.

TATE: Ruby, was Redd's gun loaded?

MONROE: Yeah.

TATE: How do you know?

MONROE: I saw Redd put the bullets in before he put it in my purse.

TATE: What did Mr. Hanson do after he slapped you?

MONROE: He said he had a few guns of his own but knew— He said he knew a better use for my gun.

TATE: Did he tell you what he meant by that?

MONROE: No, he—

TATE: It's okay. Take your time.

MONROE: Um, he—

TATE: There are tissues to your right, if you need one.

MONROE: Um, he said if I didn't act right, he'd shove the gun up inside me.

TATE: And what did you think he meant by "inside" you?

MONROE: He pushed up my skirt and said he'd shove it in down there.

TATE: He threatened to shove a loaded weapon into your vagina?

MONROE: Uh-huh.

TATE: Is that a yes, Ruby?

MONROE: Sorry, yes.

TATE: And what did you do?

MONROE: I don't know. I kind of blanked. Nobody knew where I was. It was like my worst nightmare was coming to life. I thought he was going to kill me. He was holding me down with one hand. He was kind of grinning, you know, like he was really getting off on it.

TATE: What happened next?

MONROE: He put the gun real close to me. I could feel it down there. I begged him to stop. I told him the gun wasn't even mine. That Redd made me carry it.

TATE: Did he stop?

MONROE: He said he liked the way I begged. And he might stop if I begged him for sex. He said his wife never begged.

TATE: And what were you thinking?

MONROE: That I had to get out of there. This guy is going to kill me.

TATE: What did you do?

MONROE: He was screaming at me to beg.

TATE: And did you?

MONROE: I just started crying and saying, "Please, please." I don't really remember.

TATE: So what happened then?

MONROE: He set the gun on the pillow next to my face. He was still over me, and he was trying to get his belt undone but was having a hard time holding me down and doing it, so he let go for a second.

TATE: And when he released you, what did you do?

MONROE: It happened so fast. I don't really remember.

TATE: What do you remember happening next?

MONROE: At some point, I must've reached for the gun.

TATE: Ruby, how did Mr. Hanson react once he saw you had Redd's gun?

MONROE: He buckled his belt and backed toward the sliding glass door.

TATE: What happened next?

MONROE: He started laughing at me. Said it was obvious that I'd never shot a gun before. It looked like he was going to charge toward me.

TATE: And then what?

MONROE: Then the gun went off.

TATE: Ruby, when the gun first fired, was anyone hurt?

MONROE: No, the bullet must have hit the glass door behind him. It shattered into like a million pieces. It was really loud. He kind of fell sideways and said he was going to kill me for damaging his property. He reached for his chest of drawers. I thought he was trying to get a gun.

TATE: So what did you do?

MONROE: I fired the gun. I was just trying to scare him so I could get away.

TATE: Did you hit him this time?

MONROE: No, it went into the wall behind him. I screamed for him to leave me alone.

TATE: What did he do next?

MONROE: He was so mad, and I was trying to get off the bed and yelling for help, and I don't know.

TATE: Ruby, what was Mr. Hanson doing at this point?

MONROE: Like I said, his face was really red. He seemed drunk. I didn't know what he was going to do, and I was freaking out. He was yelling about getting his AR15.

TATE: You thought he was keeping an assault rifle nearby?

MONROE: I didn't know what to think. He said he had one and kind of rushed toward me and reached for the gun. I think I scratched him on the wrist or the hand trying to keep it from him. I don't really remember. But he yanked on the end and tilted the gun sideways.

TATE: Did the gun go off during the struggle?

MONROE: Yes.

TATE: Did you intend to fire the gun that time?

MONROE: It happened so fast. I was just trying to keep him from taking it from me.

TATE: So did that third bullet hit Mr. Hanson?

MONROE: Yeah, that's when I saw the blood on his shirt. I felt something wet on my arm and hands.

TATE: And what was on your arm and hands?

MONROE: His blood.

TATE: Okay, then what happened?

MONROE: He was still fighting at first, and then he looked down at his chest and kind of had this startled look on his face. It was like he didn't realize he'd been shot until he saw the blood. He kind of fell backward through the broken glass door. It shattered even more when he went through it.

TATE: And what did you do, Ruby?

MONROE: He was still mumbling about grabbing

his gun and he was moving toward the swimming pool. I was really scared, so I fired Redd's gun as kind of a warning shot.

TATE: So, let's back up a second. You were still concerned he was trying to get a gun, even though he was outside and moving away from you?

MONROE: Yeah, I didn't know. I mean, I saw his gun in the car, and he said he owned more of them. I thought he was going to get one of his guns and kill me.

TATE: So what happened next?

MONROE: I fired a warning shot.

TATE: And to be clear, this was the fourth time you fired Redd's weapon?

MONROE: Yeah.

TATE: What happened next?

MONROE: He fell next to the pool. I took off.

TATE: Did you check to see if he was okay?

MONROE: No, I ran back inside the house. I wanted to get away from him in case he got back up and chased me.

TATE: So you didn't know whether Mr. Hanson was dead at the time?

MONROE: No, I mean, he'd kept fighting me before. I didn't want to take any chances.

TATE: Did you take anything before you left?

MONROE: Yeah, I remembered Redd wanted me to come back with cash, so I grabbed Eric's wallet off the nightstand and his keys.

TATE: Did you take anything else?

MONROE: I took his truck.

TATE: Why did you take his truck?

MONROE: I just had to get out of there. I didn't know if he was going to chase after me. I had to get out. And I didn't have any other way.

TATE: Had you ever driven before?

MONROE: Yeah, my mom's boyfriend taught me— Uh, Clay, he taught me how. Let me practice on his truck in empty parking lots, a little on the streets when he'd had too much to drink.

TATE: And where did you go when you left Mr. Hanson's home?

MONROE: I went to see Redd.

TATE: At the Super 8?

MONROE: Yeah, and I gave him the wallet.

TATE: Did you tell him what happened?

VANELLI: Objection, hearsay.

THE COURT: I'll allow it. You can answer.

MONROE: I told him I just shot a guy. I said I didn't know if he was okay or not.

TATE: And how did Redd react?

MONROE: Like he didn't believe me until I showed him the blood on me and the truck parked outside.

TATE: What did you do next?

MONROE: Redd kind of looked at me different, you know.

TATE: Different how?

MONROE: Like he admired me or something.

TATE: So then what did you do?

MONROE: Redd turned on the TV to see if there was anything on the news about it.

TATE: Was there?

MONROE: Not yet.

TATE: Ruby, who took the money out of Mr. Hanson's wallet?

MONROE: Redd did. He said I'd done good. That he'd buy me dinner. But I was feeling pretty messed up, so I told him no. My stomach was really hurting.

TATE: And who removed one of Mr. Hanson's credit cards from the wallet?

MONROE: Redd did. He said he was going to buy a gold chain with it.

TATE: Did you get any of Mr. Hanson's money?

MONROE: No.

TATE: What happened next?

MONROE: Redd told me to change clothes, since there was blood on my shirt, and to clean up. He told me I was going to have to ditch the truck. So I changed and took a towel from the bathroom and wiped the blood from my arm.

TATE: What was your mental state at that point?

MONROE: I don't know. Kinda freaking out, I guess. I couldn't get the blood off.

TATE: What about the truck, Ruby?

MONROE: Redd made me move it. He said he was worried the police would find us if the truck was parked right out front.

TATE: Did you move the truck?

MONROE: Yeah, to the Tom Thumb parking lot down the street.

TATE: Did you do anything else to the truck?

MONROE: I'd brought a towel and wiped off the steering wheel and stuff.

TATE: Why did you do that?

MONROE: I was scared, I guess. I was thinking Redd might beat me for what I'd done. But by the time I got back to the motel, he was already gone. He'd taken the money.

TATE: And, Ruby, I know this is difficult, but what have you learned about Mr. Shandler's where-abouts since you were arrested?

MONROE: He's dead. He was killed in the Super 8 parking lot earlier this year.

HERE ENDS THE EXCERPT

Fell through door

no fear

sed → Shot

JULY 13, 2023

Dear Maya,

It's been almost a week since I've written, but the trial is keeping me busy, and I'm finding it hard to know what to say. There's just so much that's happened, I don't know where to start.

Mr. Tate finished asking me questions today. It was really hard talking about everything in front of those people. There's this one jury lady with glasses. I just know she thinks I'm trash. Every time she catches me looking at her, she gives me a dirty look. She's the jury foreman. Like the head juror. They had an election and every-thing. I didn't get to vote or I would have voted for the younger guy in the back row. That guy always wears these plaid shirts, and when I smiled at him the first day, he smiled back. But he stopped looking at me after he saw the pictures of Eric.

I'm glad you didn't have to see that, by the way. It was real-ly bad how the prosecutor blew up the pictures real big. I didn't know he could do that. Mr. Tate whispered to me not to react, but it was really hard not to. There was so much blood. I wanted to look away, but I couldn't. It was like one of those movies they show on late-night TV. Except this was real. It's weird, but I don't really remember Eric looking like that. No wonder they want to lock me up for life.

You're probably wondering how I did since I've been so

worried about testifying. I did good. Those were Mr. Tate's words. "You did good, kid. I'm proud of you." Can you believe it? I was so happy he said that. He even smiled at me. He has a nice smile that makes his eyes squint in the corners. I couldn't help but smile back. Is it weird his smile means so much?

As soon as the bailiff brought me back to the holding cell, I felt like I was going to cry. There's all this snot on the walls where other inmates have smeared their boogers, and I was trying not to bump up against the wall and get my white shirt dirty. But I knew I was about to cry, and Mr. Tate brought some tissues so I wouldn't have to smear my snot on the wall too.

I just wish the prosecutor didn't get to question me too. That's coming tomorrow. Mr. Tate says if I remember what we practiced, I'll be fine. Even though it went okay today, I know I can still fuck it all up. Mr. Tate asked questions so that the jury would hear my story the way he wanted, but I'm not sure if they believe me or not. And now it's the prosecutor's turn to try to trip me up.

I guess I'll be staying up all night going over what I have to say in my head. Wish me luck.

Your friend,
Ruby

JULY 14, 2023

Ruby nervously taps her foot against the carpet as she glances around Judge Ambrose's conference room—the blue-and-white Republic of Texas flag on the wall behind Cadence, the oversize mahogany table that separates the two of them. On the other side of the window, a chirping sound calls Ruby's attention away from the room.

A red cardinal flicks its tail as it perches on a branch outside, singing. Her mom loved cardinals. She'd always point one out when she saw it, saying that cardinals held the spirits of loved ones who died. Ruby always wondered which loved one she was hoping had come back to her.

"You sure you don't want anything to eat?" Cadence asks as she carefully picks at her courthouse cafeteria salad. A small pile of tomatoes sits on a napkin to her right.

Ruby twists against the cuffs that keep getting stuck in the frills of her blouse. "I'm fine," she says, though her stomach is still churning with worry about the cross-examination, a fact that was announced to both the judge and bailiff when she walked into court this morning and puked her breakfast all over Mr. Tate's shoes.

The court granted Mr. Tate's request for a delay in her cross-examination until after lunch to give them time to get cleaned up, but that only gave her more time to worry. By the time she'd returned, Mr. Tate had already asked Judge Ambrose if Cadence could briefly take her through some breathing exercises over lunch to help calm her mind, though she suspects the real reason was that he didn't want to lose another pair of shoes.

Thirty minutes tops, the judge had said, while insisting she remained shackled with the bailiff stationed on the other side of the door. Ruby tries a breath, but the room smells stale—dust and old carpet.

Cadence forks a cucumber. "All right, talk to me. What's going on?" She pops it into her mouth and crunches.

Ruby shifts as she glances outside again, but the cardinal has already flown away. "I don't know." She sighs. "Do you think it's fucked up how she answered all those questions and didn't look at me?"

Cadence swallows. "Who?"

"My mom. The other day."

"Where is this coming from?"

Ruby shrugs.

Cadence takes another stab at her salad. "Maybe she was nervous. She had a hard time sitting still, remember?"

Ruby twists against the cuffs again, annoyed with Cadence's answer. "And why'd she cut her hair so short?" Cadence's eyes flick to Ruby's hair, which has only just now grown below her ears, and Ruby can sense what she's thinking. "I *know*, okay? But at least I didn't dye my hair blond. She looked a lot older. Her skin looked gray."

"I've never seen her before, so I don't have anything to compare."

"I don't know why she wouldn't look at me." Ruby rips the cuffs from a ruffle, tearing the fabric. "She never fucking looked at me. Why?"

Cadence lowers her fork. "Are we still talking about the trial here?"

Yes. Maybe. "I mean, why even show up if she didn't care about what was happening to me?"

"The fact that she showed up at all is something." Cadence unscrews the cap on her water bottle and takes a sip. "She didn't have to do that."

Heat blooms at the base of Ruby's throat. "I have a right to be pissed."

"You need to focus," Cadence says, pointing her fork toward Ruby. "Today is important."

Ruby huffs her annoyance; the chains clink between her legs. "You think I don't know that?" Especially when the whole reason they're sitting here is because she puked on her lawyer.

Cadence takes another sip of water and replaces the cap on the bottle. "Look, I know she disappointed you and hurt you. Many times over. But I also think she tried to help you in the only way she could."

The heat reaches Ruby's face. "If you think she cares, you're the one who's nuts."

"I agree she should have protected you," Cadence says, her voice steady. "But I do think she was trying to do that, in her own way, by testifying." She gestures toward the closed door. "Her showing up in that jail uniform and her testimony and the fact that she wouldn't look at you—even though it hurt—all of that made you appear more sympathetic to the jury."

"She couldn't have known."

"But Brian did." Cadence gives a firm nod. "He's looking out for you now. We both are. And maybe your mom didn't fully understand how she was helping you, but what if she did?"

Ruby resists the suggestion, knowing what happens anytime she's allowed herself to hope when it comes to her mom.

"They'll be calling the jury back soon, and the judge has assured us they have no idea you got sick earlier. They only know there was a delay." She mimics taking a breath. "So, all you need to do is focus on the job you have this afternoon. And maybe try another deep breath?"

Ruby clenches her jaw. She doesn't want to take a deep breath.

"We can talk more about this later," Cadence says, checking her watch. "But for right now, you should be thinking about the testimony you're about to give. Understand?"

Ruby shifts in her chair with what Cadence has left unsaid: *Don't fuck this up.* She presses the soles of her borrowed ballet flats into the carpet. "What if I don't get back up on the stand?"

Cadence shakes her head. "You're the one who wanted to tell your story, and that means it's the prosecutor's turn to ask you questions. You knew that was part of the deal from the very beginning."

Ruby shrugs, determined to match Cadence's indifference. "I changed my mind."

Cadence pinches the bridge of her nose as if trying to keep her temper. "You don't have a choice." She releases her nose. "How do you think the jury will react if you refuse?"

"They won't believe me anyway, so what's the point?" She's seen the evidence against her; she already knows what they're going to decide.

"You don't know that."

"I know I don't deserve their trust." Ruby sighs with the weight of it all. "I've done horrible things, right?"

"We all have. But you're a survivor."

"What if I'm not?"

"You are, and that means you do what you have to do to keep going, including now."

Ruby lifts her bound wrists, awkwardly holding on to the edge of the conference table. "I just can't stop thinking about how Eric wasn't nice to me."

Cadence gives a half nod, like she assumes Ruby is working through the cross-examination they've practiced. "I think you did a good job so far telling the jury."

"But everybody's mean to somebody sometimes, right?"

Cadence furrows her brow. "Where are you headed with this?"

"That doesn't mean they deserve to die."

"Stop. Just stop right now." Cadence closes the lid on her salad and pushes it away.

Ruby lowers her gaze to the shackles around her wrists. She can't keep going unless she knows. "Do you think I'm a bad person?"

"I said stop. You have one job left in this trial." There's a knock; Cadence stands. "We can finish this later."

Ruby looks up. "No, wait. I seriously want to know."

"Just a minute," Cadence calls to the bailiff on the other side of the closed door.

"You know my whole story now, all of it," Ruby says as she rises from her chair, clutching her stomach, "so I'm asking you: Do you think I'm a bad person?"

"I don't know why you're asking me this now." Cadence faces her. "Of course I don't think you're a bad person."

Ruby searches her face and nods to herself. If Cadence can truly believe that, then maybe she has a chance at believing it, too.

THE COURT: Welcome back, everyone. I trust you had a good lunch. Ready for your cross-examination, Mr. Vanelli?

VANELLI: Yes, thank you, Your Honor. Ms. Monroe, you indicated earlier in your testimony that Mr. Shandler gave you that tattoo there? Is that right?

THE COURT: Miss Monroe, do you need him to repeat the question?

TATE: Ruby?

THE COURT: Young lady?

MONROE: Sorry, yes. He made me get this.

VANELLI: And what letters are tattooed along your collarbone again?

MONROE: R. D.

VANELLI: And what did you say your full name was?

MONROE: What does that have to do with it?

THE COURT: Just answer his question, miss.

VANELLI: I'll ask again, Ms. Monroe. What is your full name?

MONROE: Ruby Danielle Monroe.

VANELLI: So R. D. are your initials, correct?

MONROE: You think that's what this is?

VANELLI: Your Honor, I'd ask that you admonish the witness.

THE COURT: Young lady, you need to listen carefully to the question and answer what he asks you. Only what he asks you. Do you understand?

MONROE: Yeah. I mean, yes, sir.

THE COURT: Continue, Mr. Vanelli.

VANELLI: So R. D. are your initials?

MONROE: Not really. Danielle is my middle name. My last name is Monroe.

VANELLI: You say your name is Ruby Danielle. That would make R. D. your initials, correct?

TATE: Objection, badgering. She's already answered the question.

THE COURT: Let's all take a deep breath. Overruled.

VANELLI: R. D. are your initials?

MONROE: Sort of.

VANELLI: All right, you indicated your father left when you were younger?

MONROE: Yes.

VANELLI: So you lived with your mom, then? With the exception of the three times you mentioned being removed from your home.

MONROE: That's right.

VANELLI: Did your mom finish high school?

TATE: Objection, relevance.

THE COURT: Overruled. You can answer the question.

MONROE: No. She dropped out.

VANELLI: Same as you, then?

MONROE: Yeah.

VANELLI: And did your mom work?

MONROE: When she could, yeah.

VANELLI: But you received welfare payments from the government; isn't that right?

TATE: Objection, Your Honor. Relevance again.

VANELLI: I can't ask how they earned their money?

TATE: There is no crime in being poor. You're out of line.

THE COURT: Thank you, Mr. Tate, but I will make that determination. I'll allow it for now, but get to the point, Counselor. Overruled.

VANELLI: Yes, Your Honor. And your mother spent the welfare payments that were supposed to be used for food and other necessities on drugs; isn't that right?

MONROE: I don't know where she got the money. Sometimes her boyfriend would give her some. Like an allowance.

VANELLI: I see, and did you get an allowance, Ms. Monroe?

MONROE: Nothing regular. Maybe a few bucks here and there.

VANELLI: Did you ever use the money you received to buy drugs?

MONROE: No.

VANELLI: Alcohol?

TATE: Your Honor. If Mr. Vanelli is trying to establish my client drank or used drugs before she was arrested, I believe we've already conceded that point. She is not on trial for underage drinking.

THE COURT: I tend to agree.

VANELLI: No, she's not on trial for drinking. She's on trial for murdering an innocent man.

TATE: Objection, Your Honor.

THE COURT: Mr. Vanelli, you will have the opportunity to make a closing argument later. For now, let's stick to the questions.

VANELLI: Yes, Your Honor.

TATE: We ask that the jury be asked to disregard the last comment.

THE COURT: Granted, the jury will disregard the State's last comment. Mr. Vanelli, continue.

VANELLI: You've already told us that you've been meeting with a social worker.

MONROE: Yeah, with Cadence.

VANELLI: Cadence Ware?

MONROE: That's right.

VANELLI: And how long have you known Dr. Ware?

MONROE: Um, we first met right before my case got moved to adult court. I was in juvenile detention then.

VANELLI: And did Dr. Ware ask you questions during your first meeting?

MONROE: Yeah.

VANELLI: And I'm assuming you answered her.

MONROE: We talked, if that's what you mean.

VANELLI: And you are not her only client?

MONROE: I don't know her other clients.

VANELLI: That's okay. And how long was your first meeting with Dr. Ware?

MONROE: I don't remember.

VANELLI: Ten minutes? An hour?

TATE: Objection, Your Honor. Calls for speculation.

THE COURT: Sustained.

MONROE: Should I—

THE COURT: We don't want you to guess, miss.

MONROE: Okay.

VANELLI: So, with multiple clients, how can
Dr. Ware possibly remember everything you told her
that first time you met?

MONROE: Uh, I—

TATE: Objection. Your Honor, again, calls for
speculation, and I object on the basis of the motion
in limine.

THE COURT: All right. Ladies and gentlemen, the
lawyers and I need to take care of a little detail
before we continue. Bailiff, will you please escort
the jury from the courtroom? This will only take a
moment. Miss Monroe, please return to your seat.
Thank you.

BAILIFF: All rise.

[THE JURY EXITS THE COURTROOM]

THE COURT: Please be seated. First off, your
speculation objection is sustained, Counselor.

TATE: Thank you, Your Honor.

THE COURT: And state your other objection for
the record.

TATE: The State's questioning is in clear violation of our motion in limine.

VANELLI: I didn't say anything about Dr. Ware's

notes, Your Honor. I asked how she remembered what the Defendant told her.

TATE: That's semantics, and you know it. You're trying to trick this witness into opening the door about these phantom notes when you already know Dr. Ware doesn't have notes from that first session.

THE COURT: I tend to agree. First, you're making arguments before the jury during cross-examination—

VANELLI: Your Honor—

THE COURT: —and I know you've been around long enough to understand that is improper. Now, with regard to Dr. Ware: as I recall, there is no evidence of wrongdoing, and this court has already ruled against you.

VANELLI: You did, but the State asks the Court to reconsider.

THE COURT: On what basis?

VANELLI: On the basis that we are entitled to any information a testifying expert witness relies upon in reaching her opinions. In her report, Dr. Ware provides a detailed summary of the events of January 7, 2022. And I don't think she or anyone could possibly remember that level of detail without referring back to notes, a recording, something.

THE COURT: Response, Mr. Tate?

TATE: Your Honor, as I said before the trial started, we've already had a lengthy hearing on this, and the State is in deliberate violation of this Court's order. Frankly, I'm offended Mr.

Vanelli insists on continuing with this rhetoric.

VANELLI: Are you seriously telling this Court that Dr. Ware took notes in every single session she had with the Defendant, with the sole exception of that first one? Look, I just want to make sure we have the full story here.

TATE: If you had been paying attention during the pretrial hearing that you made us all show up for three months ago, you would realize you have it. We don't have any notes.

THE COURT: All right, gentlemen.

TATE: Your Honor, I believe the State is getting desperate here. Dr. Ware already explained during the pretrial hearing that she was planning on taking notes during that first meeting but could see that doing so would make an already-agitated client uncomfortable. At that same hearing, Dr. Ware testified she adjusts to the needs of her clients, and in this case, it was the only way to get Miss Monroe to start talking to her. She offered her client a snack, and they talked. That's all. There are no notes, and there is no reason to drag this out any further when the State can simply ask what happened during their first meeting. It's called examining a witness.

THE COURT: Okay, Mr. Tate. I know passions are high, but let's all calm down for a second.

TATE: My apologies, Your Honor.

THE COURT: I presume you are going to move for a mistrial.

VANELLI: But, Your Honor—

TATE: Yes, the Defense would like to move for a mistrial. The State has tainted this jury when there is absolutely no evidence of impropriety.

VANELLI: May I respond?

THE COURT: Mr. Vanelli, you've put me in a very awkward position here. We are almost finished with this trial, and you have come very close to violating this Court's order.

VANELLI: Your Honor, please. The jury has only heard a question as to how Dr. Ware can remember one interview when she had multiple clients. Perhaps it raised a question in their mind, but certainly not enough to prejudice the jury and taint the entire case.

THE COURT: Okay, here's what I'm going to do. I'm going to deny the mistrial because I think we can still salvage this.

VANELLI: Yes, Your Honor. Thank you.

THE COURT: Now, Mr. Tate, I assume you're going to call the forensic social worker?

TATE: It's looking that way, Your Honor.

THE COURT: All right. If you decide to call her, I don't want anybody even whispering about these alleged missing notes again. Ask her about the report, fine. But no questions about notes, got

295

it? You do that, and I'm granting a mistrial. Do you understand me, Mr. Vanelli?

VANELLI: Yes, Your Honor.

THE COURT: See how nice it is when we all get along?

VANELLI: Yes, Your Honor. Thank you.

TATE: Thank you, Your Honor.

THE COURT: Then let's get to the facts of this case. Enough with the grandstanding, got it?

VANELLI: Yes, Your Honor.

TATE: Yes, Your Honor.

THE COURT: Miss Monroe, will you return to the witness stand, please? Remember, you're still under oath.

MONROE: Yes, sir.

THE COURT: Bring in the jury.

[THE JURY ENTERS THE COURTROOM]

BAILIFF: All rise.

THE COURT: You may be seated. Thank you, ladies and gentlemen. I apologize for the inconvenience, but I think the lawyers are on the same page now. Continue, Mr. Vanelli.

VANELLI: Thank you, Your Honor. Now, on January 7, 2022, you left the Super 8 with a gun in your purse, correct?

MONROE: Uh-huh.

VANELLI: And you claim you did that for your protection?

MONROE: I did do it for my protection. Another

girl had been killed by a john right before Eric picked me up.

VANELLI: And when the first police officer questioned you, you indicated you smiled at Mr. Hanson at the Taco Bell; is that correct?

MONROE: Did they tell you that?

VANELLI: Wasn't it actually you who approached Mr. Hanson at the Taco Bell?

MONROE: No, he came up to me.

VANELLI: He bought you a meal?

MONROE: Yeah.

VANELLI: And you said you noticed his nice clothes, his nice watch, his new truck?

MONROE: I didn't know he had a truck until later.

VANELLI: But you noticed his nice clothes and watch?

MONROE: [Witness shrugs]

VANELLI: Is that a yes?

MONROE: I guess so, yeah.

VANELLI: And while you were eating the meal Mr. Hanson had bought for you, you said you learned Mr. Hanson volunteered at Big Brothers Big Sisters?

MONROE: That's right.

VANELLI: So you thought you could prey on this man who obviously had a heart for kids?

MONROE: It wasn't like that. He asked me how much.

VANELLI: So he took you into his home?

MONROE: Yeah.

VANELLI: And you claim it was because he propositioned you for sex?

MONROE: He wanted to have sex, yeah.

VANELLI: Did he tell you that?

MONROE: He didn't use those exact words, but I saw the way he was looking at me.

VANELLI: And when you got to Mr. Hanson's home, you realized he must be a very wealthy man, right?

MONROE: I guess so.

VANELLI: So you started planning how to rob him?

MONROE: No, I just wanted to get out of there.

VANELLI: You're telling this jury that you were in such a hurry to get out of Mr. Hanson's home that you stopped to take a nap with him?

MONROE: I was tired. And I figured I'd sneak out after he fell asleep.

VANELLI: But you didn't sneak out while he was asleep, did you?

MONROE: No.

VANELLI: You shot Mr. Hanson, correct?

MONROE: The gun went off when he tried to take it.

VANELLI: And after you shot him and he was backing away through a glass door, you followed him, right?

MONROE: I don't remember.

VANELLI: So you shot Mr. Hanson, and you admitted you saw the blood on his chest after you shot him the first time, right?

MONROE: Yeah.

VANELLI: And knowing you had already shot Mr. Hanson, you decided to continue to pursue him outside?

MONROE: I didn't know what he was going to do.

VANELLI: So you pursued him and you shot him a second time in the head?

MONROE: I shot. I thought it was a warning shot. I didn't know it had killed him.

VANELLI: And even after Mr. Hanson dropped to the ground, did you try to render aid?

MONROE: What?

VANELLI: You didn't call for an ambulance?

MONROE: No.

VANELLI: You didn't call the police?

MONROE: No, I was scared. I had to get out of there.

VANELLI: Instead, you stole Mr. Hanson's wallet and keys, correct?

MONROE: I thought—

VANELLI: And you stole his truck; isn't that right?

MONROE: I thought—

VANELLI: And you gave the money to your pimp, right?

MONROE: I gave it to Redd.

VANELLI: Who was your pimp?

MONROE: I thought he was my boyfriend.

VANELLI: By then? You still thought he your boyfriend?

TATE: Objection, Your Honor. Mr. Vanelli is badgering the witness again and not allowing her to finish her answers.

THE COURT: Careful, Counselor. I agree you're getting close to that line.

VANELLI: Yes, Your Honor. Ms. Monroe, you're telling me that by the time you met Mr. Hanson, you still thought Mr. Shandler was your boyfriend?

MONROE: I don't know.

VANELLI: Based on the fact he was asking you to sleep with other men, you must have known he was your pimp and not your boyfriend?

MONROE: I'm not sure.

VANELLI: And then you moved Mr. Hanson's truck from the Super 8 motel parking lot because you were worried the police would find you, correct?

MONROE: Redd told me to move it.

VANELLI: And you wiped down the truck with a towel to try to remove your fingerprints, right?

MONROE: Yeah.

VANELLI: Did your pimp instruct you to wipe down the truck?

MONROE: That was my idea.

VANELLI: Your idea. So isn't it true that the real reason you went to Mr. Hanson's home that evening was to rob him?

MONROE: No, I—

VANELLI: And you decided to use whatever means necessary, including killing him, right?

MONROE: I was just trying to get away.

VANELLI: Did you get away, Ms. Monroe?

MONROE: Yes.

VANELLI: But Mr. Hanson will never leave his home again, will he?

MONROE: No.

VANELLI: Because you killed him, right?

TATE: Your Honor.

VANELLI: Withdrawn. No further questions.

HERE ENDS THE EXCERPT

JULY 15, 2023

Dear Maya,

My testimony is over. It didn't go exactly how we practiced, but Mr. Tate said we're still okay. If we weren't, though, I'm not sure if he'd tell me.

So, I tried something new after dinner tonight. Since you always said church was the one place you felt like you didn't have to hide the real you, I asked Liz (she's the new guard who replaced Demarcus) if I could go to the room where they hold services on Sundays. I know what you're thinking, but just hear me out.

I don't know why Liz let me. She said it was okay for a minute. Maybe she knows I'm on trial for life.

Nobody was in there, but it felt like I should shut up and be respectful like when I'm in court.

I just sat there on the back row in that empty room. There was a small wooden cross up front on the wall. It wasn't fancy but kind of nice. I was looking up at the cross, and it's the first time I ever remember it being totally quiet since I was arrested.

Being in there made me think of you. You had all this stuff going on in your life, but you still made time for me. You always gave me a hug when you saw me coming. It's like you could read my mind, knowing how bad I needed one.

I miss your hugs. I miss you telling me that you think I'm better than all this bullshit. That I could do something better. I know I always blew you off when you said that stuff, but I want you to know I heard you. I miss hearing you.

Don't judge, but I tried to pray since you said it sometimes helped. I don't know what came over me. It's not like God's been showing up for me. I always figured what's the point. I know you don't agree. You've always believed in a higher power.

I don't think I did it right. But God probably already knows what I did anyway.

It's been a long time, but I started singing too. I swear, first time really singing since I got arrested. And not quiet, either. Right after I prayed, I sang full voice, and Liz even clapped when I was done. I'm not going to say what song it was, but maybe I'll tell you sometime if we ever see each other again.

See? I heard you. I didn't want to believe it before, but maybe there is something better. If I don't go to prison for life.

Cadence told me she doesn't think I'm a bad person. I hope she's right. But if she is right, I can't help but wonder why all of this is happening to me. I just hope I deserve everything Cadence and Mr. Tate are doing for me. They've done so much for me even though they aren't getting anything in return. Kind of like you.

Anyway, thank you for being my friend. I know I didn't make it easy. Maybe someday I could make it up to you.

I miss you,
Ruby

JULY 16, 2023

Ruby's heart races as she rushes into the interview room. "What's wrong? Was there an accident? Is it Mr. Tate?"

"Everyone is fine," Cadence says, holding her hands out as if to calm Ruby. "I know it's a Sunday, but please don't worry. I'm here to talk with you about something before court tomorrow."

Despite Cadence's reassurance, the anxious feeling that has been growing in Ruby all morning has taken root—only a few more days until she knows her fate. No matter what happens, everything is about to change. And she finally figured out why.

When Dickhead leaves the room, she drops into the chair across from Cadence. "I know why this is happening to me."

"What—" Cadence asks, as if Ruby caught her off guard. "What do you mean?"

"I didn't figure it out until early this morning." Pretty much ever since she wrote to Maya, she's been thinking about it.

"I'm not following."

So many times, she'd wondered, *Why me?* She can't believe she'd blocked it out of her head until now. Ruby folds her arms over her chest.

Cadence blinks. "I still can't read your mind, you know."

Ruby hesitates when she realizes she hasn't thought this through. She wasn't planning on talking to Cadence about it. She wasn't planning on even seeing Cadence today. "Forget it. It's stupid."

"Nothing you have ever told me has been stupid," Cadence says with a firm nod. "If it's bothering you, I want to know."

Ruby shifts, still unsure how to react when Cadence says stuff like that. She sighs. "I was thinking about Clay."

"Your mom's boyfriend. The one who . . ."

Ruby shudders. "One time after, he told me how stones have different meanings. Like emeralds mean 'money.' Pearls mean 'purity' or some shit like that."

Cadence nods. "Sounds familiar."

"But rubies symbolize lust." She leans forward. "Why would Mom do that to me? Name me after sex. I was a baby, and she cursed me."

Cadence cracks a smile.

Ruby falls back in her chair. "I *knew* you would think it was stupid."

"No," Cadence says, pulling out her phone. "I'm sorry. It's just that doesn't sound right to me."

"You calling me a liar?"

"After all these months, are you really asking me that?" She types a search, nodding as she turns the screen. "Ruby means 'luck,' not 'lust.'"

"Give that to me," Ruby says, snatching the phone, reading "LUCK."

"Seems to me she named you with all the hope she could muster."

Ruby shakes her head, remembering how crushed she felt

when Clay said her mom had cursed her. That it was her fault, what he did to her. Like her name was a mark of her worthlessness, long before Redd gave her the tattoo.

Cadence returns the phone to her bag. "Better?"

Ruby shrugs, still unable to shake her uneasiness. Despite Cadence's encouragement, she still can't help but wonder if she deserves everything that has happened to her. What if all of this work has been for nothing? What if she spends the rest of her life in prison, having to be this person she's become forever?

Cadence retrieves her pen and paper. "I'm here today because Brian has asked me to testify in the morning, and I wanted to let you know what I plan to tell the jury, as I think you deserve to hear it first."

But Ruby's mind is racing with doubt. She stares at Cadence's scarf of the day—yellow silk with tiny birds—wondering if she is still hiding who she is, too. "Do you ever take your scarf off? Around other people, I mean?"

"Sometimes." Cadence brings her hand to the knot in the silk, checking its tightness. "Depends on the people. Now, tomorrow—"

"What about in front of your husband?" Ruby interrupts. "Or does he make you keep it covered?"

Cadence's expression darkens, and Ruby can tell she's hit a nerve. "That's not really his decision to make."

"Then why do you still hide your scar?"

"I think . . ." Cadence says softly. "I think you know why."

Ruby traces Cadence's gaze to the place her shirt has slipped slightly, exposing her shoulder. Her glare darts across the table. Cadence wasn't supposed to know. Nobody was. "Who told you?"

Cadence raises her hands in surrender. "Let's discuss this calmly, okay?"

"*You* stay calm. I asked, who?"

"Doc. But only because I asked."

"Bastard!" Ruby jumps from her chair.

The door flies open and bangs against the wall as Ruby grabs the bottom of her shirt. She yanks it up over her head, screaming, "You want to see?"

The guard lunges toward her.

"Wait," Cadence yells. "Don't touch her!"

Dickhead freezes when he spots the web of scars—marring Ruby's shoulders, running beneath the cotton of her sports bra, wrapping around and down the small of her back. Cadence covers her mouth with her hand.

Ruby's chest heaves with each breath as she begins to feel the goose bumps forming on her exposed skin. The buzzing in her mind quiets to a dull roar as she mutters, "Why is this happening to me?"

Cadence shakes her head.

"It's all my fault." Ruby gasps. "It will never get better, will it?"

"All right." Cadence turns her attention to the guard. "I think we're okay now."

Dickhead—the man who has chained her and caged her and pushed her and yanked her—gives Ruby a sympathetic glance. It makes her stomach turn.

"Please don't," she whispers.

He averts his eyes and silently steps into the hallway, the latch clicking loudly.

Ruby doesn't move away from the wall as she puts her shirt back on. She doesn't know where to look. Most of all, she wonders why she did that. She wonders why she's done any of this. "I don't want to hurt anymore."

Cadence releases a heavy sigh. "I know." She slowly moves toward her. "May I hug you?"

Ruby gives the slightest of nods as Cadence places one arm around her, followed by the other, and holds her. Ruby breathes in the smell of laundry detergent and perfume. The smell of safety.

"I'm so sorry," Cadence whispers into Ruby's hair, and something inside the girl breaks. She feels the wetness on her face against Cadence's shirt. Ruby can't remember the last time someone touched her without wanting something in return.

Cadence squeezes gently. "You have so much value. I wish you could see."

She doesn't believe Cadence's words—she *can't*—but she can feel that Cadence believes them. Ruby's shoulders begin to shake. "There was one night I said I wouldn't sleep with him, and he whipped me with a wire hanger. He told me I deserved it for sleeping with all those guys."

"Oh, honey," Cadence says, pulling her close again. "None of this was your fault."

Ruby presses her lips together, holding in the worst part: she still believes he was right.

"Did you hear me?" Cadence says.

"I should've just let him sleep with me like he wanted, but I was so mad he was making me be with those other guys." She trembles. "I should have let him."

"Let him rape you?"

Ruby winces against the memory. Each strike, ripping through her bare skin. Her back, on fire. Blood soaking the carpet. Redd's fingers digging into the slashes when he grabbed her and flipped her over. The hate in his eyes. "I blacked out and"—Ruby senses the catch in Cadence's breath—"I should've just done what he wanted. Maybe he would've stopped."

"You couldn't have stopped him. He beat you and raped you over and over. *He* did that."

Ruby looks up with teary eyes. "I should've just said yes."

"You did nothing wrong."

"He said he loved me." Ruby shakes her head, feeling the break in her chest all over again. "But he didn't love me. He lied."

Cadence nods solemnly.

"How will anybody love me now?"

"Someday," Cadence says, sweeping the hair from Ruby's eyes, "when you decide to show someone the real you—the person I've gotten to know—they will."

Ruby's breath quivers with doubt. She lowers her gaze. "I'm scared."

"I am too," Cadence says.

"What if I'm locked up for the rest of my life?" Ruby sniffles and roughly wipes her face. "What if I forget who I am?"

"You won't." Cadence gives Ruby's arms a squeeze. "It took me a long time to understand this: There's only one person's love you'll need. And once you earn it, you'll be able to rely on it always, I promise."

"Whose?"

Cadence gently lifts Ruby's chin. "Your own."

THE COURT: All right, I trust everyone had a good weekend?

VANELLI: Yes, thank you, Your Honor.

TATE: Yes, Your Honor.

THE COURT: Glad to hear it. Now, gentlemen, I reviewed your motions again last night, and this Court still finds Dr. Ware's qualifications meet the threshold requirements of Texas Rules of Evidence 702 and, as such, will allow her to testify as an expert witness in this case.

VANELLI: My objections still stand, Your Honor.

THE COURT: And they are noted in the record, Counselor. But I find that with over sixteen years of experience, nine of those specifically working with juveniles in the criminal justice system, Dr. Ware has more than enough knowledge, skill, and experience to testify here. That is my ruling.

VANELLI: Yes, Your Honor.

TATE: Thank you, Your Honor.

THE COURT: Let's call in the jury.

BAILIFF: All rise.

[JURY ENTERS THE COURTROOM]

THE COURT: You may be seated. Sometimes the lawyers and I have to work out a few technical matters, so thank you for your patience. The Court recognizes Dr. Cadence Ware as an expert witness in forensic social work, and you will weigh her testimony as such.

TATE: Thank you, Your Honor. The Defense calls Dr. Cadence Ware.

After being duly sworn, **DR. CADENCE WARE** testified as follows:

TATE: Please state your name for the record.

WARE: Cadence Ware.

TATE: Thank you, Dr. Ware. Can you please tell us when you came to meet Ruby?

WARE: I met Ruby right before her case was transferred from the juvenile court to the adult court system. I was asked to do an eval.

TATE: And by "eval," do you mean an evaluation?

WARE: That's right.

TATE: And what did you learn about Ruby?

WARE: Well, at first, she'd barely speak to me. She was suspicious of my motivations, and I couldn't really blame her. I quickly learned that every adult she'd ever trusted had hurt her or betrayed her in some way.

TATE: And how old was Ruby when you two first met?

WARE: Though she was arrested and entered the juvenile system when she was fourteen, I didn't meet Ruby until she was fifteen.

TATE: What did you notice about her at the beginning?

WARE: Once I started meeting with Ruby, I saw very quickly that she was a bright young lady.

TATE: And can you tell me about your evaluation?

WARE: When I first meet with a client like this, as part of my assessment, I often show them sketches of small groups of people doing something simple—say, a woman handing something to a man, two girls talking with one girl walking behind the other two, things like that. And then I ask the client to tell me the story of what's going on in each of the sketches.

TATE: And what did you learn about Ruby during this exercise?

WARE: That she viewed the world in a very chaotic way. Every situation was negative, even when the people in the sketches were smiling. She was always suspicious that something else was going on behind their smiles.

TATE: What did that tell you?

WARE: Ruby viewed the world through a suspicious lens. And after meeting with her a few times, I soon recognized the signs. She lived in a constant state of fight or flight.

TATE: How do you mean?

WARE: Through her files and talking with her, I learned Ruby had been abused throughout her life. So much so that she's come to expect abuse, whether physical or emotional. She's been conditioned to believe she can't trust anyone.

TATE: And how can that affect someone's reaction to a stressful situation?

WARE: Well, Ruby has come to expect punishment, whether it be physical or emotional or both. She's also been abandoned by those she loves. So she reacts before someone has a chance to hurt her. This condition is often exacerbated in someone whose rational brain has not yet had the chance to fully develop, like someone of Ruby's age.

TATE: Is that normal, that her brain is not fully developed?

WARE: It is. The prefrontal cortex, or the executive functioning part of our brain, doesn't fully develop until we're around twenty-five years old.

TATE: Okay, Dr. Ware. You learned that Ruby's mother drank during her pregnancy, correct?

WARE: Yes, I learned her mother drank hard liquor almost daily while pregnant with Ruby. My understanding is she also smoked marijuana occasionally while pregnant.

TATE: And what did that lead you to conclude?

WARE: That Ruby suffers from fetal alcohol spectrum disorders.

TATE: So then, does Ruby exhibit the signs of fetal alcohol spectrum disorders?

WARE: Absolutely. She is extremely intelligent, but she has poor judgment and reasoning skills in stressful real-life situations. She also has difficulty paying attention and poor memory—that, or she's subconsciously blocking out painful memories. Either would be typical in a situation like Ruby's.

TATE: Are any of these things a choice?

WARE: Not really. Ruby didn't have a choice before she was born, with her mother's drug and alcohol abuse, nor has she had much of a choice after. And when Ruby sees chaos, she doesn't respond in a way that you or I might consider proper. She can't control her impulses to react.

TATE: So during your sessions with Ruby, what did you do?

WARE: At first, I did most of the talking. Told her I was there for her and that I wanted to help her get to the root of her anger, because she seemed really angry at first.

TATE: Was she truly angry?

WARE: I realized that anger was actually a manifestation of her pain. She would lash out at others because she had not been given the tools to deal with everything wrong in her life.

TATE: It sounds like you have come to really care about Ruby.

WARE: Once you get to know her, it's hard not to care.

TATE: So I take it you've seen positive progress during your visits?

WARE: Ruby came to me a very frightened, suspicious young girl who reacted first and thought later. Now, with a reliable support system in place, she is learning how to control those impulses. I believe she will find the tools she needs to navigate her life in a positive direction.

TATE: Based upon your sixteen years of knowledge and experience, do you think life in prison is the appropriate sentence for Ruby?

WARE: No, I do not.

TATE: And why do you say that?

WARE: Ruby understands the wrong that has been done here. She's committed to work on herself, more than I've seen in many of my adult clients. I think Ruby has great potential.

TATE: Did you ever feel like you had a breakthrough moment with her, as they say?

WARE: I don't think we had a breakthrough like you're talking about. That's more something you see in the movies. But I think we gained a mutual respect for one another over time. Ruby has done the difficult work, and will continue to do that work, in order to move past the traumatic events in her life so she can become a productive member of society.

TATE: And when the State argues Ruby isn't capable of being a productive member of society, what do you say?

WARE: I'd say they haven't spent as much time with her as I have. Sometimes, I think merely showing up repeatedly for my clients can be enough to help them start to see their value. Ruby had been abandoned by everyone she loved, and I wasn't going to do that to her. Not if I wanted her to trust me.

TATE: And does Ruby trust you?

WARE: I hope she does.

HERE ENDS THE EXCERPT

about record

d about Eric

un → Eric shot

JULY 17, 2023

Dear Maya,

Trash. Tease. Whore. Pain. Bitch. Stupid. Worthless. Cunt. Nobody. Those are my words.

No one has ever used that other word and me in the same sentence before. I can't believe Cadence said it. Does she really think I have potential?

Maybe she was just saying that because it was part of the story, but I don't think so.

I'm just feeling a little weird about it all because after she said those things, she didn't smile or wave when I left the courtroom.

She looked sad.

I think she's worried about the jury. When I asked Mr. Tate, he said it would be unprofessional for Cadence to smile when I'm on trial for murder. He said not to take it personal, but he didn't have an answer when I told him she's smiled at me before.

Mr. Tate doesn't know. Maybe, if I ever get out of here, I can tell you the whole story.

Your friend,
Ruby

THE COURT: Is the State ready to make its closing argument?

VANELLI: Ready, Your Honor.

THE COURT: All right, you may begin.

CLOSING ARGUMENT FOR THE STATE OF TEXAS:

Ladies and gentlemen of the jury, at the beginning of this trial, I told you the State proudly carries the burden of proof in this case. And I am sure you can now understand the reason for that confidence. We have proven every element needed for you to find the Defendant guilty of capital murder.

Let's walk through it, shall we? First, we must prove the Defendant intended to rob the victim in this case. You heard it from the Defendant's mouth: she took Mr. Hanson's wallet and truck. Detective Martinez told you he found Mr. Hanson's wallet at the Super 8 motel. The cash was gone, and one of the credit cards was missing. It doesn't matter whether the Defendant gave the wallet to her pimp or kept it for herself; she is the one who robbed Mr. Hanson. She is the one who took his truck, moved it, and tried to wipe it down. And by the way, remember she told you it was her idea to wipe down the truck to remove the fingerprints, a conscious attempt to separate herself from what she knew was a heinous crime.

Now, the Defense would like you to believe that Mr. Hanson propositioned her for sex. But that makes no sense. Mr. Hanson was fully clothed when the police found him dead. He even had his shoes on. If he was planning to have sex with the Defendant, don't you think he would have at least removed his shoes?

We must also prove the Defendant caused the death of Mr. Hanson in the course of her robbery of him. Again, we have proven that element. The Defendant admits she shot Mr. Hanson—not once, but twice. She admitted she intentionally fired her weapon. And the bullets that killed Mr. Hanson match the bullets from the Defendant's gun. Dr. Yuan explained that the bullet shot into the back of Mr. Hanson's head was fatal.

Again, the Defendant will argue that it was self-defense. And again, that makes no sense. Shoot once? Okay, maybe. But multiple times? She was clearly chasing after Mr. Hanson so he couldn't seek help. The gun has her prints on it. The nine-millimeter bullets that killed Mr. Hanson match those shot from the Defendant's gun. She was covered in Mr. Hanson's blood. She wiped it off. She tried to separate herself from this crime, but the hard evidence won't let her, and you can't allow her to get away with this, ladies and gentlemen.

You heard testimony from Mr. Hanson's ex-wife and from Darnell Johnson. Both describe Mr. Hanson as a man who cared about his community. A man of God. He was a successful businessman who could've ignored those less fortunate than himself, but he didn't. Instead, he poured himself into his work and his community, admittedly to the detriment of his marriage. You heard Mr. Johnson's testimony— Mr. Hanson saved his life. He is in college now and will become a doctor because of the mentorship of Mr. Hanson. And we contend that is exactly why Mr. Hanson picked up the Defendant: not to have sex with her, as the Defense would have you believe, but to help her. Like he'd helped so many others before her.

The Defense has called Dr. Ware, a social worker, to manufacture a sob story about how the Defendant didn't have any choice but to kill Mr. Hanson. As you know, I objected to Dr. Ware's testimony. We contend it's all smoke and mirrors to distract you from the real evidence in this case. Because the fact remains that Mr. Hanson didn't threaten the Defendant. He was trying to help her, and the Defendant killed him in cold blood. And now he can never help anyone again.

The Defendant had a choice not to shoot Mr. Hanson, and now she's trying to fool you into believing she was innocent in all this. But you can't believe a word she says. The Defendant is no innocent. She is a prostitute who has spent her entire life around criminals and addicts. Her own mother is in jail on drug-related charges, and she came to Eric Hanson's house with a gun to rob him. She admitted to regularly consuming drank, smoking pot, and taking pills. She took Mr. Hanson's wallet and his truck. She killed him, all for a few bucks. Likely to buy drugs for her and her pimp.

The Defendant is not blameless. She's a murderer. Can you live with yourself if you let this murderer walk free? The Defendant doesn't have any remorse. Just look at her. She didn't apologize. Can you, in good conscience, free a cold-blooded murderer? Can you?

I don't think you can. Therefore, I ask that you return the only verdict the evidence demands. A verdict of guilty.

THE COURT: All right, thank you, Mr. Vanelli. Is the Defense ready to close?

TATE: Yes. Thank you, Your Honor.

CLOSING ARGUMENT FOR RUBY MONROE:

Members of the jury, sometimes people have a dark side. A side they don't show their family, their coworkers. But it's there nevertheless. And the Defense contends Mr. Hanson had a dark side.

I want you to remember that Ruby Monroe is only fifteen years old. She was only fourteen when Mr. Hanson picked her up at the Taco Bell. And make no mistake: He was the one who propositioned her. He was the one who asked if she was ready for some action. He was the one who asked her how much. He was the one who asked how much a fourteen-year-old girl was going to charge him for sex. He wasn't trying to help her. He wanted to use her. Just like she'd been used by adults her whole life.

You heard the painful testimony of how Ruby was removed from her home by protective services on three separate occasions, how Ruby's father left them when she was young, and how her mother's boyfriends had sexually abused her. How Ruby begged her mother to make one of those boyfriends stop, but instead of making him stop, she kicked her daughter out of her house when she was only thirteen at the time.

And next thing we know, Ruby is picked up by a man who acts sweet on her, pretends to be her boyfriend, only to exploit her. No, Mr. Shandler—or Redd Dogg, as people knew him—did not love Ruby. He was a man in his twenties who sold a young girl to men and then took all of the money. He beat her and threatened to kill her. Ruby is the victim of sex trafficking, a dire problem here in our city and throughout the nation. She is one of thousands of innocents.

You see her here. This petite girl. No wonder she was scared when she was trapped in a truck with Mr. Hanson, a much larger man. No wonder she didn't speak up when he decided to change plans and drive to his house. No wonder she was afraid when she saw his gun in the glove compartment.

Sure, she had a gun in her purse. But she didn't put it there. Her pimp did, for protection, because he knew how dangerous it was for girls like Ruby on the streets of Dallas.

And then you hear the horrific testimony of how Mr. Hanson slapped Ruby awake and threatened to probe her vagina with a loaded weapon. Now, the prosecution would have you believe Ruby is lying about that. But remember what Mr. Hanson's own ex-wife said? Mr. Hanson made her very uncomfortable watching pornography in which the women are being penetrated by all kinds of objects. Mr. Hanson had a dark side. You heard Ruby tell you how he wanted Ruby to beg him for sex. A fourteen-year-old girl beg a thirty—two-year-old man for sex? It's sick.

He slapped her awake, like she'd been slapped by her pimp, by her mother's boyfriend, and she knew exactly what to expect. Abuse. Sexual, mental, physical. You heard Dr. Ware. Ruby didn't have a choice. She didn't have the tools to reason. Her brain wasn't fully developed due simply to her young age and her mother's abuse of alcohol while Ruby was still in the womb. Ruby was slapped awake and forced into fight-or-flight mode.

And when she got the chance to protect herself,

she took it. She grabbed the gun and shot. She admitted she was afraid. And who wouldn't be? She was in an unknown house with a large intoxicated man who had just threatened to kill her.

Yes, she took Mr. Hanson's wallet and truck. But think about why. She was afraid, that's why. She had to get out of there and knew Redd would beat her, like he had so many other times, if she didn't bring him money. If she had gone to that house to rob Mr. Hanson, like the prosecutor suggests, why didn't she take his fancy gold watch? She didn't steal his televisions or expensive gun collection. She took nothing but the bare minimum that she thought would allow her to survive.

The prosecution likes to make a big deal about the fact that Ruby shot Mr. Hanson more than once. But you heard her testimony. She feared for her life. She says he was yelling and threatening to get a gun. She thought she was protecting herself.

I beg you: put yourself in the shoes of this girl who has been abused over and over again by the adults in her life. And despite what the prosecution would like you to believe, she is just a girl. Think of how she has been used and afraid. But think also of what her social worker said at the end of her testimony. Dr. Ware said Ruby has great potential. But only if you give her that chance.

Ruby reasonably feared for her life. Mr. Hanson threatened her, as many men have before, and she did what she thought she had to do to protect herself, to stay alive. This is a clear case of self-defense.

Therefore, I ask you return the only just verdict in this case: not guilty.

HERE ENDS THE EXCERPT

Mother Takes Plea Deal in Midst of Daughter's Trial

BY GRANT LATHAM
Staff Writer

Jennifer Monroe, mother of accused murderer Ruby Danielle Monroe, accepted a plea deal on Thursday. While the jury deliberates Miss Monroe's fate for the alleged murder of local businessman Eric Hanson, court records show her mother is pleading guilty to a felony charge of fraudulent possession of a controlled substance. The charge carries a potential twenty-year prison sentence and a fine of up to $10,000.

Despite testifying at her daughter's trial that she was not receiving a lighter sentence, it appears the Dallas County District Attorney Cheyenne Miller decided to offer her a deal. When asked about the seeming discrepancy, Ms. Miller stated, "One case has nothing to do with the other." She further explained, "Upon an independent evaluation of Jennifer Monroe's case, we believed treatment and rehab would save the voters of Dallas County tax dollars and be a better resolution in this particular case."

A source close to the Hanson family, who wished to remain anonymous, disagreed. "That [deal] was nothing more than a political move by the DA who has no regard for public safety," the source said. "How long are we going to go easy on these drug addicts while good people are murdered?"

Judge Loretta Wong of the 213th District Court is expected to sign the sealed plea documents later this week.

THE COURT: All right, I'm told we have a verdict. Everyone here?

VANELLI: The State is here and ready, Your Honor.

TATE: The Defense is also ready, Your Honor.

THE COURT: Very well, then. Bailiff, will you please bring in the jury?

BAILIFF: All rise.

[JURY ENTERS THE COURTROOM]

THE COURT: Please be seated. I understand the jury has reached a verdict.

FOREWOMAN: We have.

THE COURT: Will the Defendant please stand?

HERE ENDS THE EXCERPT

Accused Murderer of Local Millionaire Acquitted

BY GRANT LATHAM
Staff Writer

A Dallas County jury acquitted fifteen-year-old Ruby Monroe in the capital murder of Eric Hanson late Saturday afternoon, hours after telling the judge that they were struggling to agree on a verdict.

Ruby Danielle Monroe has been incarcerated—first in a juvenile detention center and later in the Dallas County women's jail—since her arrest in January 2022 for the robbery and shooting death of businessman Eric Hanson, whose body was found behind his home on January 7, 2022.

Jurors deliberated for almost four days before finding Monroe not guilty.

At 11:00 a.m. on Saturday morning, Judge Fred Ambrose received a message from the jury that they were deadlocked. He brought them back into the courtroom and instructed them to continue deliberating. They reached a verdict at 4:00 p.m.

The entire case hinged on the credibility of the accused, Ruby Monroe, who, in testimony, insisted she shot Mr. Hanson in self-defense.

The victim's family has requested space as they determine their next steps. Miss Monroe, a minor, has been released to an undisclosed ward.

DESTROY

DECEMBER 1, 2023

Ruby's gaze settles on the playground equipment outside her counselor's office window. Girls about her age play with small children in the winter sunshine. One of the girls is pregnant, her belly bulging over her yoga pants as she pushes a little boy on the swing. Ruby tugs her braid over her shoulder and nervously fiddles with the ends.

"Do you want to try telling me how you got those scars on your back?"

Ruby spots her reflection in the window—the thin-faced girl with dark hair—and slouches in her chair. She buries her hands deep inside the pockets of her hoodie. The air feels thick as she tries to take a breath. She focuses on the candle flame, flickering on the corner of her counselor's desk. She wonders if there's enough air for both of them to breathe.

"Ruby?"

She sits up out of habit, as if it was a guard from the jail calling her name.

The counselor—Janette—looks her directly in the eye. Hers are a watery blue. Gentle, but with an unmistakable sadness in the center. She wears a pink suit with an official Girls Center of Dallas name tag. The only evidence of her former involvement in the life is the money bag tattoo on the side of her neck.

Janette lets out a long breath. "That's okay." She looks up at the clock.

Ruby glances too. Time's up.

"Maybe next time."

Ruby is already out of her chair and twisting the doorknob.

Janette stands. "You know if you need to talk anytime—day or night—I'm available. You have my cell?"

"Yeah, thanks," Ruby says before she escapes.

When she's outside Janette's office, Ruby pulls the paper schedule from her pocket, even though she knows what comes next: free time. Ruby hates free time, when she has nothing to do but think.

Girls in jeans and T-shirts and skirts and sweaters smile at Ruby as she walks down the hall. She has a hard time remembering all of their names, but she's gotten better at it with time. Apparently, that's all she has now. Time.

"Ruby," a voice calls from behind her, followed by the sound of heels clicking against the tile floors. It's Ms. Graham. At barely five feet tall in those heels, the director's confidence makes her seem much taller. Rumor has it she was almost drowned by her pimp when she was about Ruby's age. The girls say you can ask her about it and she'll tell you the whole story. But Ruby knows how it feels to be asked, and so she doesn't.

"You have a visitor." Ms. Graham touches Ruby's arm in that reassuring way she always does. "Dr. Ware is here to see you again."

For the first time in a while, genuine happiness tugs at the edges of Ruby's mouth.

"She's in the lounge," Ms. Graham says. "Now, if you'll excuse me. I need to check in a new girl."

Ruby turns for the lobby, and it's all she can do not to run. She stops when she reaches the check-in desk for visitors and scans the room of sofas and chairs. A group of girls gather around the television, watching a talk show. On another sofa, a girl with mascara running down her cheeks wipes her tears with a tissue as a woman—probably her mom—lectures her.

Then she spots the scarf and the familiar smile.

"May I?" Cadence asks when Ruby has made her way over. She always asks permission first, ever since the day she saw Ruby's scars. It makes Ruby feel both self-conscious and protected. But mostly the latter.

She nods, and Cadence brings her in for a long hug. Despite her muscular frame, Cadence's hugs always feel soft. Safe.

Cadence releases her, too soon, and takes her usual seat in front of the large windows that overlook the gardens, now dormant for winter. Ruby sits with her back to the window.

"How are you?" Cadence shrugs off her coat. She then removes her scarf, exposing the zigzag down her throat. She says the center is a safe space and has made a habit of removing her scarf when she visits. Ruby is just happy Cadence has found a place where she doesn't feel like she has to hide, especially since it's with her. "You look good."

"I am," Ruby says, her last conversation with Janette still niggling her mind. "I just don't understand why I have to talk to Janette when I've already told you everything."

"Healing can take a long time. Talking will help." Cadence nods reassuringly. "She's trained for this, and besides, you're only getting started. You've been here, what? Less than five months? And how long have you been seeing Janette?"

"Two weeks. It's— I'd rather talk to you."

"I'm here, aren't I?"

Ruby shrugs. "I guess I've been thinking a lot lately."

"About Redd?"

Ruby gives a slight shake of her head. "Do you really think he would've killed me if I hadn't shot first?"

"Eric?" Cadence's voice softens. "I believe he could have, yes."

"And if I died, nobody would've cared, right? I would've been just another girl gone missing."

"You didn't die, though. You survived."

Ruby zips her hoodie up to her throat. "I guess you can't really go missing if there's nobody who misses you."

"I'd miss you." Cadence reaches for Ruby's hand. "Brian would miss you. These girls would miss you."

"Yeah, but there's nobody who knew me before who would care if I lived or died. I haven't heard from anybody since I got here. I even wrote my mom in rehab like you said. Nothing."

Disappointment pales Cadence's face. "I'm so sorry."

"And Maya . . . She never responded to any of my letters, but I thought— I thought she might at least call when I got out."

"Well, actually, that's why I'm here today." She squeezes Ruby's fingers. "I have a confession to make. I've been dishonest with you about something."

Ruby resists the urge to pull away. "What?"

"I'm not proud, but I didn't see any other way." Cadence squeezes Ruby's hand again before releasing her. She reaches into her bag and retrieves a stack of letters, bound by a thick rubber band.

In an instant, Ruby feels the weight of her words back in her hands. She flips through the stack. Her letters to Maya. All of them. Even the ones she wrote in juvie. All unopened. Unmailed.

"They're all there. Even the ones you gave to the guards, before you started giving them to me." Cadence's shoulders sink. "I know I should have said something, but after everything you told me, I was afraid they'd harm your case if they ever got out. But I didn't want to tell you that, because then you'd stop writing them, and it was clear you were working things out between our meetings. They really seemed to help you push past barriers in your own mind, much more than I was able to do at times."

Ruby presses the stack against her lap. All those words. All that fear and anger. Her confessions. So many lies.

"I hate that I did this." She reduces her voice to a whisper. "But if the prosecutor got his hands on these, he would have used them against you, to attack your character, and if Brian found out . . ."

Ruby can see the guilt weighing on Cadence. For not telling her. For not telling Mr. Tate the truth.

"You trusted me," Cadence says finally. "I'm so sorry."

Ruby takes a deep breath, and then another. If she's honest with herself, deep down, she suspected there was something off all along, a feeling that Cadence wasn't mailing her letters. At first, she'd even asked her if she would read them; Cadence didn't say no. How could she be angry with her now, after everything that's happened? "You said you'd help me, and you did."

Cadence opens her mouth to speak, but then Janette calls her name from across the room. Cadence holds up a finger, as if asking for a moment.

"I still wanted to make things right," she says and gestures over Ruby's shoulder toward the window.

Ruby turns in her chair, and on the other side of the glass, Janette escorts someone with curls, loose around her face, into the garden. The girl, with her head held high, sits on a bench beneath the boughs of a leafless tree. She looks older now, somehow even more beautiful in her Vassar sweatshirt and jeans, but still unmistakably her.

"Maya," Ruby breathes.

"You just can't—"

"I know. I won't." Ruby's heart beats with hope.

Cadence takes the stack of letters from her and nods toward Maya. "Then what are you waiting for?"

A grin spreads wide across Ruby's face. "Thank you," she says before hopping from her chair and hurrying toward Janette, who waits at the door with Ruby's coat. But Ruby doesn't need her coat, not really. She doesn't feel the cold air outside either.

Instead, warmth envelops her as she runs into the arms of her friend.

JANUARY 6, 2024

Dear Maya,

By the time you get this letter, you should be back at school. Thanks for visiting over your Christmas break so I wouldn't be all alone. And for the rainbow scarf you knitted for me. Everyone keeps telling me how pretty it is. I only wish I'd had something to give you.

Also thank your sister for me. I know she's never really liked me, but it was nice she sent that box of cookies. I've already shared them with the girls down the hall, the ones who didn't have any visitors over the holidays, so they could at least have something sweet.

Speaking of sweet, Cadence just left. She brought me a huge bag of M&M's and a package of Double Stuf Oreos. So good! She was glad to hear you came while you were here on break. I probably won't tell her I'm writing you now. I know I said it was okay she didn't send my letters to you, and I understand why Cadence only wants me to look ahead, but a part of me wishes she hadn't destroyed them.

I'm outside now. You know the garden where we talked that first time? I'm under the large tree again, and the cold air is stinging my cheeks, but I love it. It reminds me I'm still alive. Does that sound weird?

Mr. Tate visited with Cadence today. He almost didn't recognize me! I know it's strange, but his smile still means a lot. He brought me another calendar for my room. This one has girl-power quotes from all these famous women. It's totally corny, but I'm still going to use it. He was excited when I told him I'm starting life-skills classes this month and am going for my GED. He even asked if I was going to go to college. I thought you'd like to hear that. Sometimes I have to pinch my arm just to remind myself this is my life now and I'm not dreaming back in my cell.

It's weird how writing to you makes me think of all the things that got me here. Remember what a mess I was? Even though you never read my letters, I got used to talking to you through them. I guess that's why I'm writing now. I wanted to tell you something when you were here, but I couldn't say it to your face. Too weird. So here goes.

I know you did all you could to help me when Redd was trying to get me to go with him. I just wasn't ready to listen to anybody then. I still don't totally understand how, but the letters I wrote to you helped me get unstuck. When I put down the words, it's like something opened up inside, and I could start talking about things with Cadence. I'd never done that before. Talked about my shit like that with somebody I hardly knew.

Cadence is always telling me the things we tell ourselves and others are important. "Words matter" is what she says. I think that's another reason I wanted to write to you now. I want to tell you every-thing even though I know I really shouldn't. You were my friend when there was no one else, and you deserve to know the truth.

Please don't be mad, but what I told Cadence in that first meet-ing was different from what the jury heard. Believe me when I tell you that we had to tear up my story and make up a new one. Mr. Tate didn't know. He trusted us, and he never questioned. I almost gave up when that judge transferred me from juvie to jail. But Cadence wouldn't let me, and when the trial came around, I almost knew the story better than I knew the truth.

But that's all it was. A story. A piece of the truth. A story changes depending on who's telling it. Depending on how much that person is willing to tell.

I know you do that too. Change your story. I think it's the only way girls like us can survive.

So I'm trusting you to keep this to yourself, okay? I promise I'll tell you more next time I see you. Until then, thanks for being there for me always.

Love,
Ruby

"Then let's get started." Cadence nods toward Ruby. "Tell me about the day you met Eric Hanson."

"Can't I finish my Twizzlers first?" Ruby says through a mouthful.

With the rainbow mural to her back, Cadence considers the girl as she chews the last of her candy. For a moment, her tough shell has fallen away, and all Cadence can see is the child dressed in the oversize T-shirt and sweatpants—pants rolled up at the bottom and the V of the top gaping to reveal her sharp collarbone and the tattoo.

Cadence knows exactly what that tattoo is. And exactly what it means.

She feels the singe of something familiar—hatred, disgust, for the men who do what they do to girls like Ruby. Just looking at her stokes a fire in Cadence, one she's tried years to forget but can't. The girl really does look like Cadence's mother, with those haunted eyes and sloped shoulders. A vulnerability that shows through when she lets her guard down, as she has now, shoving candy into her mouth like there will never be enough.

"Finished?" Cadence asks.

Ruby gulps her soda and belches with a closed mouth. She crushes the can. "How about another Coke?"

"Let's talk first." Cadence props the notepad on her lap and, above a few details she's already jotted down about Ruby's case, writes the date: *10/18/22*. "How about we start with the first thing you remember about January seventh?"

Ruby shoves a finger inside her mouth and digs at the candy stuck in her back teeth. She eyes the notepad in Cadence's hand again, but she doesn't say anything.

"Did you know Eric Hanson before that day?"

The girl's finger emerges from her mouth, wet with a red bit stuck under her fingernail. "Does it matter?" She sucks the dislodged bit from her fingernail and chews. "Mr. Tate already told me that prosecutor wants to lock me up. And they know I was at his house, right? They probably have my fingerprints or some shit."

Ruby has already accepted the worst. Cadence makes a note: *History of violence?* "I definitely can't help you if you don't talk to me."

Ruby wipes her wet finger on her pants. "Look, lady, I don't know what you want from me. But if you'd like to get something else from the vend—"

"As I said, you can call me Cadence," she says, cutting her off. "And we might be able to find a way to keep you from getting transferred to the adult jail if you tell me what happened."

Ruby rolls her eyes.

Cadence resists her frustration bubbling just below the surface and changes tactics. "You're right. The prosecutor has a story to tell about what happened in that house."

"And you believe him?"

"Should I?" Cadence tilts her head, examining.

Ruby slaps the table. "What the hell do you want from me?"

Good, she's angry, Cadence thinks. She can work with anger if it gets the girl talking. "I want to know why Eric Hanson is dead."

Ruby crosses her arms over her chest. Her tattoo is more visible now. Cadence makes a quick note so Brian can cross-reference the database for any matches later: *Tattoo—RD?* "Does it matter? He's dead."

"For your case, it could matter very much. I want to know why a young girl kills a prominent member of the community in his own home."

"He was the one who took *me* there."

"I see," she says before scribbling *Victim.*

"What are you writing?" Ruby asks, craning her neck. "I knew you were gonna get all judgy."

Cadence shields the notepad on her lap. "I'm just keeping some notes for myself. I'm not judging you. He was a grown man, and you're a kid."

"I'm not a kid." Ruby angrily pushes the crushed Coke can from the table. It clangs across the floor. "I've been taking care of myself for a long time."

Cadence chooses to ignore her outburst. "I'm sure you have. I assume it wasn't your first time selling yourself for money?" she asks, writing *Ruby + sex* and *$$$* underneath.

Ruby huffs, but she doesn't deny it.

Cadence looks up from the angry dollar signs she's scratched onto the page. "That must have been hard."

"Why are you looking at me like that?" The girl's eyes dilate like an animal stuck in a trap.

"Like what?"

"Like you feel sorry for me."

Cadence knows what Ruby thinks about her: that despite what

she's told Ruby about her job, she's just another barb in the trap. Kind words will only make the girl less trusting, and a wounded animal is always more likely to bite. "Does it bother you that I feel for you?"

"You don't even know me." Ruby continues to writhe in her chair. "What are you looking at?"

Cadence shakes her head. "You just remind me of someone, that's all."

"Who?"

Cadence silently chastises herself. "It doesn't matter. Someone I knew a long time ago."

"Is she dead?"

"Yes," Cadence says. "Overdose."

"Sorry," Ruby says softly.

Cadence clears her throat. "So, Eric Hanson brought you back to his house. How did you meet him?"

Ruby sighs. "I was out walking, okay? I'd seen this really nice truck in the parking lot of the Taco Bell. Silver rims. Expensive. I was hungry, so I went inside to see if I could get whoever owned the truck to buy me lunch. That's the first time I saw him."

Cadence nods. "How did you know he owned the truck?"

"I didn't." Ruby shrugs. "But he was dressed real nice, had an expensive watch. A guy like that is kinda out of place in that neighborhood, unless he's looking for—" Ruby cuts herself off but quickly adds, "He didn't have any food in front of him. He was looking at his phone and was kind of intense about it."

"Intense how?" Cadence makes a quick note: *Intense*.

"Like he was upset. So I went up to him and asked if he was okay."

Cadence tilts her head. "Why would you approach someone you didn't know?"

"Like I said, I was hungry." She narrows her eyes, and a smile crosses her face. "And he looked like the type who might buy me lunch if I asked nicely."

Cadence shifts uncomfortably.

"As soon as he saw me, his whole face changed. He liked me."

"How could you tell?"

Ruby lifts an eyebrow. "He stood up and I could see."

Bile rises in Cadence's throat; she swallows hard, forcing herself not to cough. "Did he buy you something to eat?"

"Yeah," Ruby says, nodding like she's proud. "He asked if I'd mind if he kept me company since he'd had a stressful day. He wasn't a bad-looking guy, so I decided, why not?"

"What did you two talk about?"

"Mostly I ate while he talked about how his wife left him. He was still wearing a wedding ring, and his fancy phone kept lighting up with emails and texts—like he had all this work to do. He seemed like somebody important, and he knew it."

Cadence scratches an arrow in her notes, connecting *Intense* to *Arrogant*. "So how did you end up leaving the restaurant with him?"

"He was saying I was a good listener and started telling me about this volunteer stuff he did on the side and how he liked helping kids. He said he wanted to help me, like with food and stuff, so I went with him. I thought he might give me money, and I could give it to my—this other guy I know who really needed some then." Ruby shakes her head. "I didn't know we were going to end up at his house."

Cadence knew it: Eric Hanson lured her. "What happened after you got there?"

"I think he was trying to impress me, showing me around his house and shit. He made himself a drink, asked if I wanted one, but I kept yawning." She drums the table with her finger. "He said I could take a nap, and we could talk more about how he would help me after I got some rest."

"Did you take a nap?"

"Yeah." The drumming stops; Ruby's expression shifts. "He got into the bed with me, but he didn't do anything. Not until he apparently found the gun in my purse and woke me up."

Cadence freezes, her pen hovering over her notepad. "You had a gun?"

Ruby kneads her lips. "Can I have that Coke now?"

The air-conditioning pops on, filling the Rainbow Room with the smell of mildew. "Could you tell me what happened after Eric assaulted you?"

"Assaulted?"

Cadence knows she can't be wrong on that point. "He tried to hurt you, right?"

Ruby's legs bounce under the table, her Crocs tap-tapping against the floor, and Cadence knows that look. The look of someone remembering.

"Ruby? Did Eric rape you?"

Her legs still. "He tried."

Okay, Cadence thinks. *Self-defense. Maybe.* "What happened then?"

"I don't know." Ruby's focus drifts to the mural on the wall behind Cadence. "I remember I was lying on the bed. I just wanted to get away. I'd stopped moving, and I guess he thought he could put the gun down. And so I grabbed it."

Cadence quickly scribbles: *Ruby gets gun.*

"It went off."

"Did you pull the trigger?"

Cadence notices how Ruby studies the mural. The rainbow and the animals marching two by two. She's taking it all in.

"I wouldn't let him have the gun," Ruby says eventually. "It went off. . . . Eric looked pretty freaked by all the blood."

Cadence's heart catches. *Did she intend to shoot him?*

"It felt . . . weird."

"Weird how?"

Ruby's gaze creeps from the mural to Cadence's face; her eyes go cold. "I wasn't scared anymore."

Cadence forces her breath to remain even.

Ruby shrugs. "So yeah, Eric was backing up and fell through the glass door."

Fell through door, Cadence notes, her hand shaking a little. "And what was going through your mind when he fell through the door?"

"I don't remember. I kind of blanked." Ruby looks somewhere over Cadence's shoulder for a moment. "I felt better then. I do remember that part."

Cadence's pen stops scribbling; she looks up from her notes. "You felt better?"

"Yeah. I mean, he lied to me. He said he'd help me, but then tried to screw me and throw me away. He thought I was trash. It fucked with my head, you know?"

Cadence nods, knowing Ruby is doomed if this is the story the judge hears. *But there has to be more*, Cadence thinks. *A reason she would have shot him again.* "After Eric Hanson fell through the door, did you think he was going to get up and try to hurt you?"

"Not really," Ruby says, still cold. "He was crying and begging me to call 911."

"Did you call 911?"

"Hell no. No one ever called 911 when I got the shit beat out of me. Why should I do it for him?"

Cadence writes *no fear.*

"Then he said he was going to try to get help on his own. He started to get up and—I don't know—it pissed me off. Why should he get help when he lied about helping me?"

"And so what did you do?"

"I shot him again."

"But you didn't realize you had killed him," Cadence suggests, offering the girl a lifeline. *Take it.*

A wry grin crosses Ruby's face. "I shot him in the back of the fucking head, so yeah, I figured."

The pen slips from Cadence's hand and bounces against the linoleum. When she spots Ruby's eyes following it, she quickly bends over. But Ruby has already snatched it. She lifts it up, her fingers wrapped around the shaft.

Cadence doesn't dare move. She wonders if a guard could get to her before Ruby does. Why'd she let that guard go on break?

Just as she's about to call out, Ruby carefully places the pen on the table between them. "Thanks for the snack," she says, looking no older than fifteen again.

Cadence opens her mouth, but nothing comes out.

"Are you mad at me now?" It's not remorse, exactly—not for what she did to Eric—but she does seem concerned about having upset Cadence. She sounds . . . vulnerable. "You don't really think they can move me to the women's jail, do you?"

Reminded of her mother once more, Cadence shakes her head clear. She quickly reviews her notes—what Ruby's told her and, more important, what she hasn't. She's read Ruby's files, some of them. There's more to her story. More even that Ruby isn't telling her.

The girl is motionless, staring.

"I'm not angry," Cadence finally says.

It's a lie. Cadence *is* angry, but not with Ruby. She knows with every fiber of her being that Ruby is a victim. She would know that even if she hadn't been doing this work for years. She recognizes Ruby's story, and Cadence knows how it ends.

She retrieves the pen and scribbles a few more notes about the sequence of events Ruby just told her. Ruby admits she was looking for Eric at the Taco Bell. She admits she shot him intentionally. At least once. Maybe she did it on purpose both times. She chased after him when he was bleeding and begging, and she shot him.

Cadence wonders if she would have done the same to all those men who hurt her mother. Who hurt her. God knows she tried. She touches the fabric wound tight around her neck.

"You're mad," Ruby says, and it's not a question this time. The girl shakes her head. "You're gonna leave now, aren't you?"

Cadence realizes how dangerous this is, but—

"Your story is wrong."

Ruby's eyes narrow; her tough shell immediately returns. "You don't believe me?"

Cadence makes a quick note at the top of her notepad—*DESTROY*—before shoving it into her messenger bag. "No, I do. And that's why you have to listen to me." She struggles to get Ruby to look at her. "You want to spend the rest of your life in prison?"

"What kind of a fucked-up question is that?"

"Because if anyone else hears that story you just told me, being moved to the women's jail is going to be the least of your problems."

Ruby freezes, but only for a moment. "What do you—"

"I'm only going to say this once." Cadence sees she finally has Ruby's attention. "You shouldn't have your life taken away for this. What you did is not your fault. Not after what you've been through."

"What I've been through?" Ruby sucks her teeth with impatience. "What do you know about what I've been through?"

"Let's just say I've heard your story before. But you have a decision to make. Only *you* can make it." Cadence's gaze flicks to the door and then back before she lowers her voice another notch. "All of this will come down to you, so I want you to think carefully before you answer, okay?"

Ruby nods.

"Can you forget your story?"

"Why would I do that?" She looks under the table and back to Cadence, suspicious. "You wearing a wire or something?"

"I wouldn't do that. I want to help you."

Ruby scoffs. "You don't know me."

"I'd like to get to know you."

"Right," the girl says, crossing her arms over her chest.

"Listen, this is as big a risk for me as it is for you." Cadence shifts in her chair, feeling the weight of what she's proposing. "What I'm about to suggest wouldn't mean I'd lose my job—it would mean I'd go to jail."

"Why would you do that?"

"Because I believe you deserve a chance."

Ruby seems to consider her for a moment. "What would I have to do?"

Cadence swallows her resolve and looks Ruby straight in the eye. "Do you think you can trust me?"

AUTHOR'S NOTE

Although Ruby is fictional, her story is all too real.

When I worked as a lawyer at the Dallas Court of Appeals, I reviewed criminal cases involving murders, robberies, drug offenses, and more—but in my time at the court, I was most disturbed by the overwhelming number of cases on my docket involving sex crimes against children. According to the Polaris Project, the average age a girl becomes a victim of sex trafficking is fifteen. Texas ranks second in the country for human trafficking with approximately three hundred thousand children at risk. In my city of Dallas, sex trafficking is a $99-million-per-year "business."

Texas is not alone, and the law has been slow to protect these victims. Statutory rape laws vary by state, with some states having a single age of consent, while others consider age differentials, minimum age of the child, and the minimum age of the defendant. However, if money changes hands in the same sexual encounter, the child can be convicted of prostitution in many states even though the child cannot legally consent to sex. These children can't legally buy alcohol or cigarettes or vote, but they can be convicted of prostitution. While Ruby is white, like many victims, it should be noted that girls of color represent a disproportionate number of these arrests.

As of January 2023, twenty-seven states, plus the District of Columbia, have passed so-called safe harbor laws that prevent minors from being charged with prostitution. In the 2019 session of the Texas Legislature, House Bill 1771 passed with unanimous support in both the House and Senate and would have removed children from the definition of prostitution in the Texas Penal Code. However, *The Texas Tribune* reported that Governor Greg Abbott vetoed that bill, which would have provided the same protection from prosecution to children under seventeen in Texas, claiming it would have "unintended consequences."

Recently, however, Texas became the first state in the nation to make solicitation of prostitution a felony offense. Effective September 1, 2021, a john can be convicted of a felony pursuant to Section 43.021 of the Texas Penal Code. This legislation is a step in the right direction, but it's only one of many needed to help put an end to sex trafficking. Time will tell if this law is actually used to convict buyers of sex or if it is, instead, a policy written by politicians to win elections with no actual enforcement.

It is important to note that victims of sexual exploitation can be of any race, age, ethnicity, sexual orientation, gender, social or economic group, or any level of academic achievement. However, some communities are disproportionately targeted, particularly Black communities. In 2023, the National Center on Sexual Exploitation reported that 40 percent of sex trafficking victims in the United States are Black, despite Black people making up less than 14 percent of the population. In Louisiana, Black girls account for nearly 49 percent of child sex trafficking victims and 84 percent in King County, Washington, though Black girls only comprise 19 percent and 7 percent of those populations respectively.

Many mistakenly believe if these girls—most of the victims are girls—are unhappy with their situation, they can just walk away.

The illusion of choice is a huge obstacle in getting the public to see these girls as the victims they are. But to have "choice" requires that you have *options*. No girl chooses between turning tricks and having a comfortable life. Most girls on the tracks are running from something worse at home. Statistics show that prostituted children suffer prior abuse at a much higher rate. And many of the children don't even "choose" to flee their abuser but are kicked out of the house by a parent or guardian.

It is then not uncommon for victims of abuse to bond with their pimp. Teens who are forced into prostitution may possess a blend of determination and recklessness. They are often too young to realize they are being manipulated but too old to see themselves as vulnerable. Therefore, they come to accept their sexual exploitation because they cannot envision an alternative.

Physical abuse combined with mental abuse are common methods of control for a pimp. He uses love as a tool to manipulate his victim into cooperating with her own exploitation by making her think that he and he alone loves her and that he has her back. Then he brings out the weapons of fear, drugs, shame, and violence. The abuse makes the girl feel weak, so wherever she goes, she is always afraid of her pimp. As one pimp summed it up: "Fuck the head, the body is going to follow." Therefore, this leads to one of the main problems: most girls don't see themselves as victims.

According to the FBI, given their daily exposure to violence at the hands of both their pimps and their johns, life expectancy after becoming involved in the life can be as little as seven years. But I didn't want Ruby's story to end that way. I didn't want her to be, as she says, "just another girl gone missing." Instead, I chose to challenge traditional notions of victimhood and asked myself, what

354

if the victim also committed a crime? Can a person be both a victim and an aggressor? What about Eric? Was he both?

Under the statutory definition of capital murder in Texas, Ruby has violated the law. If a child is between the ages of ten and seventeen at the time an offense is committed, their case may be transferred from the juvenile court to an adult court under certain circumstances. Here, Ruby was a candidate for transfer because she was alleged to have committed a capital felony offense due to the concurrent robbery. As a minor, she would not be eligible for the death penalty in Texas but would be subject to a mandatory life sentence if convicted. However, Texas law also allows a person to be absolved from criminal responsibility if her actions are deemed self-defense. In Ruby's story, the jury believed she was a victim of sex trafficking and that she did what she had to do in order to survive and escape. Therefore, she was acquitted.

In other words, Ruby was lucky. Her actions landed her in the criminal justice system; she received a caring and competent attorney, a protective—though misguided—social worker, and a sympathetic jury. Ultimately, she was matched with an organization that assists girls who are victims of sexual exploitation. None of these things are a given, and Ruby, like most girls in her situation, could have very easily ended up in prison for life, or back on the streets, or dead. Cadence would have known the statistics, and it is perhaps what led her to make the choice that she did.

Thankfully, safe houses and organizations now exist to help victims of sexual exploitation throughout the United States. Although their numbers don't yet match the pervasive need, these groups do everything from providing basics, such as food, clothing, toiletry items, and shelter, to services such as trauma-informed counseling,

GED classes, classes on financial literacy, conflict resolution, mindfulness workshops, and more. Many of these centers offer victims an opportunity to process the trauma they've experienced and help them envision a new possibility for their lives.

There is hope for a better future for those who have been sexually exploited, and it starts with us. We can offer our time, our talent, or our resources to support organizations that help victims or change laws to bolster them. We can learn the signs of trafficking and speak out against the injustices of abuse. We can condemn and punish the johns who create a market for child trafficking. We can recognize our shared humanity with these victims, because they are victims. They are kids, and they need our help.

RESOURCES

If you or anyone you know needs help escaping commercial sexual exploitation, you can contact your local police or one of these national agencies for immediate assistance:

National Human Trafficking Hotline
1-888-373-7888 or text "BEFREE" or "HELP" to 233733

National Runaway Safeline
1-800-RUNAWAY (1-800-786-2929)

If you or anyone you know needs help finding local anti-trafficking organizations that offer emergency, transitional, or long-term services to victims and survivors of human trafficking, you can search for them here: humantraffickinghotline.org/en/find-local-services.

For more information about domestic and international human trafficking in general, you can visit these websites:

Polaris
polarisproject.org

Coalition Against Trafficking in Women
catwinternational.org

ACKNOWLEDGMENTS

First and foremost, thank you to Jordan Brown for loving my wonderfully complicated Ruby as much as I do. You helped me to think of her story in new ways across the many layers of this book and inspired me to elevate each one. I'm immensely grateful for the care and compassion you provided to Ruby, Cadence, and especially me.

So much gratitude also goes to Jonathan Rosen. Thank you for your assistance in making this book possible and for your continued kindness and friendship.

Many thanks to my new agent, Elisa Houot, for taking the reins midway through the process and for your dedication and excitement about the kinds of stories I write.

Thank you also to Andre De Freitas, for your beautiful cover art, and to Corina Lupp, for your arresting design both on the cover and throughout the book. It is everything I imagined and so much more! Thank you also to the HarperCollins marketing, sales, and publicity teams and to all the amazing librarians and booksellers who are helping me bring Ruby's story to light.

A huge shout-out to my Hamline MFAC family, especially my talented cohort, the Joyful Resistance! I wrote this book while earning my master's degree in writing, and from the faculty to the alumni to my fellow students, I couldn't have been part of a more supportive community. A special thanks to my advisers, who all had something to say about Ruby's story: Lisa Jahn-Clough, Brandy Colbert, and Meg Medina. Your combined wisdom sustained me through the beginning, middle, and end of this book, and I'll be forever grateful to each of you for your valuable feedback and our Zoom calls, which always left me feeling inspired to keep doing the work.

Also, a massive note of thanks to Anne Ursu, one of the most talented, kind, and generous writers in publishing. Thank you for your wisdom, your encouragement, and your enduring support.

Thanks to my mom, my first cheerleader, for always being available to chat about our shared excitement over books. Also, a major thank-you for walking me back from the edge a couple of times when I called you in a pinch, needing to know more about how social workers think, along with their training and approach to teens like Ruby. Any errors in this book are mine and mine alone.

To Madeline, the first reader of Ruby's words in a draft that was absolute garbage. Thank you for encouraging me in spite of it all. How did I get so lucky to have such a brilliant and beautiful person like you in my life? I love you, love you!

And finally, to Shane. This one has taken a lot, hasn't it? Thank you for supporting me in my writing—through the ups and many downs and through earning a master's degree during a pandemic. I know it's not always easy being married to a writer, especially this writer, but I'm so grateful I get to travel this strange and wonderful journey with you by my side. I love you always!